Love, Lust and Combustion

Mingo Moran

Copyright © 2023 **Mingo Moran Books**

All rights reserved. No part of this publication may be reproduced, distributed, or transmitted in any form or by any means, including photocopying, recording, or other electronic or mechanical methods, without the prior written permission of the publisher, except in the case of brief quotations embodied in critical reviews and certain other noncommercial uses permitted by copyright law. For permission requests, write to the publisher, addressed "Attention: Book Rights and Permission," at the address below.

Published in the United States of America

ISBN 978-1-960159-05-2 (SC)

Mingo Moran Books
222 West 6th Street
Suite 400, San Pedro, CA, 90731
ihmcss111@gmail.com

Order Information and Rights Permission:

Quantity sales. Special discounts might be available on quantity purchases by corporations, associations, and others. For details, contact the publisher at the address above.

For Book Rights Adaptation and other Rights Permission. Call us at toll-free 1-888-945-8513 or send us an email at admin@stellarliterary.com.

Dedicated to Hard Working Drag Racing Innovators that hold down regular jobs, work long hours, and still find time to build World Class Cars to compete with sponsored backed giants

TABLE OF CONTENTS

CHAPTER 1: THE EARLY YEARS 1

CHAPTER 2: LIFE IN THE PITS 8

CHAPTER 3: THE FIRST CLEAN PASS 15

CHAPTER 4: THE LITTLE WAVE PITS 21

CHAPTER 5: THE START OF THE REAL DREAM
AND THE NIGHTMARE IN THE MIDDLE 28

CHAPTER 6: THE DREAM CONTINUES 36

CHAPTER 7: OH, MY GOD! 45

CHAPTER 8: THE WORLD LOOKS DIFFERENT 52

CHAPTER 9: TRAVEL IN THE NEW RIG 60

CHAPTER 10: IT'S ALIVE 70

CHAPTER 11: THE FINAL ROUND 78

CHAPTER 12: THAT'S NEXT? 86

CHAPTER 13: DID NOT SEE THT COMING 94

CHAPTER 14: A VERY CLOSE CALL! 103

CHAPTER 15: A BREAK IN THE ENGINE GENERATES
A BREAK FOR THE CREW 110

CHAPTER 16: A NEW FIRE BREATHERS IS CREATED 120

CHAPTER 17: READY TO ROCK AND ROLL 128

CHAPTER 18: PUT THE HAMMER DOWN 135

CHAPTER 19: TAKING A BREAK 142

CHAPTER 20: LOADED FOR BEAR 148

CHAPTER 21: LIFE SHIFTS INTO HIGH GEAR 160

CHAPTER 22: AN UNEXPECTED SURPRISE 172

CHAPTER 23: A SUNDAY TO REMEMBER 182

CHAPTER 1:
THE EARLY YEARS

It was a crisp early summer day in 1980 in Cheyenne, Wyoming. The sun was shining in a spotless blue sky. As usual, the air was a bit crisp, a chilly 52 degrees. Cheyenne is over a mile high in elevation, and even in early June, the morning temperatures are in the forties and fifties. The air, however, gave you a fresh, clean feeling. It was clear and unusually quiet, as the normal howling wind was still. Wyoming weather is as unpredictable as a teenage girl. One minute a calm beauty and the next a raging storm. I have seen it 60 degrees and sunny at noon and then a raging snow blizzard at five in the afternoon. This could even happen in June. Today, however, the weather was projected to be clear and calm, and we were loading the racecar to try a new combination at North Denver Dragstrip in Denver, Colorado. We had about a two hour drive to get to the track. Once we arrived, there was always the normal pit set up which took about an hour.

We had worked on the 23 T Altered drag race car until about 3:00 AM in the morning. We grabbed a couple of hours of sleep, a quick shower, dressed and were ready to depart at 6:00 AM. As usual, I had trouble finding enough help to go to the track and act as crew. Zed Black, my 19-year-old neighbor, was the only one I had found with enough drive and energy to keep up the rigorous pace that it took to help maintain a racing operation. My name is Travis Richard Davis and I had been attempting semi-professional drag racing the last couple of years.

The current engine combination used a big block 440 Mopar composed of some 426 Hemi parts and a heavily modified reinforced cross bolted 440 block. This motor used a unique casting aluminum head and twin turbo chargers. The dyno time, I had acquired, at great personal cost, indicated that there could be as much as 1500+ horsepower . We were still struggling with the mechanical injection system because the class we are running NCRA (*National Championship Racing Association*) required a mechanical injection system without electronics. It was the 1980's, so not much electronic engine controls existed yet anyway. It was still a carbureted world out there. We were using a series of by-pass valves and mechanical fuel pump pressure curves to try and transition the fuel metering to the airflow. The problem with turbos in drag racing is they run off of exhaust gasses , which is a derivative of load and fuel in the exhaust header. The engine needed load before boost could be built. No problem for the Heavy equipment diesel engines that Travis worked on for a living, but a real challenge for a drag engine that only runs about two minutes during a 1/4-mile pass down the strip. In fact, the whole event took less than 30 seconds from the water box to the finish line. You need to be able to run through the water box, make a low powered burnout to heat the tires and then transition to an idle state. After the burnout, you back up and get staged in the starting line staging and timing lights. There are two staging lights, pre-stage, and stage. This is where it became tricky with turbos. With a turbo car, you had to ease into the Pre-stage light and then power brake the car. Power braking is a process where you put one foot on the brake or in the case of the Altered, one pulling on the hand brake lever holding the car tight. The driver then starts to ease down on the throttle. The engine now starts to work against the torque converter, which is called "stalling against the converter." At this point, the load on the engine is causing enough exhaust gasses to push on the turbine wheel of the turbo which then spins the turbo compressor wheel. This function is called "spinning up the turbos!" The compressors start to suck in massive cubic feet of air and compress it against the intake valves of the engine. This pressure is called "Boost." The boost will start to build and the engine gains in torque. Too much boost and the car will surge forward and be disqualified because the car has broken out of the staging beams. Not enough and the car will stumble out of the gate. Running the engine "fat" or rich was the safe play, but it was a careful balance. Too much fuel and it would foul the plugs. Travis had to have a boost coming up before the green light came on or the car would fall flat on its face. Once the boost came up, he would have to modulate the brake lever just to let the car inch forward into the starting beam. Later as turbo cars became more popular, this would be called bumping in. Once the second stage light came on, Travis had to apply the transmission brake, which locks the transmission in reverse and 1st. Now the accelerator goes to the floor, and the engine goes to max boost. Getting a mechanical injection system to make all this happen was a real challenge. It was complicated, but Travis liked complicated.

They had the boost wastegate set at 30 PSI which is almost two additional atmospheres and would triple the horsepower of the engine compared to natural aspiration, if it did not blow the heads off that is. An instant later the green lights would start down. Now the engine and turbos were screaming to be released! Both competitors had to manage this process, but it was far less complicated for a Naturally Aspirated (No Boost) car. To make things even more stressful, you have to leave on the green light with a better reaction time against the competitor in the other lane. Reaction times are measured in tenths of a second. Once the green light comes on, it would take less than 10 seconds for the whole race to be over. This all happens in an extremely stressful short period of about two minutes.

We also had to worry about engine temperature. Travis used waste gates to control the boost. Waste gates are adjustable valves that allow the engine exhaust gas to bypass the turbos once the boost pressure setting has been achieved. If he used too much boost, the engine would detonate and blow the piston into pieces or rupture the head gaskets. The engine drives the torque converter and provides massive horsepower into a two-speed semi-automatic transmission.

It is fascinating that drag racers had evolved the simplest automatic transmission that Detroit has ever put out, the two-speed Powerglide, to be able to handle well over 1000-horsepower. Even today, this basic transmission configuration out of 1960's engineering is still the foundation of effective racing transmissions. Of course little or nothing was original, not even the case is stock for high horsepower applications. If all went well in the staging process, the engine would leave with 80% boost. We had accomplished getting the motor to 100% boost before leaving the line, but the engine built too much power and quickly overpowered and blew off (Spun) the 17-inch wide tires into smoke leaving the starting line.

In their test runs out on a country road and using a track event stopwatch, they knew they had the potential to set and maybe blow away the national record of mid 7 second ET (Elapsed Time in the 1/4 mile) and 190+ MPH record. The car was massively complicated. The mechanical injection system had a multiple series of valves and orifices (pills) that worked in conjunction with a mechanical fuel pump that had a volume curve driven by engine RPM.

Travis liked complicated. He was not one to sit in a chair and watch Jeopardy. If he was awake, he wanted to be thinking about how to harness combustion. Even when he slept, he was solving mechanical problems.

The trip to Denver was a quiet one due to the lack of sleep. Travis was lost in a million technical thoughts about possible ways to make the engine combination even better or to modify the delivery and suspensions system to be able to transfer the massive power from the engine to the ground. The only occasional distraction was to glance at Zed's 20-year-old beautiful blond girlfriend sleeping curled up in a ball next to him. She claimed to love helping and drag racing in general. She was extremely smart and Travis was always impressed with the observations she made.

She lay on the truck seat with her head in Zed's lap and her beautiful tanned legs and behind pointed towards Travis. She also had a taut stomach leading up to a shapely set of firm breasts ending with a beautiful face with a pert little nose and deep blue eyes. Zed was only 19, but he was already 6'2" and a hard 190 pounds. Zed and Travis had both been lifting weights and Zed was an excellent gymnast. Travis struggled with an extra 50 pounds, which had kept him focused more on cars than women. Female relationships came harder to Travis than they did to Zed. Zed would date this girl for a while and then cast her aside for someone else that would chase him. He was a nice guy, but young, very smart, and very fit. Who could blame him for playing the field?

Travis, now 35, had been married once already to a religious woman who spent her whole life in church. He had not had a lot of time for women in his life after his first marriage ended. His ex-wife was a very nice lady, maybe too nice. They just lived in two different worlds. She dedicated her life to God. Travis believed in God, but he believed that God helped those that aspired to make things better. Travis would rather bury his efforts in steel. If steel failed to do what Travis wanted, he could bend it, weld it, or better yet throw it away and get a stronger piece. You could not do that with people. They could not be modified like a car engine. Too many people get into relationships thinking they could change the other partner. Travis was not naive about women. He loved women, but would get mad at himself, when he allowed them to distract him from his mechanical goals. He could not deny however that they were wonderful complicated beings that he never quite understood. Maybe that is why he could never make a relationship work. Most women were not mechanical or logical. Travis was driven by whatever had his attention. In fact, when a woman got his attention, he found that he would overcompensate for his perceived weight problem. He would try to make his women happy with monetary things. This meant he had to work even more hours to make more money to try and meet all his commitments. For now, he got a lot more out of putting his mental and physical efforts on his racing. Because of that, he had no woman in his life at the moment, and that was OK with him.

Later in life Travis would wake up to how desirable a motivated, enthusiastic, and passionate a man he was to the right women… Travis was very energetic, financially stable, smart, motivated and currently very unaware of his attractiveness to women.

April, Zed's girlfriend lying next to him, looked too good to be true. April was never far from Zed. Zed and April were both sleeping and Travis allowed himself a few glances at April. Never too long a look as he respected her and his friend. That said, her flat stomach moving up and down as she breathed in a deep sleep that only the young seem to be able to do. Travis rarely slept for more than two hours at a time. He was perplexed with ideas about work or racing constantly running through his mind. Currently his mind was not on business or even racing, instead it had drifted to questions like, what was April like when passionate? Travis had always noticed how April was always touching or massaging Zed. Travis would sometimes walk into the shop and Zed would be kissing April with deep passionate kisses. Damn, it must be nice to have that young passion. When this happened, Travis would always quickly start a discussion about something about racing. April did not seem to be modest around Travis. Often she would bend down and hand Travis a tool exposing, briefly, her firm breast. He would always quickly look away. She sure seemed to be around a lot. Travis did not mind, as not only was she beautiful, she was smart, and ambitious.

Travis was a loyal friend to Zed, and appreciated all of his help. Both worked hard to make their dreams come true. Travis would have to keep his emotions and desires in check when it came to April. Travis was a bit surprised that inside he had a burning growing envy of Zed and his relationship with April. He would make a better effort to avoid glances at April, and keep his mind on the engine and car. Yes, that was the ticket, bury yourself in the car. Still, they were both sleeping and what would it hurt for Travis to steal a few glances at that magnificent girl lying next to him on the seat? Travis began to reflect on the night before when April had worked with them until 2:00 am and then fixed breakfast for everyone. She truly is ambitious, beautiful, passionate, and damn smart. In fact, April was the one that suggested the bump start process using the hand brake! She actually started college at 17 and was close to getting her Associate two year business degree.

Travis hoped to blow the record away soon in hopes that he could get the attention of a sponsor. So far Travis had spent every waking hour for four years either working on the motor combination, the car, or working overtime at the heavy equipment dealership to make money to feed the unrelenting appetite of the racecar.

As the sun began to rise and shine through the windshield glaring in their faces, they headed east. April stirred and shifted in the seat. April's new position allowed Travis a voyeur view of her beautiful behind. They were on a straight stretch of highway and Travis allowed himself an extended look at that beautiful sight. As he raised his gaze he discovered, however, April was no longer sleeping but instead staring right into his eyes and watching his longing stare. Travis immediately flushed red, as he was sure she would be upset. Wow, this could turn into a real mess. The one longing look could offend the wonderful girl and maybe even cost him his best friend! Zed would not be too fond of this old man ogling his girlfriend. However, to Travis's surprise, April just smiled and winked! She then closed her eyes and drifted back to sleep.

This left Travis confused. What he did not realize was that April was spending time with Zed not just because she liked him, and he was very sexy, but she also wanted to be closer to Travis! She found the older man exciting and very powerful, because of his knowledge of mechanics, drag racing, and his energetic productive lifestyle. Zed was driven as well but many times immature. April knew Zed would soon blow her off for some other hot chick. She could only hope that when that happened Travis would allow her to stay involved in the racing business. Yes, she was young but she desired a special someone in her life that was mature, ambitious and knew what he wanted out of life. When she looked at Travis, she did not see the extra 50 lbs., she saw a smart and driven competitor.

CHAPTER 2:
LIFE IN THE PITS

The sun was higher in the sky now, and both Zed and April were waking up. April spoke first, "I am hungry, and can we stop for something to eat?"

Travis was only mildly annoyed at the thought of taking time away from the track, surprising to both April and Zed, Travis said, "Sure, I see a truck stop sign." We can get fuel for the truck at the same time. By fueling now, it would keep them from having to stop as they left the track tonight.

It was always a long process to get loaded back up and headed home. After the race, the adrenalin will be gone from the excitement of racing. What will be left is the realization that Travis would have to find more overtime or take on some more government work to pay for whatever they broke. Hell, they would use over $200 in racing fuel alone, and the tow truck would use $300 in gas. Travis swung in and handed April a $20 to get food for everyone.

Travis did not have to tell April what he wanted for breakfast, she knew. Travis would want two sausage biscuits, with cheese only, and a large diet soda. Travis was predictable. She ran Zed down as he was headed to the restroom and asked him what he wanted. Travis started to pump gas into the truck. He watched his hard work click away on the pump meter. Pulling the open trailer, which he and Zed had built, caused the truck to get about five miles to the gallon.

The trailer had a storage box on the front that contained a generator, an air compressor, a makeshift bench, some lighting, and a place for a portable tool box. Behind the box was an open trailer that held the precious race car. It always took a couple of hours to load and unload the tools and boxes of spare parts. The storage box protected the race car from bugs and other debris, but also caught the wind which made it tow like a brick. Both Zed and Travis hoped to have time someday to build an enclosed trailer with shelving and storage.

The gas pump kicked off at $66.00. Damn, gas was getting expensive. This load of premium was $1.35 a gallon. Travis was a master mechanic at $20.00 an hour and $30.00 an hour overtime. Fuel would take a major bite out of his racing budget. Racing gas had to be bought by the barrel, and it ran $3.50 a gallon.

Travis went in and paid for the fuel, made a quick pit stop for some personal relief and to wash his face and hands. Washing his hands, he looked at his hands with disgust. They were rough, beat up, and stained with black diesel oil from working on the massive heavy equipment engines that supported his livelihood. How could he ever expect beautiful, soft skinned women to let him touch them? Surely they would take one look at his ruff exterior, his extra fifty pounds, and his often-unshaven face and be turned off, or even worse not notice him at all. He was just a tool to get things fixed. Forget that, get your head back in the racecar. If a car disappoints you, you can fix it, or park it until you have the time, energy, or money needed. It would sit patiently, under the car cover until Travis could get back to it. However, he did know women were like sports cars, high performance meant high maintenance.

Everyone piled back in the truck, and Travis attacked his food while guiding the truck back on the highway. He did not have time to eat what April had prepared for him last night because he was having trouble winching the car up onto the trailer. By the time he got back to the pancakes April had made, they were cold. He quickly discarded them so April would not notice. Now he was starving. Maybe it was the fact that he had not eaten since… Wait, when had he eaten last? Was it yesterday? No, he had put in a twelve-hour shift at a customer's site to get an oil field drilling engine running. It had been the night before at a dinner shack at one of the rigs he was working on. The drilling rig cook had made him a big steak and fried potatoes. The fried potatoes reminded him of Travis's dad who had died recently of a heart attack. His dad loved sliced potatoes fried in butter. He would get up in the middle of the night and make them in a cast iron skillet. It was these eating habits and that damn smoking habit that killed him. Travis washed the biscuits down with some icy cold diet soda.

In the twelve hour work shift, Travis had put new turbos on the drilling rig's engines. They had shut the engines down without cooling them down a bit after a drill pipe trip out. This meant the turbos, which spin at 70,000 RPM under load, ran several minutes after shut down. This would fail the turbo shaft bearing because they were spinning at high speed and with the engine not running, there was no oil flowing into lubricant or cooling. Once the bearing fails, excessive shaft orbiting would take out the seals, and the turbos would push oil out the exhaust seal. They had to be changed out before they failed completely and trashed the top end of the engine. The toolpusher at the rig had tried to claim warranty on the rebuilt engine but it was one of Travis's engines, and he knew it was right. Travis quickly disassembled one of the old tubes and showed the Tool Pusher the quench marks on the turbine shaft from where oil had dripped down on a still hot shaft after a hot shutdown. Travis was patient with the Tool Pusher as he was one of his good customers. Travis ended up leaving the rig with the Tool Pusher thanking him for coming out in the middle of the night to get him up and running. Travis was also leaving the rig with a signed invoice for the $7800 repair.

Travis was a bit embarrassed at the savage way he attacked his food April had gotten until he noticed that Zed was doing the same. Zed was a bottomless pit. He worked out so much that he was a carbohydrate junky. Zed did ok in school, mostly because Travis refused to let him go racing unless he maintained a B average in school and no flunking grades. After school, Zed would spend an hour in the weight room and then another hour working on the parallel bars, rings and mat exercises. He was strong dark skinned and hard as a rock. Travis had been amused last night when Zed grabbed the engine hoist frame and performed his gymnastics routine. Travis was afraid that Zed would slip up and crack his skull on the hard shop floor. Zed dismounted perfectly, impressing both Travis and April. No wonder April loved being with the hard bodied Zed.

Travis navigated back onto the highway and began watching for the exit to the track. Upon arrival at the track, they went through tech (Safety, technical, and rule compliance) where they had gotten some strange glances and prodding safety questions about the odd turbo powertrain combination. The car drew attention but had no problems passing. That was a big load off Travis's mind, as he was not sure the new heat shield around the turbos was going to meet NCRA approval.

When they selected their pit site close to the end of the track, everyone fell into their job assignments setting up camp. An hour later, the site was set up and the car was propped on jack stands ready for the pre-warm up that Zed performed before Travis took the car up for the first run. Zed loved this part of the day as he got a chance to sit in the driver's seat and feel the thundering motor under his heel as it warmed up. Often he would blip the throttle to check the response of the injectors. Travis was always fiddling with something during the ten minute warm up. Today he was observing the exhaust with a fuel to air ratio meter. Travis was troubled, the ratio was reading 18:1 indication of a very lean situation. This would burn pistons during the run. They would need to adjust the primary stage relief valve to a higher pressure. That would require a pill change in the valve. The air here must be denser because of the looming clouds on the horizon. Travis was concerned as he did not think they had the right orifice to fix the situation. They would have to make one, and they only had thirty minutes until the first round time runs.

Travis gave Zed the cut off signal of a hand across the throat, which made Zed's heart jump as he was afraid that Travis had seen a large problem that would keep them from running today. This was the fifth time this summer that they had been to the track and the car still had not made a clean full pass. Travis was moving quickly now, and yelled back to Zed indicating the problem. Zed, "Get the generator fired up and recharge the car battery. I will need to make a new orifice."

Travis quickly went to the trailer and flipped on the outside working lights. He knew where every piece in the trailer was. He pulled a blank orifice from his spare parts box and set it up in the jig while he waited for the car to cool down a bit. He grabbed the 7/8 and 1 inch wrench he would need to pull the valve apart. He also grabbed some rags and a coffee can to catch the fuel. They did not need a fire at this point. The relief valve was only inches away from the 1100-degree exhaust manifolds.

April had changed into her coveralls that had their race logo on it. She had altered the outfit to make them shorts. Zed wolf whistled as she came out of the truck, which made her smile. It quickly faded however, when Travis screamed at Zed to get moving. April could tell that there was trouble. She could see visions of working all-day again on this damn car.

Travis pulled the orifice from the valve and took it to the trailer. He measured the orifice hole, which was .130 of an inch. Travis calculated the flow rates of the pump at idle and used a written table he had built to calculate what the new orifice should be to obtain a 14:1 ratio. It would have to be .120. The smaller orifice would be more restrictive on the return side of the injection system and raise the fuel rate. The next drill bit down from 1/8 inch (.125) would have to work. They had twenty minutes before the first qualifying round. Travis grabbed the bit and put the jig on their portable drill press. He started to drill the orifice, when Zed walked by and bumped the jig. The drill bit broke! Travis had a strained look on his face, but did not say a word. Zed had been with him all summer, and never complained or asked for pay. Zed looked back and said, "What the hell are we going to do now?" Travis thought for a moment, and grabbed the original orifice. He put it in a vise and grabbed a center punch and preened it shut on two sides. He had the orifice back in the car before Zed could even get in the seat to fire it up. They fired it up and the ratio was at 16:1. Travis pulled it hot this time putting first degree burns on his arm. He preened it once more and back in, it went. It was now 15:1 still lean but it would have to be good enough, as they barely had enough time to go to the lanes.

Travis was pulling on his fire suite and Zed was hooking up the tow car. April already had Travis's helmet out. Holding it, she jumped on the back of the truck and placed her foot on the tow rope the way Travis had shown her to keep slack out of the rope as they slowed down. Travis was in the car, and Zed climbed into the truck to pull Travis to the lanes. Travis had a good feeling of completeness. Often at this point, he had a hole in the pit of his stomach as he would be concerned that something was not quite right, or that there was something they had forgotten . It would be very disappointing and embarrassing to break down in the lanes or worse in the burnout box. Today however, that feeling was gone! In fact Travis even had time to daydream as he longingly looked at April's dangling legs. He knew later he would be envious of Zed when the race day was over and all Travis had to show for his efforts was a broken car, an empty wallet and a head full of dreams. Zed, however, would have sleeping with April to look forward to.

Back to the race, the car was turning into the lanes and everyone snapped to their duties. Several racers nodded as they came into the lanes but Travis was focused on his checklist. To outsiders it might seem that racers are assholes, but the insiders know that they are just focused. There is often no second chance at 165 MPH or 7500 RPM, and Travis had over $50,000 in his race operation. Every last cent he could find in fact. Travis was in the seat, belts and helmet on. He patiently waited for the other lanes to make their passes. However, he was baking in the 7-layer fire suit and helmet. Would this be the day he would make a full pass or would there be another disaster like the rod failure the last time. That failure had cost him over $2800 in parts to repair. Travis's lane started to move up one car at a time. Now he could feel the knots in his stomach start. Anticipation was always the worst. Thoughts would start like, what if it did not start? Would they get shut down because of a leak? Did Zed get the tire pressure right? Would it stall after the burnout? All of these things had happened before. Travis could see the car before him roll into the burnout pit. He saw the car in front of him light up the tires for a burnout to heat the tires. It sounded like a Big Block, Travis thought, very throaty. The rope was unhooked and Zed was pulling out next to the track ready to follow Travis down the strip to pick him up after the run. Sweat was dripping in Travis's eyes. April reached in and gave Travis a kiss on the helmet for luck! She had never done that before? Travis hardly noticed. He was focused on the starting procedure. Would it start? He flipped on the ignition toggle switch. April pulled the safety rod on the parachute, and Travis hit the starter switch. The engine roared to life in less than a half turn on the crankshaft. Oh my God, here we go.

CHAPTER 3:
THE FIRST CLEAN PASS

Travis noticed as he moved into the burnout box, that this time it felt different. Nothing seemed out of place. April was moving to the starting line to guide Travis into the burnout box, just like he had shown her. Travis eased the car into the burnout box and felt first the front tires dip into the water box then the rear tires move in. Travis snapped the throttle to half position. The engine coughed a split second and then he felt the rear tires start to spin. He felt them grow as the tire speed came up and the smoke haze started to roll off the tires. He watched the engine tach climb quickly to 6500 RPM. Now the rear tires were billowing smoke. When Travis saw the engine temperature gauge come off the cold peg he lifted the pressure off the throttle. He was sideways, and about 100 feet down the track. As the tires began to dry he could feel them start to grip the sticky treated concrete track. As he felt this, he removed pressure from the foot throttle, he heard the loud chirp and the tire speed matched the ground speed. He carefully applied the brakes. He quickly put it in reverse and started to back up. April quickly appeared to his left and guided him back to the starting line. She signaled for him to stop. He checked his position and did a dry chirp blipping the throttle to clean off the last bits of water and dirt from the tires.

Zed had been watching the process from behind and came up and did an overview of the car. He signaled thumbs up. April motioned Travis forward into the initial lights. At the first one yellow pre-stage light, Travis paused and cleaned out the engine by blipping the throttle to 6500 RPM again to clear the throat of the engine. It was ready to sing now! He then opened the second power valve lever and power braked forward into the second light. The boost was building up. Travis had used a waste gate of a Diesel V8 engine used in Scraper tractors. It was dependable and easy to adjust. The waste gate has a signal line coming from the boost manifold that when max boost has been reached it bypasses exhaust gas straight into the exhaust headers instead of pushing it through the turbine wheel of the turbo. Travis knew that he had to get to the stage light first and apply the transmission brake. The turbos provided almost a 200% power gain but required exhaust gas to spin. He would have to get staged, transmission brake engaged (locking the transmission in first and reverse) and the torque converter to a full stall producing the 30 PSI of boost needed. They had the wastegate set for 30 PSI which would give the car the power to launch with the 17 inch drag slicks they were using. They had done much testing and 30 PSI was all the engine could hold. Any more than that caused too much cylinder pressure during combustion and they would blow a head gasket. They had even broken a block! That's why they had built special billet steel main gaps, and modified the block with side bolts into the caps.

The turbos were now screaming, but there was no stumble this time. Travis had the car staged and up to full power when he saw the first two lights flash. He released the transmission brake switch when he saw the last yellow come on. It would take the car an instant to react. He then felt a sensation he had never before experienced. Sheer massive acceleration like being launched in a rocket sled! The only way he could describe it later was pull, real hard pull.

The car seemed to leap off the line and then the rear drifted slightly to the right. Minor loss of traction, quickly corrected, and the tach shift light screaming SHIFT. Travis banged high gear and he felt another sensation of acceleration. That feeling of scoot came as he hit high gear. It almost felt as if the car was going to drive out from under him.

Then the finish line was on him and the tach was at 7000 RPM. Had he not shifted? Why did the finish line come up so fast? Had he staged wrong, it couldn't have been that fast...could it? Travis popped the chute and felt the sudden pressure on his shoulders from where the belts dug into his body and the car violently slowed. Travis was surprised at how hard the chute had deployed. Travis hit the brakes and then checked all the gauges. All seemed OK, but the coolant temperature was over 250 degrees. He let the engine power down, slowing the turbos and he shut it off. Travis noticed that he had run past the first two turn out return lanes and had to use the last return road. This seemed odd as the last return road was usually only for the 150 MPH and faster cars. Travis's fastest pass to date was a 9.3 at 145 MPH but he had never had any trouble making the second return road. The car came to a stop and for a few seconds there was a funny silence. He could hear the engine making popping sounds as it cooled down. With the helmet still on all Travis could hear was his breathing, which was very fast. His heart was pounding. Wow, what a rush!

The next few minutes were a blur. Travis started to get out of the car and pull off his helmet, but before he got it off Zed and April had arrived in the tow vehicle, horn blaring, and before he knew it, they were beating the top of his helmet. Travis was a little annoyed at first, because he was aware that they had to get the car hooked up and cooled! Why were they messing around? They needed to get the track clear for the next racers. They were jumping around like their pants were on fire. He could not understand them at first as he was still trying to get his helmet off, but then the words sank in. Zed was screaming at the top of his lungs, "You set a new track record. You set a new track record." Travis's heart jumped and he whizzed around to look at the time clock. He could not believe his eyes. It was still flashing a 7.89 time and the MPH was 173 MPH. The announcer was screaming that we had just witnessed a new gas track record for North Denver Dragstrip. It hit Travis all at once; he had hoped someday to break the 8.0 range but not the first clean pass, and certainly not a track record. Travis was stunned. He just stood there, holding his helmet just taking it all in.

Oh my God, the car had finally come together. April and Zed were hugging and kissing. Travis joined them for a group hug. Travis, usually a very intent technical person, could not hold back the emotion. Tears welled up in his eyes, and he was weak in the knees. He leaned back against the racecar and just let himself take it in. Many people said the combination would never work. He was determined to prove them wrong. They said never, never with a Big Block Mopar. This would prove them all wrong. The team had done it with an independent race team, with private money with no sponsors. A 7.89 at 173 MPH. Travis also knew that there was even more to get!

As Travis finally started to peel off the fire coat from his chest and his emotions began to subside, he looked back at the car and said out loud, "I think if we install a timing retard switch we can get another 50 HP (Horse Power) out of it." Zed laughed out loud. Only his friend, Travis Richard Davis, could move so fast through success to look for the next progress steps. Travis set his coat and helmet in the back seat of the truck and got in the driver's seat. Travis commanded, "Zed, you drive the racecar back to the pits." Travis knew that as they were pulling the car back, there would be tremendous glory and admiration from the other racers displayed. Travis had his glory in the time slip that he now had in his hand. April had gotten it from the time shack as she went by in the back of the tow truck. April again took her position on the tailgate. She would keep her foot on the tow rope to keep the slack out of it and yanked the front end of the car. They all had trouble concentrating, but safety and car must take priority. They needed to get the car back to the pits and check some things out before the next round.

Several years ago, Travis lost the front end of a dragster to an overly aggressive tow vehicle taking off too quickly without a foot on the tow rope. The slack came out all at once breaking the front spindle off.

Zed anxiously jumped in the racecar in a semi-standing position. He could still steer the car and run the hand brake, but be in full view of those he went by during the victory return to the pits. They were not disappointed, as folks were lined up on the fences cheering and waving all the way back. They had stopped further passes from happening as the whole facility knew that the new gas track record holder would return to the pits. As they entered the pit the car was swarmed with racers and spectators. The local news media had even shown up! Travis stumbled out some words about how he knew it could be done and then he thanked his team, friends, parts stores and local machine shop for believing in him. The cameras and requests to sign autographs overwhelmed Travis! That was a first for him for sure! The track ended up selling out hats and tee shirts and later Travis stayed to sign for everyone that wanted it. Travis also promised Zed and April a night on the town but right now he wanted to check the car, especially the engine. He wanted to cut the filter open to make sure the bottom end had no damage. He wanted to pull the plugs and read them to see if their mixture was right. They had decided to go ahead and run the bracket racing in the fast 16-car field.

Travis hated Bracket racing. It was a way that cars of any ET could race each other. The racer makes time trials and decides on an ET that their car can run consistently. They put their ET on the window or side panel. If you were a poor boy like Travis, you use white shoe polish. Then, when they are paired up with another car, they stagger the tree lights so that it lets a slower car leave first. In a perfect world, if both drivers' reaction times are perfect, they would be dead even at the end. Of course, nothing is ever perfect, and if you go .001 of a second faster than your dial in, you lose. It is called "breaking out." If both cars break out, then whoever breaks out the most loses. Now Travis had two big problems. First, the next closest competitor was a second slower. This means he was going to sit there, for what would seem like an eternity. It is very frustrating to sit and wait, watching the other car speed towards the finish line. He was going to have to catch up. Travis loved coming from behind, but he hated the break out rule. He was going to have to get out of it early to keep from breaking out. Wait, catch up and then back off just right so you stay ahead of the racer you just passed! This was just not in Travis's nature and this was the wrong car for that type of racing. Door slammers or rear engine dragsters with carbureted motors always did the best. There were racers that had this down to a science. Women are almost always in the finals. They had great reaction times and did not let their egos get the way. The second problem is that the engine would get red hot sitting on the converter stall that long.

Travis liked Competition Eliminator, where you ran against an ET index and a tight set of rules such as cubic inch to weight ratios, engine size and other factors. It was like bracket racing where cars would spot each other using the tree again, but this time you can go faster than you index! No break out rule. It was a class where the best mechanic won instead of just the best driver.

He did go out in the second round of bracket racing. Travis Red lit against a fast rear engine dragster. The guy told him later that he could hear the turbos coming chasing him down. He said it sent chills up his spine. The turbos just screamed when at max boost. Travis caught the guy 100 feet before the finish line. He had already Red lit, so he let it all hang out. It was another new track record: A 7.45 at 187 MPH. This was a great day. The race team did not realize just how radically their life would change after that day's events. Travis would never again have to use the last dollar on his credit card credit limit to buy a needed part or gas. Instead, he would have to fend off calls from sponsors wanting him to use their parts at no charge. He also did not realize that his last pass had indeed set a new track record, at 7.45 and 187 MPH. The car was so fast that North Denver Dragstrip's insurance would not cover them! Their limit was only good for 180 MPH and a 7.50. This would stop Travis from running there again. The track record set that day would hold until the drag strip closed a few years later. It was his second track record, and it was his last bracket race. It was Competition Eliminator for them now.

CHAPTER 4:
THE LITTLE WAVE PITS

On the trip home from Denver, Zed and Travis realized their turbo-Altered combination was a full .7 a second under the NCRA index! This would give them a real advantage in their point's pursuit. In their case, they would have almost a half-second advantage over the competition. They also knew the advantage would be taken away with a change in rules or weight breaks one year after they hit the competitive circuit. Travis knew there was more power to be had, but he also knew the iron block he was using would not take much more. They were stressing the limits of the short block now.

The crew arrived late getting home at 4:30 AM Monday morning. Travis barely had time to shower and grab a bite to eat before going to work on his 6:00 AM shift for 12 hours. He knew he would be dragging by the end of the day. Zed and April were already asleep in Travis's spare room before Travis came out of the shower.

Travis could do almost anything if he could get a shower. Something about the hot water cascading down his hair and face renewed his energy. The warm water opened his veins and the blood flow to the areas that were in pain from overuse and abuse. It always relaxed Travis and gave him energy. He noticed as he stuck his head under the shower that the water coming off his hair was dark with soot, sweat, dirt, and lubricants from working on the car in the heat. He quickly washed the race dirt off his body and climbed into a fresh pair of blues jeans and a biker shirt. He went to the house garage and looked at the transportation options to get to work. There was the truck of course, but it was still hooked up to the trailer, the 67 Corvette, but it was pretty dirty, and he did not have time to clean it up. The 1939 Humpback Dodge, a blown street rod, but it was out of gas. It was cool but nice out, and the sun was hinting at the horizon. Travis turned to the two motorcycles on the left side of the garage. The choice became simple, there was the hard tail chopper, which offered an exciting feel of power, or the Glide, which was comfortable and had a stereo to keep him awake.

He jumped on the Glide and headed out. He was sure the thunder from the big drag piped V-twin would not be appreciated by his neighbors, but they should realize that there would be plenty of time for sleep when they were dead. Travis moved onto the highway and quickly found himself at 90 MPH. Man, he just loved acceleration and speed. It was a drug to him. The Glide had a 124 CI Big Bore kit on it and a monster 44MM carb. It pulled 110-foot pounds of torque and would lift the front end off the ground in first and second gear simply by opening up the throttle. Not bad for a bagger. The key to this bike is to roll the throttle on not snap it open unless you like riding wheelies on a 700 pound bike. The brisk morning air and turning on the stereo to some rock tunes helped Travis stay awake. It was the song about how a guy first liked the wild tendencies of his girlfriend, but then they became old, and he became tired of her continuous party girl attitude. He began to get a picture in his mind from the music when brake lights on the car in front of him flashed on. Travis quickly realized he could not stop soon enough, and he would have to take the ditch to avoid hitting the car in front of him. He was going way too fast. There had been an accident, probably because someone had fallen asleep. Travis was lucky it was not him that had fallen asleep. He hit the brakes hard, but not hard enough to lock them up. A motorcycle with locked up brakes was going down. He also released them just before he hit the ditch. It was better to roll in and concentrate on keeping it upright.

Travis was lucky. The median and ditch had just been mowed, and there were no big holes in his path. Down in the ditch, Travis went. The Glide handled the rough terrain well, because of the large front touring tire. Travis was lucky he had not picked the chopper. The skinny front tire would have dug in and flipped the bike. Travis would have been lying in the morgue in an hour. As Travis came out of the ditch, he glanced at the vehicle almost not recognizable now. The SUV was smashed into a concrete embankment. Strange, even in its current state it looked familiar. Has he seen it before? It was a large black SUV. It would haunt Travis all day…where had he seen that before? Travis made it back to pavement just in time for the exit ramp to the dealership. Travis eased the bike off the highway. He pulled his bike next to the building instead of the way out of the parking lot. The owner rode as well and had created a "Bike Lot" right next to the service entrance.

Travis headed in, and as he approached his toolbox, he got his first surprise of the day. Someone had taped the front-page news article in the local paper to the front of his box. "Local racer unofficially breaks a national record at the weekend event." Travis had not even thought about that! Had they really broken the national record? It would not count, as the race was not an actual point's race, and their time passes were not in competition. But had they really gone quick enough? Travis had not checked the racing publication "National Digger" to check the current class record ET and MPH. The National Digger was the NCRA publication that came out once a week with current information on all classes. They posted the latest articles on drag racing, and had a section with all the Class Index information and also the class record for each class. If the class record was too far under the Index, they would either adjust the index down closer to the record, or they would change the weight break. A weight break done with a pound per cubic inch table. This would slow down the field by requiring them to add weight to the car. Mass in motion, and the more mass, the more power it would take to get it in motion. It was Basic Physics.

Travis quickly found a paper and read the entire article. As Travis read the article, a crowd of local company supporters gathered. It was true they had recorded times that were a full .02 under the record at the unofficial event. Travis had a real concern in the back of his brain that the NCRA officials might also see the unofficial record. The key to Competition eliminator was to keep your advantage to yourself for a bit and only roll out as much as you need to win for a while. The work and cost effort to be this far under in a class was tremendous, and a racer wanted to enjoy the advantage to build up the bank account!

The article shocked Travis so much that he had not seen the company owner, Matt Edwards, walk up behind him.

Matt slapped Travis on the back and said, "Damn the company name looks good on the paper." Sure enough, the opening statement called out where Travis worked. Matt stated that several of Travis's customers had already been calling to inquire if it was true. They were excited that their favorite mechanic had been successful, but concerned that they would lose his services. They considered Travis not just a technician, but a consultant on their operations. Matt said, "Travis, congratulations! After you get settled can you come up to my office? I have an idea I have been considering, for a while, that I would like to share with you."

Travis's heart jumped at the thought of going up front. He did not like walking across the clean carpets in his work boots. He would have to pass the sales and executive offices, and the "suits" would stare at him wondering why they had let a "grease monkey' up front. Funny, they sure did not mind him around when they were at one of Travis's customers. They would give the customer the perception that they and Travis were long lost buddies. But here in the dealership, they would act like they did not even see him. Oh well, Travis had come to terms with that a long time ago.

After a few more congratulations from the other technicians, Travis headed for the locker room to change out of his work boots. He kept a pair of clean boots just for these occasions. Matt was a race and motorcycle fan and would occasionally ask Travis up after hours for a "bench racing" session. Matt had a 1969 Charger with a 440-6-pack, a four speed, and a Dyna 60 with 4:10 rear end gears. Travis and Matt had overhauled everything in the car together at Travis's home shop. They had even used the company paint booth to spray the Hemi-Orange paint on the Charger. It was truly a unique and beautiful car. It was damn quick too. The motor had one of Travis's special combinations in it for street use. Travis had found a special combination of camshaft and compression ratio pistons of 9.5:1. He would advance the cam timing 4 degrees, which closed the intake valve sooner, resulting in more of the compression stroke with a closed valve to build pressure against. It basically made a low compression motor think it has higher compression characteristics. The motor would also run on pump gas! Compression means more combustion…a bigger boom, which forces the piston down harder. More torque per revolution. (Torque * RPM) / 5252, is the basic equation of Horse Power). The more torque you build per revolution, the more horsepower you can deliver.

The whole horsepower thing was a marketing ploy by Fulton to help him sell steam engines against horses a hundred years ago! Travis washed his hands a third time and headed up front. Luckily it was still early, and the suits were not in yet. As he approached Matt's office, he paused as Matt was on the phone. Matt motioned Travis in, and Travis overheard Matt say, "I agree it would be great promotion for our products as well. I am glad you can support the idea. It would be perfect for both of our companies to be associated with the innovation needed to establish a national record." Again, Travis's heart jumped.

As Matt hung up the phone, he looked up at Travis, smiled, and said, "Travis, you really know this stuff don't you?" Travis did not reply, turned a bit red, and waited in anticipation, not knowing what he was doing up here in the suit zone. "Travis, if you are interested, I want you to take the next week and set up a race office in the old back shop."

Travis sat quietly with huge wide eyes. Was he hearing things? He needed the hours in service to pay for funds to support his race habit. Matt continued, "I am going to have the entire facility cleaned out, painted, air-conditioned, and the heating upgraded. I am going to have all the windows and doors repaired or replaced to make it airtight. In fact, I would like you to create a clean room secure area for special development. I want you to create a capital and annual operating budget to cover turning your race operation pro. I want you to make it your full-time job to make that national record of yours official and then see how many more times you can break it. After you get a reputation built up for us, I would like to expand to restoring autos the way you and I did the Charger. We can add sales staff and technicians as needed when the revenue grows. I would start you out at a monthly salary of $10,000 a month, and you would keep any prize money. The money coming in from sponsors or contingency funds (Manufacturers will pay for stickers on the race car when you win) would be brought back into the operating statement as revenue. If all goes well, it will break even after the first year and give me some interesting tax advantages. The company will have to take ownership of the racecar, as it would be considered a company asset. We can discuss a price for the car, but I was thinking it would be around $100,000. Are you interested?"

Travis froze and blinked wondering if this was really happening. He was still standing as he hated sitting down on the clean, lush office furniture. He decided to sit down before he fell down! Travis had that same emotional feeling again. Is this really happening to him? He had worked so hard and spent every last dollar he had to pursue a dream. Would it finally get easier?

Travis had not even recovered enough to respond when Matt surprised him again, "Oh, and bring in any receipts of last weekend's expenditures as we will consider this retroactive to last Friday. I will also have our company lawyer draw up an agreement and make sure that you retain all engineering design rights and control." "Of course, you will be the 30% owner in the new venture as you will own the intellectual property." "We can split any profit or loss at a 70 -30 split after three years." "You will need a pit crew and shop staff. You should also consider someone as an office manager to take care of the office work and maybe act as a parts runner. I know how you hate to stop in the middle of a project to "chase parts." "Make sure you pay them a top wage, as we need to keep a high profile image and we want people with the same passion for this that you have. We need people who will stay with us and not jump ship. Are you interested?"

Travis could not speak. His mouth was too dry. He found the power to nod his head, " Yes."

Matt continued, "Good, we will need to repaint the car and add some advertising for us. Is it alright to repaint the car? Would you want to do that yourself, or hire it done?" This snapped Travis back into reality. No one was going to touch his baby. He might let them do some lettering, but he would paint it.

Travis quickly responded. "Wow Matt, this is fantastic. I will paint the car. You can spray part of it if you like."

Matt smiled at this and said. "Yeah that would be cool." Matt was glad to see Travis quickly recovering to the confident master mechanic he was. Matt continued. "Our manufacturer has already offered one of their older Stock Car haul rigs for you to transport the car. They will repaint it of course." Travis had stood up to shake Matt's hand in agreement, but this last part put him back into his seat again. Travis finally managed to get out, "Matt, I don't know how to thank you."

Matt replied, "No thanks necessary, you earned it, and we are both going to make money on this."

As Travis left the office, the suits were coming in. They gave him their normal glare. Fuck'em, Travis thought, he was on top of the world. How many people really get to do what they love for a living? He had to call Zed and April and ask them if they were interested in jobs, as a pit crew member and office manager. April had six months left to finish her Bachelors business degree. She would also be 21 by then and could become a Public notary. Maybe she could finish school and work at the same time.

CHAPTER 5:
THE START OF THE REAL DREAM AND THE NIGHTMARE IN THE MIDDLE

Travis told the shop foreman that he was taking a Personal Leave day off. All the technicians received 10 PL days and Travis had built up 4 weeks' vacation every year. All of which was used for something to do with racing.

He could not wait to get to his Glide. He had decided to go back to his place and break the news to the crew face to face. He passed where the Black SUV had been wrecked, and it was gone, but there was still clean up taking place. There was antifreeze, oil and a red substance all over the concrete highway. Travis did not want to think about the red substance. It was transmission fluid, yeah transmission fluid. Racers never wanted to think about what could happen in an instant. Sure he had a roll cage that was double reinforced with gussets even beyond what NCRA (National Championship Racing Association) required. He and Zed had argued about that. Zed said, "Come on man that is adding weight." But Travis had seen first-hand how metal can fail due to inclusions or other stress risers that couldn't be seen. If that car rolled, he wanted it to be as strong as he could make it. He did not care if it weighed another 100 lbs. He would just build more horsepower to compensate. Every joint was reinforced with angled gussets.

He made the final turn. He saw a police car sitting in front of his place. Zed was sitting on the porch with his head hung low, and April was nowhere to be found. Travis knew this was all too good to be true. Life is like balancing an engine. If you add weight using stronger rods, metal has to be added to the crankshaft to compensate. As it turned out, the Black SUV that Travis had recognized belonged to April's parents!

Zed said, "April's dad had fallen asleep at the wheel and ran into a concrete embankment." Neither of April's parents used seat belts. They were both instantly killed. Travis glanced at his pager and saw that April had paged him. He kicked himself for not being there for her. She never asked for anything but how she could help.

Travis said, "Where is she?"

Zed said, "She is in the spare room and the door is locked." The police had informed her, and she had started crying out of control.

Zed said, "She would not even talk to me."

The police were leaving, and Travis went inside not sure what he could do but knew he had to try. He approached the door and called her name. The door flew open, and a distressed April flew into his arms and broke into tears. Travis held her and felt her whole body shaking violently. He moved her to the couch and let her get it all out. Zed came in and was a bit surprised at April's reaction, but was glad to see that she was allowing herself to start the grieving process.

It would be months before April would function at full capacity. It was a very long night, and Travis did not reveal his good news. It did not seem appropriate in the current setting. The next week was full of unspeakable responsibilities. The week after that, April pretty much stayed held up in Travis's spare room. Travis could hear her crying from time to time, but when he would ask if she needed anything she would say, "No but thanks." April was an only child. What made matters worse, her dad had not left a very pretty financial state. Travis went in and explained the situation to Matt, who was very understanding, and said he would have some of the guys get started on the new shop clean out and that Travis should help when he could.

Matt also said he would have his company lawyer look into April's financial situation and make a recommendation of how best to clean it up.

After the funeral, Travis and the company lawyer helped April sort through the finances , and it appeared that there was a way to pay all April's parents debts, but it would require the sale of the family home. They had no life insurance. April was very financially savvy and quickly concluded that she was going to be out of a place to live. To complicate things she and Zed were fighting a lot. Zed was young and moved to closure quickly. He was very consoling for a while, but could not understand why April did not want any physical attention. Travis understood both sides. Zed was very young and headstrong , but April had to grow up in a hurry. Women are emotionally driven, and the last thing she needed was to be pushed or pressured by Zed at this point.

Zed also kept pushing Travis asking why he was spending so much time at work even on weekends. They needed to work on the race and tow vehicles! Travis had been going to work and quietly working on moving to the new shop. It was taking shape quickly, and he had been surprised to find out that the new tooling would include a new engine dyno, glass bead machine, a press, floor grinder, drill press, work benches and they had access to the company's machine shop. They were even going to add machining capabilities for block, crankshaft and balance work to the existing machine shop. Matt figured the relationship with a record holder would bring in new gas engine machining business.

The race operation had an internal account that they could open work orders to so that everything could be kept accounted for accurately. Travis had been working with Brenda in accounting to set up an operating statement. Travis was learning a whole new side to the service business. He found that he really liked understanding the financials furthering his quest for knowing how things worked that went beyond mechanical things. He was good at grasping new concepts, except for women. He could never really figure out how they worked. Each time he thought he was beginning to figure them out, they would do something different. The new race shop floors were now all sealed and painted. There was also lighting in the shop that resembled the sun! The heat and A/C had been upgraded, and there was even a "Clean Room" for final engine and transmission assembly. Travis's toolbox had been moved over, and Travis had used a portion of the tool budget to get Zed a brand new smaller set of tools and boxes. Actually, the Tool dealer had agreed to provide new boxes for both Travis and Zed in return for some A&P using the new record holder car including maybe a calendar!

After a month of getting the shop ready, Travis decided it was about time to cheer his teammates up so on a Friday afternoon he asked the pair to join him for dinner. After work, Travis picked Zed up at his house, and Travis asked where April was.

Zed said, "Hell, I don't know. She does not seem to like me much these days. Besides, I have been seeing Sandy." Sandy was a buxom redhead that ran a 1969 Pro Gas Camaro. In fact, she had been begging Travis and Zed to build her a new motor. She had a trust fund from daddy and spent her time going to college and racing her car. It was an OK ride, but needed lots of work and broke down a lot. It appeared that Zed had used his promise to "fix it up" to fix himself up with her company. Zed was extremely bright and already knew more than older race mechanics. Travis frowned but understood that when you are 19 a month is a long time.

Travis asked, "Well, where do you think she is?"

I don't know" Zed said, "but if I had to guess I would bet that she was over at your house." Travis had given both of the crew member's keys a long time ago. They drove to Travis's house and sure enough April's old but clean looking high mileage Duster was sitting behind the house in the driveway of the shop. The car was always clean inside and out, but it had 165,000 miles on it and gave a hint of blue smoke when it started . It was a slant 6 with a three on the tree manual transmission.

The shop lights were on. When Zed and Travis went in, there was April sitting behind the wheel of the racecar. She had on a biker shirt and blue jeans that had holes in them. She had to pay special, to get jeans with holes in them. Travis had holes in his jeans also, but he did not buy them that way. They were worn out from working in them.

April said, "I need a place to live and all I want to do right now is race. I want to quit school and help you, Travis."

Zed yelled out, "Fat chance, we can't even afford to buy race fuel right Travis."

Travis just smiled and said, "Well you're not quitting school, but for now you can move into the spare room in the house or we can build you something out here in the shop. It is heated and has a separate bathroom. By the way, be careful what you wish for, someday it might come true!"

Zed and April looked puzzled over that comment. But they both knew that when Travis talked half the time they did not understand what he meant. Travis added, "Running a race team is a whole lot of work."

They both shook their heads and blew Travis off with a, "yeah ok." April was very relieved to have a place to stay. As she jumped out of the car, Zed tried to slap April on the ass, as he usually did, but April dodged his swat and said, "Hold on mother fucker, you have felt this ass for the last time." That caught Travis by surprise. April was usually very soft spoken. She really had grown up in a hurry this last month. She continued, "Go find Sandy if you want a hand full. I am sure she would love to facilitate."

Oops, it looks like the cat is out of the bag Travis quickly said, "OK people, enough for now. It has been a rough couple of weeks for everybody, but tonight we turn the corner. Let's go get a pizza and some beer and come back to the shop and think about where we want to take our new record holder to kick some ass!"

Both April and Zed liked that idea. April called in two large pizzas for pick up, one pizza for Zed and one for her and Travis to split. After April had hung up the phone, the crew headed for the dually. However, as they got in, this time April got in front and stayed on the passenger side instead of sitting in the middle. She made Zed get into the back seat! Yep, looks like they are toast Travis thought. Travis hoped it would not affect them as a team as he had grown quite fond of this troop.

They headed towards their favorite pizza place, which was about a twenty-minute drive. Travis pulled through the corner liquor store and got two six packs of light beer. April looked funny at Travis, as he usually did not allow her to drink as she was still under age!

Travis saw her look and said, "It is time to move past our troubles and remember we have a bright future ahead!"

They headed towards the pizza place and both Zed and April opened a beer. The truck had tinted windows, the crew rarely drank while traveling as it was usually going to a race, and everyone knew better. HorsePower and alcohol do not mix. The racing track is way too intense to be intoxicated. Things moved too fast, and there was always too much to do. Travis did not drink while driving. He really preferred a hot tea with Irish Cream liquor rather than beer. It was a drink he had picked up down under in a "Best Practices'' Maintenance Seminar he participated in for the heavy equipment company Matt owned. The Aussies had taught him very quickly not to try and drink with them. They would put you under the table, stay up late, and then get up in the morning and work 12 hours just to start it all over again.

Tonight, both April and Zed took deep long pulls from their cold frosty bottles of light beer. Travis actually saw April relax for the first time in a month. Poor kid, she really had a rough month. Travis had to give her credit as to how well she was handling all this.

Travis, of course, had made it a point to get to know both Zed's and April's folks. If she was going to run all over with the racecar guy, he wanted to make sure they knew he was an ok guy. They had also made sure that both of Zed and April's family's cars were well taken care of. They had even rebuilt an automatic transmission in April's parents SUV. They were very impressed when April helped pull it, and did most of the overhaul to the tranny, with Travis's help of course. Her folks were a bit shocked when they picked it up, and Travis just said, "No Charge, and thanks for letting April hang out with us."

It was a damn shame they were gone and did not get a chance to see her graduate college and take over running the race operation from a business perspective. She had really handled the last month well, but had been forced to grow up in a big hurry. She really did not seem like a 20 year old anymore. She was going to be 21 in two months. She had proven that she had an old sole in the last month in the way she cleaned up her father's financial mess. Travis reminded himself that Sandy, Camaro girl, would just have to keep her distance for a while. Travis made a mental note to coach Zed, a bit, to have fun, but not rub it in April's face.

They picked up the pizzas and Zed had two slices eaten before they got out of the drive through! Wow, that guy was a vacuum cleaner. April was about done with her first as well.

Travis complained, "Hey, you guys! Save some for me." As Travis pulled out, he turned right instead of left to the house.

Zed said, "Hey old man, did you forget where you live?"

Travis said, "Fuck you dude, drink your damn beer, keep your pants on and give me a slice of pizza. I forgot something at the dealer that I need to pick up to work on the car tomorrow."

In a few miles, Travis grabbed a second slice of pizza, and they continued the twenty-minute drive to the shop. By the time they got there, the pizza was gone, April was on her second beer, and Zed was on his third. Travis felt an excitement in his gut just like before the first run of the day in the car. He could not wait to see their reaction. Travis and a couple of the shop mechanics had been busting their ass to get the new shop completed. It was almost all done, and it was incredible.

Travis pulled into the automatic gate, hit an opener and the gate started opening. This was no surprise as April and Zed knew Travis had run off the dealership. Travis turned left towards the new shop. A puzzled look was on both April and Zed's faces. They had come with Travis many times to the large equipment store but had never been to the back lot. Their puzzled faces quickly changed to disbelief. Travis pulled around to the front of the back shop, and they all could see the new professional neon sign that said: T, A & Z RACING ENTERPRISES. PROGRESS OVER PERFECTION BUT PERFECTION ALWAYS IN MIND.

Zed and April both turned to Travis and Travis said, "Be careful what you ask for you might get it. April you still need to finish school, but you are the new office manager. Zed, let's take a look at your new toolbox! Oh, and those two new red Dodge ½ ton trucks over there are your new shop trucks." April had tears in her eyes, Zed's mouth was open, and for the first time in his life, he had nothing to say.

CHAPTER 6:
THE DREAM CONTINUES

The team loved the shop, and Zed quickly found the big projection Screen TV and accompanying stereo. He had the VCR going with the Movie "Vanishing Point." Now roaring engines were blaring from all four corners of the shop with over 500 watts of power behind it. In fact, Matt called down from the main facility and said he could hear it from his office! He was working late with the Director of sales on a fleet sale of large mining trucks to a large coal mine. He said he hoped the team was enjoying their new facility, including the entertainment systems, but make sure it stays at a low roar during dealer operating hours! The entertainment center was Matt's idea. He was insistent that the demographics had to attract young people. Hell, Travis did not even know what demographics meant. Was there graph paper involved? All he knew is that Zed was in heaven.

The team went through the whole facility. The huge box of tools blew Zed away. He especially liked the click type torque wrenches, mics, and dial indicators. There was even a dial bore gauge. Zed had been trying to talk Travis into replacing his old snap gauges for several years.

Travis always said, "I have been doing this shit for 20 years, and my stuff is always right on the money. I can do the math. I don't need a tool to do it for me. They both got new handheld calculators, which were very cool! It might be better, but Travis would keep his slide rule. Travis remembered the first time he pulled the speed/power slide rule from his toolbox when setting up the rear end geometry on the first racecar. Zed was only 16 then but rolled on the floor in laughter when he saw it.

He said, "Next you will pull out your pocket protector"! He really did die when Travis then pulled out a gasket maker named pocket protector! Man, this was one old guy, he even still built model cars in his rare spare time.

Back to the present, after Zed and April got a full tour of the shop including the mini machine tools, engine dyno, head flow bench, clean room, car and motorcycle hoists, heavy and light cranes, and heavy cleaning equipment, they all went into the office. April's mouth dropped open when she saw the complete office computer monitor and dot matrix printer. Matt had asked the computer department to set them up with a terminal to the main frame. They had their own mainframe partition and April would have access to a programmer so she could work with the operating statement and direct expenses. She also had a desktop PC with an internal hard drive and a new state of the art 3 ½" floppy drive. There was a shop intercom and 6 line phone system.

She walked over to the intercom, pushed the button and said, "Asshole Zed you're wanted in the office."

She also noticed that there was a separate TV and stereo setup for her, as she enjoyed the car stuff but also liked the conventional television. She also had a weird love of oldies rock and roll. Damn, she really got to Travis playing that stuff. He would like to see her in a mini skirt or short shorts! She went over, fired everything up, and flipped on Tommy James and the Shandell's, "I think we are alone now."

Travis's eyes glazed over as he remembered cruising Main Street to the song with his buddies. Wow… That was a long time ago. That was back in the day when you could cruise all night on $5.00 of gas!

April was engrossed in her new computer and entertainment system. Travis said, "Well Zed, let's go look at the new trailer and hauler."

Zed's eyes got wide! "We have a new trailer?"

Travis replied, "Yep, and a rebuilt Semi-truck to pull it."

The truck had a scroll mechanical fuel system 3408 as power. It is rated to 500 HP, but Travis had put the super tune to it, opened the rack, installed a 992 Wheel Loader Turbo and it now pulled 800 HP at 1900 RPM. That meant that it had over 2000 foot lbs. of torque. If they wanted to get home quick, this would do the trick! With that much torque, they would snap the 15 speed transmission if they were not careful. They would also have to watch the pyrometer to make sure it did not stay over 1200 degrees for more than about 5 minutes. At exhaust temperature at 1300 degrees, pistons and valves burn pretty fast! As they walked outside Travis flipped on the outside mercury vapor lights, and there was a Bright Blue Truck and Trailer. The trailer had sleeping quarters, bathroom, and a complete shop inside! There was even a lift to raise the racecar up and store transportation below. Travis thought they could get a mini shop truck or maybe a pair of motorcycles. Wow, what a way to make a living. The trailer had complete climate control so there would be no more working on the car in a dirty environment. There was also a full hydraulic actuated canopy that deployed off the side for an "outdoor shop" where the fans could interact. Man, Matt had done it right! The trailer also had a full set of hand tools, power tools, a state of the art compressor, generator, and again a mini machine so they could make or repair parts! Yes, there was also a Mig/Tig welder and torch as well. There was even a spot for a spare long block engine and transmission. When Zed noticed this, Travis said, "That's right, tomorrow we get started on the spare components. I have some ideas on how we can change the cam timing. I also have some ideas on how we can eliminate some overlap in the clutch sequencing in the transmission to speed up the high gear shift." Even the slightest of clutch overlap at 1000 HP would burn the transmission up."

Travis told Zed he would have to show up on time and work at least eight hours now as he was now making 14.00 dollars an hour.

Zed blinked, and said, " That is master mechanic wages!"

Travis replied, "Not quite, but you are worth it." They both went in, and Travis told April that she was on salary at $1500 a month. Would that be OK? She was speechless. Also, all her books, and tuition were covered as well. Travis said that she would stay in college and get her degree. Travis and Matt even hoped she would get an MBA later.

Travis and Zed went back into the shop and April was still engrossed. Zed said he was tired and wanted to know if he could take his new truck and go home. Travis went into the office, grabbed the keys and tossed them to Zed. Travis said, "Be careful they are tuned for torque. You lose your license, you lose your job!" Travis also threw April her keys and said, "Come on kiddo, I am tired too, we need to be here by 7:00 AM tomorrow to get started!"

April reluctantly shut down her systems. Wow, the system exceeded her expectations. Zed took off in a cloud of smoke as he left the lot. Travis had turned down a new truck. He had hand built his dually and loved it. Maybe he would ask for a budget to upgrade the engine.

He saw April pull out and she was not quite as aggressive as Zed, but defiantly left in a spirited style. She had more finesse. She eased the truck out onto the road. April then looked to make sure there was no "Johnny Law" lurking about before she found the bottom of the throttle.

She loved the feel of V8 horsepower under her foot. She did not bury the throttle, as she knew it was a new truck and she was new to it. She would wait to mash the pedal to the metal until she knew more about what it would do. But for now, she was urged to feel the power. She wanted it to come through the accelerator pedal and up her leg letting it flow all the way through her mind, allowing her to forget the past for a few minutes. She felt the acceleration push her back in the seat. It was like she was driving into her future. There was still a resounding roar of the truck as she left the lot. Travis could hear a very crisp chirp as she hit second gear. That girl was alright.

Travis smiled and began one last walk through of their new shop. It would be a great venue to launch their new lives. He knew that he, Zed, and April would use this fantastic facility to build a championship team that was going to set the world of drag racing on its ear. Travis had to pinch himself mentally. Has this really come true? How much better could life get? He walked through the facility, turning off lights, making sure the air compressor was off, pushing chairs up to the desks, picking up a wrench that was left out, and placing it back into the right slot in his toolbox. Just before he went out the door, he turned and took one more look at their dream come true before turning off the last breaker for the overhead lights.

Travis headed his dually onto the road and could not resist the urge to lay into it as well. He usually saved it for the track, but this had been a beautiful day. As he rolled the pedal on the twin turbo diesel that Travis and Zed had transplanted into it, the truck answered with an incredible torque. The truck went sideways and lit the tires up instantly. The four 750-16 tires were no match in traction for the 600 HP twin turbo diesel engine. Travis had a Marine application engine in his truck. The temperature gauge started to rise quickly, and Travis slipped the special industrial automatic transmission into second gear. Travis pushed it a bit further and then eased out of the throttle. Travis had noticed that the pyrometer jumped up quickly. They had the injectors set a bit on the lean side to maximize fuel economy. He knew that exhaust heat was necessary to get the turbo's spinning, but he also knew that heat could cause massive damage if it came at the wrong time.

The truck quickly settled down, and Travis's mind drifted into how he could use an alcohol/water system to cool the intake charge to keep heat from building quite so fast. Wait a minute! He could do the same thing with the racecar. If he did that, he could eliminate the after cooler! That would take 30 pounds off the car! Travis flipped on the voice recorder on his mini cassette to capture his idea. He carried his recorder everywhere as he had to get these thoughts out of his head. He had read that capturing ideas on a pad or in a recorder would help let your mind rest. If he did not do this, he found ideas kept running over and over in his mind. Travis only slept 4 to 6 hours a night. The combination of a mind that never slept and a body that was getting old had taken its toll.

Travis oftentimes would slip out into the Hot Tub outside his bedroom door in the early morning hours. He had built a privacy fence around it so he did not have to worry about wearing swimming trunks. The hot, swirling water helped him relax and felt good on his sore muscles and tired mind. Travis was heavy, but he was also a huge man. Occasionally he and Zed would hit the weights and Zed was always amazed at how much Travis could lift for an "old man" especially with Travis's legs. He had tree trunks for legs. Not too pretty, but he could body press over 600 Lbs. up to 50 reps. After a long day at work, or racing, the Hot Tub was the one place he could really feel his mind and muscles relax. He would hit the tub tonight to help him relax and get a good night's sleep. Tomorrow, he would tell Zed about the water/alcohol injection idea.

A short time later, Travis arrived at the house. April's truck was already at the house. When Travis entered the door, he heard April's bedroom TV, and it sounded like it was the evening news. The weather was on. Tomorrow was going to be a beautiful day the forecaster projected. "Yes, it was", Travis said to himself. He figured April was already out for the night. She often left the TV running all night. The noise helped keep her mind off her loss. On several occasions the last couple of weeks, Travis would have a restless night and would go out to the kitchen and get a drink and he could hear April sobbing. She had had some tough breaks. Travis did not disturb her. He knew from going through his own folk's nasty divorce, and his father's death, that sometimes you just have to let yourself experience the emotional steps of denial and anger.

Travis was not trying to minimize April's grief, she was dealing with a tremendous loss, and he would do whatever he could to help her through this. Travis desired to know how things worked, including the mind. It was rare that he took time to read, but when he did, he tried to read something that would increase his intellect. He was reading a new book about the habits and behaviors of successful people. It had spurred Travis's fascination to learn. Travis had been reading several articles about family loss to try and help April through her ordeal. He knew from his reading that the steps for grief and change, in general, were much alike. People have to pass through the stages of denial, anger, and then acceptance resulting in a new emotional state of awareness. Travis knew that someone like himself would move through these steps quickly, to get to the next state. He also knew that people had different rates of change. He had read that in the case of loss of a loved one, that there was another step in the process, grief. Travis and Zed would have to let April experience that emotion for her to heal. He and Zed would be supportive of April. He knew she was very motivated and now had a lot to look forward to. She had a great opportunity to finish her education without fear of economics. She also had a great new job, which may or may not end up being a career. The new job would definitely give her the opportunity to use her new skills.

What Travis did not know was that April was now anxious to get started on a new life. She had accepted that she had lost her family and realized that they were not coming back. She was determined to remember her great parents, but to work on closing that chapter, turn the page, and immerse herself in her new life. Travis, and even Zed, had been very supportive of her, but it was time to move on. She was surprised and pleased that Travis and Matt had given her new opportunities to pursue a happy life.

She had a solid education and a career path, but she had a desire for more. She had done her best to hide her secret desires. At Matt's suggestion, she had taken some counseling after her loss. She was careful not to move too fast towards any new relationship, and she wanted to make sure that her emotions were real and not mistaken gratefulness. She did not want a codependent relationship with anyone. The feelings she had for Travis before that horrible night had not subsided. Travis was a complicated guy, and she was not sure that he would be interested. She also knew that their age difference would be perceived as a roadblock. Travis might be older, but he was one of the most dynamic people April had ever met. She knew deep in her soul that she loved this big bear. She had been wrestling for a couple of weeks now as to how best to approach him and let him know how she felt. Even now as she lay in her room with the TV playing as a distraction, her heart pounding, she was trying to work up the courage to let Travis know how she felt.

She heard Travis's truck come in the driveway. She heard him come in and quietly move past her door. She heard him go into his room. Damn, she had hoped he would knock on her door. She finally drifted off into a light sleep. She remembered thinking just before she lost consciousness, tomorrow, tomorrow she would tell him…

Travis headed off to bed, tossing off his clothes down to his jockey shorts. He paused in front of the full-length mirror in the bathroom. Wow, he was getting old. Too many pizzas, long work nights, and gravity had not been kind. Travis could even see age creeping into his face. He was starting to see lines in his face. That face reminded him of someone? Wow, was that his dad looking back at himself! Travis fell into bed and sleep came quickly. He went straight to sleep, which did not happen very often. Travis slept almost 5 hours straight. This was very uncommon for him.

He woke up and began thinking about yesterday's events. He could not wait to get back to the shop. It was only 3:00 AM, and he thought for a moment about going to the shop. He often went in early when he could not sleep. He was always surprised how much he could get done when no one else was around to bug him. Matt had given him keys to the dealership years ago and let Travis work whatever hours he wanted. Travis always got things done on time, on budget and with impeccable quality. Now he was working for himself! With that thought there was no going back to sleep. Travis rose and felt all the age of his body at once remind him how old he was. He decided that he would go to the spa and let his aching body and mind soak a bit.

Travis slipped out to the kitchen in his underwear to grab a can of diet soda. April's room was around the corner from the kitchen, and he did not hear the TV. He hoped she was getting some needed sleep. Travis slipped back to his room, dropped the rest of his clothes and went out the sliding door toward the Hot Tub. He lifted the lid and steam rose from the hot water into the cool night air. A slight smell of bromine and aroma treatment hit his nose. He also used Lavender smelling salts. The hot tub smelled clean and fresh. He eased down into the water and felt the delightful hot water surround his aching muscles. He could feel his muscles melt especially around his neck, which always seemed to carry the tension of the world.

He kept it at 101 degrees year round. In the winter it was a wonderful place to soak the coldness out of his body from working outside on heavy equipment. Whoever designed the first hot tub deserved a metal. This was about the best feeling a person could have with their clothes off. Well maybe not the best feeling. Travis did not have time for chasing women. They were way too complicated and time consuming for him. He knew that he could not stand to have a normal life of raising kids and weekend barbecues. He eased further down in the tub. He went deep enough covering everything except his head. He took a deep hard pull on the soda, set it on the side of the tub, and closed his eyes. All he could hear was the swirling sound of the pump and water. Wow, how could life be this good! How had he been this fortunate? Other than a bit lonely he had it made. Good friends and people to work with, a national record, a killer shop and all the parts he…. Travis drifted off to sleep again…

Travis did not hear the sliding door open… He did not see April slip his biker shirt off which she wore as a nightgown because it smelled like him… He almost did not feel her crawl into the spa until her leg brushed his….

CHAPTER 7:
OH, MY GOD!

Travis was startled and embarrassed as he awoke. Had April just climbed into the spa with him? Did she not see him out here? He felt April's leg brush his as she entered the tub. Travis did not say anything as he was almost afraid to talk. He could see in the early dim light that April was naked at least from the waist up. He could see her ample perky breast floating in and out of the water line. He was afraid to look, hell he was afraid to breathe.

A few awkward minutes passed, and April finally spoke. "Travis, I hope you don't mind. I could not sleep and wanted to talk with you. I came to knock on your door, but it was open. I heard the spa running, and it struck me how good it would feel. I know you come here when you can't sleep. Is it OK?"

Travis's mouth was dry. His thoughts raced, of course it's OK…was it OK? He was not sure. A beautiful young lady was at least half naked next to him! No… wait a minute, this was April. He wanted to make sure she knew he respected her as a friend, a person, a team member, and contributor. Travis did not know what to say. Finally, he stammered, "Sure that's cool. It does feel good."

He thought a few more minutes and then told her how much he respected her and her abilities…he could not keep himself from staring into her beautiful eyes. The face of an angel, but he could see a bit of devil in her smile in the pale gray night just before the sunrise.

April smiled and said, "I know that, relax Travis, I am a big girl, and I know what I am doing. I want to be next to you and I am very aware we are both naked as the day we came into the world. It just feels natural somehow."

Travis's mind was reeling! He did not want to even move. His mind was not on racing now. He could feel his heart pounding. She is naked under the water! What did she look like…? He immediately stopped expanding on those thoughts. He decided to close his eyes and think about what he wanted to do to the car. He could still hear his heart pounding. Blood was rushing to every part of his body and I mean every part of his body. Yeah, that's it...think about the racecar, and how the water injection would work. This worked for a few minutes. He was keeping his eyes held shut tight. He had to respect this girl. She had just experienced a life changing event. He was a good guy. He must control his urges.

Suddenly his thoughts interrupted with April's voice, "Would it be OK if I moved closer to you? I really need you to hold me right now." Travis hesitated, and considered his options. He decided to warn her that while he respected her, and cared for her, he was a man and she should consider her actions carefully.

He decided on his words and said, "April be careful what you ask for, you might get it." Travis used that statement a lot so April knew exactly what he was talking about. She did not hesitate, and moved quickly next to Travis. She raised his arm and April tucked into that tight nook under his arm. She pulled his arm down with his hand, placed his left arm around her body, and made a special point of putting his left hand on her left breast!

She had thought about this moment for months. She wanted to make sure that Travis knew that this was her idea, not his. She had secretly loved this man. He had more compassion, brains and more mental and physical energy than five guys her age. She knew he thought he was old and ugly, but all she saw was character, wisdom, and strength. Travis sat very stiff and careful for a few minutes, but finally the smell of April's soft blond hair, her tight, ample body pulled close to his and the feel of her delicate ample breast under his ruff mechanics hand forced him to give in. He finally melted into her presence.

He turned towards her to say one final protest of respect and she did not let him get it out. She immediately pressed her lips to his. The kiss started as lips only and then she parted her lips and pushed her tongue first against his lips, which quickly gave way to his open mouth.

Travis was a light switch type person. He was either on or off. He had done everything he could to keep the switch off, but the damn thing was on now. It was a closed circuit and the electricity was flowing. "Be careful what you ask for, you might get it" echoed in his mind.

Logic now gave way to passion. He had secretly loved and desired this girl for about a year now. Only in his deepest hidden thoughts had he dreamed about this moment. He would worry about downstream ramifications tomorrow. In fact he did not want this night to ever end.

He quickly reached over and pulled April onto his lap facing him. The kiss now became very passionate and almost violent. Combustion! He could now feel her beautiful shapely legs that were freshly shaved hug his body tightly. He was locked into a position between her thighs. The kiss broke, and Travis instantly moved his mouth to her neck, her breast, then back to her lips. Deep, hot, wet, sloppy kisses with darting tongues. He could hear their breath heavy and hearts pounding. While he was burying his mouth to her neck, her hands pulling him towards her, he heard her whisper in his ear, "Travis, I love you, and I have loved you for a long time now. I did not know how to tell you."

Travis stopped and looked deep into her eyes and spoke from his soul, "April deep down I have tried to fight this, but I love you too."

April said," Quit fighting it."

Travis again pulled her to him. Now he was at full attention and his piston and connecting rod quickly found her cylinder. He heard himself say. "Oh My God nothing can feel this good!"

He heard her gasp and say, "Yes it can and it is all yours Travis, take it."

Energy came from somewhere deep inside Travis and he began to shove his piston deep inside her cylinder. Natural lubricants started to flow. The RPM began to build until there was a frenzy of water spilling out the spa. April now leaned back still holding onto Travis's upper shoulders. Her long hair was touching the water and after several minutes of thrusts from his piston she felt the start of an orgasm that was like no other she had experienced. It was an orgasm driven from not only passion but true love making with someone you genuinely cared about. She could feel Travis deep inside her. She was surprised at just how deep his piston traveled. Still waters truly ran deep and large with Travis. This guy was definitely a high-powered big block... She was holding her breath now. Finally with four hard deep thrusts, Travis opened the door and April experienced streams of pleasure rapturing over her entire body. Her whole body had an orgasmic spasm and she could feel fluid rushing past his piston into the Hot Tub. Her orgasms came in multiple waves and each time she had a huge exasperated rush of air come from her body creating deep-throated moans.

April passionately said, "Travis don't stop, don't, oh my god NOTHING could FEEL THIS GOOD."

The intense spasms of her body were squeezing his piston. The friction was incredible, and only the lubrication of her fluids kept his piston from seizing. Travis could no longer take it and with a final stroke of his rod, and with his tongue deep in her mouth, he began flooding her with his own thick lubricant. He came and came and came until he was empty. They both felt not only the spasm of orgasm, but the release of sexual and life tension.

In Travis's other relationships the aftermath of sex was always how fast could he get out of there and back to his shop. In this case he did not want to let go of April. They both held tightly to each other like they were afraid to let go.

Travis looked deep into April's eyes and said," Did that just happen or am I in the dream of all dreams?" She did not say a word but instead buried her mouth on his in another deep kiss.

She responded, "Oh yeah, it happened."

Travis could not believe that his connecting rod was starting to get hard again… April suggested they go inside as the night sky was starting to turn gray as the sun was starting to come up.

She could not believe how passionate Travis was! How old was this guy? She had never seen anyone recover so fast. Travis did not want to let go so he picked April up from the spa, stepped out and carried her still kissing her into his house, his bed and his life. He held her tight and vowed never to let her go, and she was making no effort to get away. They made love twice more before the sun was fully up. Travis called Zed and said that they would not be in until noon and then returned to bed, the lovers wrapped themselves into each other, and both fell into a deep, deep sleep that neither of them had experienced. They both needed that sleep.

Several hours later Travis woke and saw that the clock was at noon! He first wondered if it all had been an intense dream, but he quickly realized April's soft, warm leg was wrapped around him. He could also feel her arm tucked under his and had her hand buried in his chest hair. He could feel her nestled into the nook of his neck. He moved and felt her tighten her grip on him. She did not want him to leave. He turned toward her and buried his tongue deep into her sleepy mouth. She opened her eyes and smiled while he was kissing her. She had worried as she drifted to sleep that Travis would have remorse in the morning. It was evident that this was not the case. Her tongue eagerly accepted his passion.

She felt him break the kiss and he threw back the covers and began exploring her entire body with his mouth and tongue. He quickly had his face buried deep in her. He had wanted to taste her for months. He loved her taste and the smell of their raw sex from the night before. He did not care, as they were both now beyond sharing everything with each other. As he buried his tongue into her beautiful woman, he quickly felt her spasm and pushed nice warm fluid from her body. It tasted almost like fruit juice! It was sexy and sweet. He lapped it up eagerly and dove in for more.

After she came several more times, he moved down her legs, licking her inner thighs. He then kissed her knees and finally, he pushed her legs giving her indications that he wanted her to roll onto her stomach. Travis wanted to explore every inch of this beautiful young woman. Travis then worked his way up her beautiful soft shapely legs to her beautiful ass. He then started to stroke his tongue along the crevice of her beautiful behind each time just a little deeper. As he heard her moan indicating that she was enjoying his efforts he licked deeper into her until he finally had it buried deep into her! Even here in her forbidden spot she tasted delicious. How could a woman taste so good? While continuing to bury his tongue in her beautiful ass he eased his thumb up into her in search of her "G" spot. He began thrusting his hand in and out with the same tempo as his tongue and made sure he used his thumb stroking her "G" spot and his other fingers on her clitoris.

He had studied women's anatomy just like he studied an engine. Soon he again felt her spasm over and over. The orgasm was not slow, but instant and violent. She was openly gasping and pushing her body against his mouth and hand. She thought, it felt so good, couldn't he go deeper. She loved the loving, and the lusty feeling of him ravaging her body. At that moment she knew what she wanted. She wanted to feel his seed in every orifice of her body.

She turned over and pulled Travis's head up and said," Kiss me and let me taste us! Please bury that rod of yours into me! Travis did not hesitate and shoved his rod into her tight wet body. She gasped for air at first and then loudly announced another orgasm.

Spasm of pleasure spread through her body opening her body into an accepting mode. Travis grabbed her by the ankles and spread her beautiful legs so he could see her whole sexy body. April looked deep into his eyes and said," Go ahead, push into me!"

Travis buried himself deep into her, both of them let hot air out of their lungs as they did. Finally, he could feel himself bottom out on her beautiful body. He could feel her soft silky legs in his hands. He began pounding into her with all of his strength. Each time he thrust he could feel her body pull him in. She kept repeating the word, "Yes, Yes, Yes," as he continued pounding her. He could feel sweat start pouring from his head. He could feel another orgasm deep inside him. He looked deep into April's eyes and he said, "Cum with me honey." He instantly felt her push her body harder against his thrust and her body squeeze his manhood.

April yelled loudly, "Fill me up Travis, please spray your cum inside me. I want all of it." With several more hard quick thrust, he exploded inside her with a loud moan from both of them.

Juices flowed from both of them into mutual hot love nectar that gushed from her warm body.

Travis collapsed on top of her. He was careful to keep his hands on her sides so that his weight was not fully on her. He was still inside her and they could feel their hearts pounding from the sexual work out. He had never felt so close to anyone before. They truly were one. He rolled off of her and she rolled with him so they were still in a tight embrace. They again fell fast asleep.

I guess Zed would have to be the only one in the new shop today. April and Travis both slept hard the rest of the afternoon. They slept a very deep cleansing sleep that would wash frustration and pain from both their minds.

They would make love four more times in a more traditional fashion that night. April would move into Travis' room and life the next day. They would start a spring /winter relationship that would last both of them the rest of their lives. Neither would ever feel lonely again. Tomorrow morning would start an entirely new chapter in both of their lives.

CHAPTER 8:
THE WORLD LOOKS DIFFERENT

Tuesday morning came too quick. Travis awoke and had to pinch himself to make sure it had not all been a very wonderful and erotic dream. However, as he opened his eyes, there she was curled up next to him! Her hair was hanging over her face, but he could still see her pert lips slightly parted as she was breathing heavily . Wow, he still did not believe what had happened the day before. As Travis moved she moaned a bit, and her sleepy eyes came open. Travis was a little afraid that when she woke she would have remorse about sleeping with this old guy and scream!

April opened her eyes and said, "Hi honey, I have not slept that good in a long time."

Travis replied, "Yeah, me neither." Travis could not help but say, "Are you sorry now?"

She blinked several times, "No, are you?"

Travis replied, "No way, I am just trying to convince myself that you could be interested in a guy like me."

April replied," Well, come on back to bed, and I will prove it to you!"

Travis started to push back and say they both better get their butts to work, but then thought, "Am I nuts?" He then came back to bed for one more taste. He was always ready in the morning!

April pushed him back, crawled on top, and mounted quickly. No foreplay this time, as she was still hot from last night. April was also anxious to get to the new shop. Travis thought, damn she was so tight! He was a little raw from the night before as he was sure she was also. He knew the blood would quickly rush to both their private parts making the soreness a memory. She hammered down on his morning hardness. He could quickly feel her warm fluid flow down onto his male member! She started with her legs lying flat where he could caress them. They were so soft but firm. He matched every push down on his rod with an upward thrust so he could have maximum penetration. Each time he bottomed out he could hear their bodies slap together hard. She leaned down and gave him a long wet deep kiss without missing a beat.

Both Travis and April were moaning loudly. After the deep kiss, she paused for a minute and got up on the balls of her feet squatting over his hard cock. She used her beautiful legs and feet to now bounce quickly up and down on his rod! She was speed humping him! It was like she had kicked on the nitrous!

After she started that, the session only lasted a few more minutes. She had sweat rolling down her face from the sex work out. The last few cycles were deep, and finally, he again exploded into her with warm wet lubricants. She also came as soon as she felt the warm flood in her cylinder. When both were drained, Travis pulled her down to him for one deeper kiss. It lasted quite a while, and he could feel his manhood shrink and fall out of her warm body.

She rolled off and instantly headed to the bathroom and said, "Come on old man, you can wash my back."

In the shower, they had a bit of fun scrubbing the right places. Both were very satisfied and sore from all the activities. They quickly dressed and jumped into Travis's truck. April scooted right next to Travis. She was wearing jean cut offs, and she put his hand on her beautiful silky thigh. She pulled it right up to the top of her inner thigh, up against her shorts. He could feel her inner heat! Was he ever glad he had not ordered captain's chairs? As they rolled through their normal fast food joint, the drive through lady taking his order seemed a bit surprised that the order was not just for one! She even repeated it twice to make sure.

As he rolled to the window, he thought it unusual that not only the normal little gal collecting money was there, but other employees lurking to see who else the order was for. They were both surprised to see April next to him in the truck. April had her hand on his leg so that it was very plain to everyone that Travis was hers. The collection gal seemed disappointed in this! Wow, Travis was always kind to her but had no idea that he would have had a shot. It was too late for them now, as Travis had very little interest in the rest of the female world.

They rolled to the food delivery window and again to a gathering to see the "new girl." Travis was getting a bit embarrassed by all the attention, so he quickly grabbed their food and drink, and they headed off to work. Travis just looked at April and shrugged. "I had no idea," he said.

April said, "You always were a little blind at what you had to offer." She then stated, "You are off the market now, bud!"

Travis just smiled and said, "Ok, by me, babe." He was one happy man. They slammed down the food and drink as both felt like they had not eaten in a week and were very dehydrated! They had drained much fluid in the last 24 hours!

As they hit the gate, they could see that the lights were already on at the shop. Travis, then, began to worry how Zed was going to accept April and his newfound relationship. It did not take long to find out as Zed came out of the shop as they pulled up. Travis watched his face carefully as he turned off the dully to read his reaction. Zed quickly had a broad smile and said, "Damn April, do you have to sit in his lap?"

April turned red, and Travis blinked a couple of times. Had Travis really been missing the signals all this time? It sure did not seem to surprise Zed. As Travis got out of the truck, he asked Zed to join him in the office. April picked up on the signal to get lost and said she was going to get the mail. Travis followed Zed into the office, and they both sat down.

Travis broke the awkward silence by saying," Zed, I hope this is not something that comes between us as our friendship is vital."

Zed said, "Chill out, old man, I knew she was in love with you a year ago! When we were together all she talked about was how hard you worked, how smart you were, and how much she cared for you." Zed continued, "You have done a lot for both of us and the team really works."

Travis, again, blinked a couple of times and fumbled some words like, "Well, it has always been a joint effort and he could not have done it without the team."

Zed never had much time for drama then said, "Yeah ok, now let's build some race cars ." With that, they both headed for the shop.

Travis said as he was walking, "I want to try using window washer fluid in a water injection system. I think it will give us better intake cooling and a little bit of a power adder. If that works, we can play with adding more alcohol to the mixture." They might be able to bend some rules in gas only classes! They headed to the engine dyno to make the modifications. They fabricated a window washer pump into a water injection system using weed sprayers for nozzles! The whole thing cost less than $50! After completing the modifications, they made a dyno run and sure enough, the intake charge after the turbos dropped about 150 degrees! The exhaust dropped about 50 degrees, but the HP jumped almost 70HP! Wow, usually they were happy with a 3-5 HP gain. The combination produced more torque and at a lower RPM so it would require a torque converter change to a lower stall to take advantage. They would order up the converter, but would not install it until someone got closer to their new record. No use unveiling a competitive advantage until they needed it.

OK, next step: get ready for the Denver Drag Fever Race. Denver Dragway was all pro, no Mom and Pop operation like North Denver Dragway. It was a world class, all concrete, ¼ mile track. It has state of the art timing equipment and is an excellent venue. The Wyoming/Colorado racers always had an advantage at national events as they knew how to race high altitude. While overcharged engines were not as sensitive as naturally aspirated engines, a couple more degrees of cam and ignition timing made a big difference. It always took the coastal and Midwest racers a couple of days to get things sorted out. By that time they were usually on the trailer.

Zed and Travis decided to install the window washer injection system under the seat where no one could see it. No use giving away their secrets. If they used it in Denver, they would only use it in high gear as they did not want to optimize the torque rise till they had to. In racing, it is all about combinations. It is not just an engine thing. The whole car has to match. Engine, converter, transmission gear ratio, differential gear ratio and tire size all had to match. You wanted your engine 500 RPM over peak horsepower at the end of the track.

The challenge was converter stall out of the hole and top end gearing. Build too much power, and you will blow off the tires and run out of RPM too soon. Travis had found himself on the red line several times and still be 500 feet short of the finish line. That meant a rear end gear change. Not hard with a nine inch Ford but it still took an hour to swap out the pumpkin. A "pumpkin" is a drop out third member that held just the Ring and Pinion, as well as the possi or spool unit that locked up both the rear tires, so they turned at the same speed. Conventional cars use a "Differential" spider gear set which lets you turn one tire faster than the other when going around a corner. If you think about it, it makes sense when turning right that the left tire has to travel twice as far as the right tire going around the corner. It is the same for turning left. However, when you are trying to go straight down a race track, you want both tires to get the power equally, and you want the car to lift to transfer weight onto the rear tires for maximum traction. Oh yeah, you also had to have a spare pumpkin set. In fact, optimal is two, one lower and one higher gear ratio. Then you can match peak horsepower to the track. Altitude atmospheric pressure changes the torque curve. The parts to build a strong pumpkin were about $1500 as Travis used nothing but the best gears, nickel hardened, and special bearings. They also used a nickel alloy aluminum case to reduce weight to be strong and take the shock load of a 1500 HP engine unloading via a transmission brake all at once.

The transmission brake is what is used to power up and stage a drag car to be ready for launch. Back in the 60's and 70's, it was a manual transmission and a flywheel clutch assembly. Here you disconnected the engine from the transmission by pushing in on the clutch. You then raised the RPM of the engine up to a maximum in free rev and then "let the clutch fly." Racers used a pressure plate with heavy springs to engage the clutch as soon as the hammer dropped. This sent huge shock loads to the transmission and everything behind it. Racers were very good at finding the weak link between the engine flywheel and the tires that were sitting on the sticky concrete. You often find U-joints, transmission parts, drive lines, and even clutch parts embedded into the track or protection walls on the starting line. In fact, when Travis was still a hobby racer, he had to rebuild his manual transmission three times in one weekend! That's when he decided to move to an automatic and use a Transmission Brake.

Transmission brakes were now standard practice. It locks first and reverses gears inside the transmission and then you release the reverse clutch quickly. The first systems they built did not release fast enough and reacted too slow. Travis's team had been able to improve the solenoid technology by using some heavy equipment clutch modulation solenoids that were used to control rise and decay times for automatics in heavy equipment. They made a big improvement by just applying common sense engineering. The reverse clutch just could not "bleed off" pressure fast enough. They drilled the bleed off port out with a drill bit. It made the reverse a little sloppy but who cared. Reverse was only used in this application to get the car back to the starting line after a burnout. They would just raise the engine RPM up off idle, so the transmission pump provided more fluid. No real load, just move the car back after a burnout.

The automatic transmission brake system still shocked the rest of the powertrain, but Travis stalled first with a hand brake, to get the turbos spinning up. He knew that this would take all the slack out of the driveline and rear end before they unloaded at full torque. This is a much softer approach than a clutch car but still let the car leave very hard. It was less violent and with more control. Still, the fans would miss those giant wheel stands that were the signature of a stick car. An added feature of this trans brake set up is that in stage you could lock the transmission and throttle up so that the converter stalled and allowed the engine to build boost from the turbo exhaust backpressure. You could be at almost full boost leaving the line. In this case, the torque converter, transmission and rear end they had in the car would work just fine.

They would leave the 4:10 rear end gears which were really too tall for the Denver race track. They would just not use the full RPM band of the motor. In fact, Travis would short shift first gear (shift early) and save the motor. Remember, this was before the area of electronics and PC laptop tuning. You had to "feel" your way around the tune and Travis had a natural talent for knowing the sweet spot of an engine and a car. The dyno runs showed "Peak Torque" happened between 5500-6500 RPM. They would run a 1:73 first gear transmission, a 4500-RPM converter and 4:10 rear end with 17-33 tires. That should put them in the high 7's which adjusted for the 5000 feet of elevation would be mid 7:50 at sea level.

It took them several days to get the car just right. They would make a couple of different pumpkins and a shorter set of tires just in case. Next, they would have to set up the new truck and trailer, and they only had two weeks till the Denver event. They decided to buy a second set of tools for the trailer, because they were tired of loading and unloading the trailer every time they went to a race. Travis and Zed agreed to split the cost. Their sponsor had done enough. They made sure they were outfitted but did not replicate the entire shop capability.

Travis had been down the "Thrashing Mode" at the track before and learned a long time ago that rather than fighting it out on the track, it was sometimes better to watch, learn and regroup for the next race. A lot of money and resources could be burned up in a hurry by trying to make things work. As stated before, early in his racing career, Travis overhauled a four speed three times in a weekend! He had a solid transmission mount in an old Camaro and did not figure out for a couple of races that the clutch unload at 7000 RPM was too much shock for the u-joints without a rubber transmission mount to absorb some of the shock. Even though they were using titanium u-joints, it was not until they used a spare rubber mount to replace a cracked solid steel one out of desperation that they figured out it was enough cushion to soften the blow and that the u-joint would live.

The new trailer had everything it needed to overhaul the engine and transmission, but not enough to rebuild the whole car. It also had room to store a neat little surprise that Matt had included in the deal. A Golf cart that looked like a 40 Willys Pickup truck! The back was open and had a tailgate that could be let down to sit on. It was a retro cart with a warmed over two-cylinder engine that they could use to tow the car. Since horsepower was no longer an issue, Travis had installed a fully on board cooling system in the racecar as well as a 100-amp one-wire alternator. His goal was to keep things simple and self-sufficient, and the amount of power it took to run these things was a couple of pounds of boost at the worst. They would win many races because their turnaround time was much less than the other teams between races. Travis could be sitting back in the staging lanes in less than 10 minutes between rounds! They could check everything over, add a splash of fuel, perform a tweak or two, and then back to the lanes! Last but not least, the hauling trailer also had enough room for a small pit car or two full dressers! Of course, the team usually preferred the bikes.

CHAPTER 9:
TRAVEL IN THE NEW RIG

The night before the trip to Denver Drag way was uneventful. Travis, Zed and April all slept like logs. It had been a very emotional and physically challenging couple of weeks for all. Travis did his normal and woke up multiple times at night with his mind on nitrous running a million miles an hour. This time, however, he had April's tranquil, peaceful, beautiful face to look at which distracted his mind instantly. Although, when he first opened his eyes, it seemed like a RIM sleep dream state. Was she really lying next to him? How could he be that lucky? He fell back to sleep every time with a peaceful smile on his face.

He woke up 10 minutes before the alarm went off at 5:00 AM. Before Travis could get out of bed, April latched on to him and said, "Nope, you are not leaving yet, we have to sneak in a quickie so that you will be calm today! " Who was Travis to argue? He was very "ready" as sleeping next to her in a spoon position had his body almost always stiff and ready! This time, Travis was behind April lying sideways. The spooning position was a bit lazy, but very comfortable. As he entered her, she quickly became very wet, and he loved the way he bottomed out on her beautiful body. This morning they took it very slow, and Travis massaged her neck and back as they made love. He could feel her tighten and orgasm a couple of times. Finally, she pulled his hands around to her ample tight pert breast and said, "Squeeze them tight, squeeze out my orgasm."

Sure enough, as he gently applied pressure to her breast, he could feel her cylinder muscles contract and flood her channel. This sensation also sent him over the edge, and he pushed hard a final couple of strokes. While not fast and furious, the quality was every bit as good. The event ended in a flood of both of their lubricants. No time for the bed cleanup, they would just leave the covers open to let nature take its course! It's funny how even these natural acts took an engineering view in Travis's mind.

Travis and April showered together to save time, and that plan almost went to hell! Interestingly, April was the one pushing Travis to finish up as she wanted her man to concentrate on the upcoming race. That was the whole point of the quickie, well not the whole point! April was finding out that she had a whole new level of passion welling up inside her after she had come out of the closet with her love for Travis. Zed was a very virile young man, but his sexual skills were a bit selfish. It was lusty sex, but lacked the passion and longevity she and Travis had.

They finished up and headed for the loaded rig. They jumped in and headed down to the local fast food joint for breakfast. This time they had to go in as there was no way the new track rig was going through the drive up! As they went in, the morning crew recognized them but was surprised to see them. The regular young attendant said, "Taking it slow today?"

Travis answered," No, it is to go, but we have a new rig that won't fit through the drive through." Breakfast, of course, was delayed as the morning crew had to slip out and take a look at the new rig.

The manager stated, "Wow, the rig would look pretty cool with our store's logo on the side." He then said something fascinating, "Fast Food for Fast People" as a slogan! Travis did not mention anything but would file that in the back of his mind in case they ever needed a sponsor. OK, loaded up and finally on the road!

Travis was amazed how easily the new rig picked up the load. The turbo boost was picking up the load quickly and before he knew it, it was time to move up a gear. In fact, the engine was building so much torque, he was able to skip gears! Even coming to a stoplight, he often could just leave it in a higher gear and, as long as they did not come to a full stop, the engine would pick the load right back up. It seemed that 1100 RPM was the sweet spot. Travis would have to check the Air Fuel ratio of the turbo exhaust housing and compare it to the compressor wheel to see what ratio was most effective at spinning up. If they could apply this to the racecar, they could use an even lower stall tighter converter and give them more top end. This might allow them to narrow the RPM power band of the race engine, which would enable them to build more power, and maybe even use a lock up clutch in the converter to give them a synthetic third gear out of their two-speed transmission! Direct drive is the most efficient power transfer state, and this would provide them with a top end advantage that might surprise some folks. He opened his voice recorder to remember this. Zed overheard him and said, "Yeah that could work!"

There was good music coming out of the state of the art sound system in the truck. Zed was soon fast asleep in the back seat. It was a mid-sized diesel rig, but it was an extended four-door cab. April had her bare legs on Travis's lap, and he was finding it a bit difficult to concentrate on driving! He had his hand on her leg, and he soon began softly stroking her leg. It did not go unnoticed that his third leg was getting stiff as well. After a couple of hours of driving, and when April was sure that Zed was fast asleep, she began to rub her foot up and down Travis's member playfully! Travis surprised himself by feeling the flushness of red on his face! He quickly glanced in his cab mirror, and he could also see that Zed was fast asleep. Travis did not really know what to do! They did not have time to stop for a quickie as they had to get to the track in time for tech today. If they missed it they would not be able to hit the lanes early tomorrow morning for a test and tune. He decided to try and ignore the activity. It only took a few miles for him to decide that was not going to work very long. He looked over at April and sheepishly smiled and shrugged his shoulders. April smiled and stopped for a little while but soon found herself drifting back to her old habits. Oh man, there was the song again. "I like the way you…!" Now he really could not think!

When April had Travis's "full attention," she made a bold move. She switched ends and traded her legs for her head in his lap. Next thing Travis knew his connecting rod was hanging out! OMG, she now placed it firmly in her beautiful firm lips! She was an expert and slow deep, methodical strokes with just the right pressure applied by her soft wet, warm, pink tongue. As Travis could feel his human boost building up in his lower end, he quickly reached down the back of her shorts and found his way to her well-lubricated cylinder. Just a few thrust of his finger had very fluid rushes of her female lubricant rushing from her cavity. He moved his finger quickly the full length of her crevice. He knew the motion was the right one to make more rush of fluid, and he could feel her guttural moan while her lips were still around his pulsating rod. The combination of wild sensations pushed them both over the edge! Explosions of pleasure happened in both bodies! April swallowed every drop and looked up and said," Thank you for that salty treat!" Travis' face again flushed red. She was going to kill him, but what a way to go.

As the passion subsided just a bit, Travis glanced in the mirror, and Zed was still out like a light bulb turned off. Next, he glanced at the gauges and had another rush of shock come through his body. He was doing over 100 MPH!!!!! Wow, no speed governor on this rig! He quickly backed out of the throttle and glanced in the exterior mirror. They had been lucky, it was early, and the traffic was light. There are no red or blue lights behind them! As a side benefit, they were only 30 minutes from the track. Somehow… they had gone 100 miles in just over an hour, oops! As the truck slowed, they heard Zed begin to move around in the back seat. He sat up and blinked the sleep from his eyes. Once he came around, he looked around and realized that they were close to the track! Zed said, "Wow, how long was I out?"

Travis recovered nicely, by simply replying, "Zed, wait till you drive this rig! It drives itself."

Zed's young mind moved forward quickly. Zed's next statement validated this, "I'm hungry."

April's face had a big smile and she said, "Well I am pretty full, but could stand a bio break." Travis just rolled his eyes and started watching for the next quick on/off truck stop. Travis had discovered a long time ago that picking the right exit for breaks could take 30% of the time spent in traveling. Everything to Travis was a process that could be improved! He saw a sign alongside the road, "Biggest Truck Stop in Colorado." That would be the target! Travis loved truck stops for some reason. Perhaps it was that they meant that they were on the road either headed for a racetrack or some big biker rally or car event. Besides they seem to know just what food you wanted, stuff to have for sale and all was available at a reasonable price and for a quick transaction.

He eased the rig off the highway and onto the off ramp. They pulled up in the trucker's area where it would be easy in and out driving. There was already a crowd gathering around the truck. The crew climbed out of the rig. Travis could see the trucker's attention quickly shifting to April's lovely, silky smooth body and beautiful blond hair. He did not blame them. It was nature at work. Men just did not have a chance. He could not keep his eyes off her either. He did, however, slip up and grab her hand. This show of affection surprised her a bit, but her grip tightened quickly. He made it very apparent to all that were looking that she was off the market. Zed had stopped to bullshit with a couple of the drivers, especially a rough but shapely female truck driver who had taken an interest in the rig, and April!

The rig drew extra attention as there were placards all over it stating, "Private use only, not for hire." This allowed Matt, the owner, to reduce insurance, taxes and licensing costs. Zed quickly finished up his conversations and caught up to them. "Let's eat, I am hungry." Travis smiled, and they all headed to the truck stop. Travis now had his hand in April's back pants pocket! He liked the feel of her soft behind through the denim cloth. This was a very different but nice feeling for Travis. Usually it was Zed that had the beauty in tow. They decided to grab a couple of burgers and some fries and get headed out. Travis had a diet soda, and Zed and April had sweet tea. Travis paid the bill and kept the receipt! This would all be covered by traveling expenses now! Wow, this was just pretty cool. Next, they emptied out the body tanks, topped off the rig tank, and were ready to roll. After a quick peek at the load, including the new golf cart to make sure all was secure, they jumped in and headed back out.

The entry to the highway was a smooth transition skipping gears as they accelerated in a mild but firm fashion back on the driving lane. Travis had never lost his appreciation of how well the diesel engine picked up the load. As he let the clutch out and applied throttle, he could hear the boost spin up and push massive amounts of air through the air-to-air after cooler and then stuff it down each hole of the engine. The engine governor measured RPM and the throttle applied spring pressure against the flyweights giving the injectors just the right amount of rack scroll to push just the right amount of fuel to the engine. There was also an Air Fuel Ratio (AFR) valve that had spring tension on one side and boost on the other. This kept the engine from over-fueling and pouring black smoke out. Travis always laughed when he saw a big rig with black smoke pouring out of the stack. He knew the trucker had taken the AFR out of the circuit as they thought it would give them more power. It did not. Max fuel was max fuel. The black smoke was just wasted partially burned fuel going out the stack. They were literally burning money. They also thought that you had to keep the engine wrapped up to make power. These supposedly hopped up engines were loud, burned oil, and wasted fuel.

Travis knew that if you used torque instead of just horsepower, you could move to the next higher gear quicker and actually accelerate faster. This was typically about 200 RPM above peak torque. The engine turbo would spin down as you let off the throttle and pulled the transmission out of gear. Travis had the timing perfect between shift points. He could hear the engine and just knew when to push the shifter into the next gear as the transmission speed matched road driveline speed. It was an art to shift without a clutch but one that was fun to learn. It was kind of like conducting an orchestra. The driver is the conductor telling the entire powertrain how to "play" the power music. Truly a sweet song when it is performed well.

It was another hour till they reached the track and it was very quiet as everyone had their own thoughts on what the next couple of days would bring. They had arrived early enough to get a good pit location where they were close to the end of the track. Travis would have no problem turning off the racecar at the finish line and then coast right into their pit. They would not even need to tow the car if they were lucky. Complication is your enemy when you are racing. The car is complicated enough to worry about. Keep everything as simple as possible around the act of running the car down the track. While they were unloading and setting up, the new rig drew lots of attention. It was truly a sweet rig, and Zed had the tunes cranked. There was a hydraulic fold out awning over the car that gave nice shade and protected the car from sun heat or rain if they were that unlucky. They set out the chairs, unloaded the car, covered the tires and had their entire camp set up in about 30 minutes! Wow, this was a nice rig! They had the car up on jack stands and had done an initial walk around to make sure all was ready to go.

Zed checked the tire pressure front and rear. He left the slicks at 10 psi and they would not do the final tire pressure setting until 15 minutes before the lanes opened. Then they would warm up the car including spinning the rear end to get the oil warm. Again, consistency, consistency, consistency was key to winning races. Control everything you could. Travis had been asked many times why he loved this all-consuming sport. Part of it was that you had the challenge of controlling the uncontrollable. Every racer will tell you that the car is right when you are just barely on the edge of control between traction and power. The rest of the process was technical design, innovation, competition and of course, most racers struggled with economics.

Most drivers liked one thing the most, the opportunity to show off. Travis loved that part too, especially the burnout to heat up the tires. He had a tendency to hang on to the throttle a little longer than most. He loved the way the car sounded and slid sideways during the burnout. He also liked when he lifted the pedal, the tires would rotate about two revolutions and then grab like crazy as the RPM dropped to match tire and road speed. You knew it was right when you heard that loud chirp at the end of the burnout as the tires engaged the pavement. That moment was still a couple of hours away.

The team usually had no time, but this time they actually had time to chill out! They set the chairs in front of the racecar and actually had time to watch the racers coming in. Zed had already run the car down and had the technical inspection completed. Travis was a 6.90 ET license driver, so all was good. April sat in the middle, and she and Travis held hands. That was different but felt very good for Travis. He did get some funny looks from the folks that passed as it was a bit of a spring, fall relationship! The racers that knew him all had big smiles on their faces as they knew that Travis worked hard, was a fierce competitor, but a good guy and was the first one to help another racer in need. The common knowledge was that Travis deserved something like this. Zed set out a fourth chair, and when Travis had a questioning look on his face, Zed just replied, "Hey gotta be ready" with a big smile.

They were positioned high on the track. The return road had been built with an intentional 3 % grade up to help the racers slow down after completing the 1/4-mile. Because they were close to the end, they were high enough to have a venue that overlooked the whole track. Watching the activity was fascinating. The racers were unloading their cars and setting up their camps, all around them. Sometimes Travis missed the open trailer grassroots days where they, many times, surprised much bigger operations from the platform of their home made built tandem axle trailer! Travis put his head back and his greasy old "I Love my Hooker Headers Hat" slid down over his eyes. He could smell his own sweat in the sweatband of his old hat. It was his lucky hat, and he had been very fortunate lately.

April was rubbing his neck, and it had become one of those rare times when Travis felt truly content. He felt her soft hands on his neck. He could hear the sounds of race car engines starting, and the cool breeze of late morning, He even dozed off for about 20 minutes. He came to life when he heard a very familiar voice call out "Holly Shit what the Hell is this?" He did not even open his eyes, and he knew it was his friend of 20 years, Bubba Greenwood.

Travis replied, "Well the only competition here is that piece of shit Vega some big guy has. We all know that is nothing to worry about so might as well take a nap!"

Bubba kicked his buddy's feet from under Travis and Travis jumped up and tackled Bubba. "How the hell ya been man?" Bubba took a long look at the new rig, and his eyes settled on April for a little too long of a look.

Bubba replied, "Not near as good as it is for you!" April blushed and gave Bubba the bird, at which he laughed. Actually, Bubba had heard about April's folks and sent a huge arrangement of flowers and called to offer his support right after it happened. Bubba and April were close friends, and they were always joking around. Bubba gave April a Bubba hug, and you could see it was very welcome. Travis could count on his right hands the people in his life that he truly trusted and Bubba was number one on the list. Bubba said, "OK, come show me this rig…" Travis gave him the grand tour including getting him a soda. They all sat down, and Bubba took the extra chair. Not exactly what Zed had in mind, but he loved Bubba too. There was only a few minutes left until they would have to start getting the car ready for time trials. Bubba asked, "Anything new on the car?"

Travis just smiled. Yes, Bubba was a very close friend, but not that close! Travis just said," We might have a couple of surprises for you. "

April came out and sat on Travis's lap. She was still in her cut offs and Travis put one hand on her bare leg and the other in her pants pocket. He wanted it very clear to anyone around that this was his territory! Bubba looked at the scene and shook his head and said, "Lucky bastard."

There was a call on the loudspeaker that their class was being called to staging lanes 7 and 8. Travis and his crew snapped into action. Travis started putting on his seven-layer fire suit. He always waited until the last minute to put it on because it was very hot to wear. It had saved many racers' lives, but it was a beast to wear. To boot, Travis had gotten black for a color so it would not show the grease from quick changes to the car. He completed lacing his shoes, and then went over and started to ease himself down in the car. The car was a tight fit, which was not comfortable but a safe, tight fit. The frame had been custom built for Travis's larger frame and ample body. In the event of a wreck, and you do go over the high side (Wreck and roll), you don't want to be bouncing around inside a loose cockpit. NCRA rules meant that you had to wear a six-point harness. A 3-inch lap belt, 2-inch shoulder harnesses, one for each side, one coming up from the floor via the middle (Anti-Submarine belt), and the last one attaches to the helmet, so your head is limited from bouncing around. It takes a while to get all of this done, and April helped get Travis in. April kissed him on the helmet when done.

Travis was all business now, so it almost went unnoticed but he did look up and smile at her beautiful face. Travis is a fortunate guy indeed. Zed was bringing over the golf cart to hook up and tow the Altered to the staging lanes. Travis always wanted to be one of the first in line, so he did not have to be in the back of the line too long. Even up here in Colorado, where the air is cooler and very little humidity, the suit is very hot. Travis could not even imagine racing in high humidity, like Florida or the Midwest. However, he did not want to be first as he wanted to watch a few racers make runs so he could size up the track.

As Travis watched Zed hook up the golf cart, Travis had to smile. The golf cart is a kick in the ass! It was the pit and tow vehicle that came with the new rig. A company out east makes a Golf cart body kit that has a 40 Willis pickup look. The bed was open on the back with a rumble seat. There was room for two up front and two in the back. It had a small toolbox area as there was always a chance for last minute adjustments. That was rare, and Travis wanted predictable consistency. The guys that were always messing with their cars in the lanes usually ended up on the trailer in the first round. When it is right, just leave the damn thing alone. April sat in the back and kept her foot on the tow rope to maintain the slack as Zed towed the car up. It was a smooth operation with everyone knowing how it works and what to do. They were in line third from the front. Travis refreshed himself on all the controls in the cockpit. He was ready.

He did not plan to hit the water injection on the first pass. They wanted a track baseline first. He had a limited view of the track as the slower cars ran, but he did not see any burnout oil downs. Damn, he could feel his bladder filling up! He should have emptied it one more time. Luckily the cars moved quickly, and Denver DragWay was a very efficient operation. He could see the lanes next to him empty, Zed and April were getting ready and making final tire pressure adjustment. Zed came up and said, "Still pretty cold, so I dropped to 9 ½ PSI in the slicks." Travis gave him a thumbs up. It was time to start it up and be ready to move on to the race track.

CHAPTER 10:
IT'S ALIVE

As Travis pulled on the hand brake and eased the transmission in gear, he felt a solid engagement and eased up on the brake handle. All gauges are normal. He eased into the burnout box watching Zed's instructions and hand signals. He felt the bounce of the water trough and then just pulled to the edge of the burnout out box till Zed waved to stop. Perfect…what a team. Travis pulled hard on the brake and started to stall the engine up a bit against the torque converter until he saw the boost start to climb. He was in second gear. He released the brake and punched the throttle to about halfway. The engine responded instantly and boost rose to about 15 PSI. He felt the car move up higher as the tires began to violently spin and grow from centrifugal speed. He could smell the tire smoke. The back of the car made a little jig to the left, and Travis could hear the engine and turbos scream as they spun up! It was an incredible feeling. When he again saw the temp gauge come off of the cold peg, he eased off of the throttle and got that satisfying jerk and load tire chirp when the hot tires engaged the track as he was slowing.

He came to a stop and started to back up. He was not to the 1/8-mile marker, but he could see it! He began to back up, and April appeared on his left side as always. Even though she was tanned, in her tight fitting shorts, and white tennis shoes, it was business for both of them. She backed him up right into his tire tracks. He could see the lights again now. He slipped it in neutral and cleared the engine out with a quick blip of the throttle. He did not even look at the other car. His process would not be rushed, and he would be consistent.

It did not matter if it was a time trial or an elimination race. He used the same process every time. Consistency was the name of the game. He dropped it back into low. He would power brake it up against the converter by holding the brake while pressing on the throttle. He eased into the staging lights. When the first light came on, he jammed on the brakes, and ran the throttle up a bit more to build more boost. He could hear the turbo's spinning up, and the starting official was waving at him impatiently . Patience guys, it will be worth it. The second light came on, Travis slammed on the transmission brake and buried the throttle. The boost gauge was bouncing off 25 PSI. His eyes instantly went to the second of the three yellow lights on the tree. As soon as he saw the second light go off, he let go of the transmission brake. The car leaped out of the gate, and again the shift light came on way too fast it seemed. Travis hit the air shifter button, and the transmission slammed into second gear. He felt a slight jig to the right as it hit second, but nothing too scary. Before he knew it, the tach was at 7000, and the shift light was on again as he was going through the traps. He was flying down the track. Never saw the other car. He eased down on the brake and popped the chute, and killed the engine. It was easier to slow down this time as the 3% uphill grade shut down area helped. Travis eased the car around the second turn off lane.

There were four turnouts at Denver Drag Way as they ran Top Fuel cars here and needed more run out room. He had used the third. Hopefully, it was not because he had gone slower! Travis's mind was racing. How did it do? It sure felt good. The car came to a stop and for a few seconds, Travis could again only hear his heart pounding and his hard breathing. Damn, that was fun, almost as good as sex! It took a few minutes for his crew to catch up and he instantly knew that it was a good run as his team was smiling ear to ear. Travis snapped off the belts and eased up out of the seat. He pulled his helmet off just in time to hear the announcer say, "Well, that was worth the wait!" That pass was .02 under the national class record! They had run a 7.35 and 180 MPH at 5500 feet of elevation! Wow, Travis had not even used the water injection yet. Maybe they would save that for a later date down the road. April gave Travis a big wet kiss, which he gratefully accepted. Zed again steered the car as April drove the golf cart. Travis sat on the back and used his foot to keep the slack out of the rope. It was a short tow, and they were in their pit. Travis was peeling off his suit when Bubba showed up.

Bubba said, "What the hell, you set a new class record for your first pass! Really…did you have to let it all hang out on the first pass? Don't you think you should sandbag a bit?"

Travis looked up with a shit-eating grin and said, "Who says that is all there is?" Travis asked," How did you do on your first pass?"

Bubba had a door slammer 1970 Vega wagon and ran the slower class. Bubba said, "I was on the money at 9 :90 ET at 120MPH."

Travis said, "120, how soon did you let off to get that low a MPH." Bubba just smiled and started back to his pit. Both teams had to get ready for the next runs.

In the next two time trials, their car would run a 7:30 and a 7:40 all around the 180 MPH mark. They had backed up the first pass, and it was a national event so the new record of 7:30 was set which was a full .06 under their index. This would give Travis a huge advantage if he could repeat it over his competition. In the first elimination round, Travis pulled a door slammer for a competitor. This would be hard to do. Travis ran AA/Altered, which is in the NCRA competitive eliminator group. Competition Eliminator was a set of high tech classes, where you were allowed to use all the innovation, physics and tricks they could to build odd, but fast combinations. You had to build by the rules but, unlike bracket racing, you were allowed to run under the established index for your class. All the cars have specific weight breaks (LBS per cubic inch), and specific rules for building the car. Competitors could pay a fee, $2000, to challenge another racer. If challenged, there would be a teardown and car inspection to make sure it met the rules. The car was also weighed to make sure the LBS per Cubic inch were met as well. All national event winners were torn down and inspected. Competition Eliminator classes, of which there were over 30, ran against each other using an indexing system set by NCRA. Again, much like bracket racing except you could run under your index as long as the car met the class rules! When the record became too far under the index, the index would be adjusted. That's why you wanted to keep a little in reserve if possible.

In today's case, Travis's Altered was running under the record, and about .06 faster than the index. This would give him a huge advantage, but it was no time to sleep. In their first round, they would run a 69 Camaro, running BB/ Gas with an Index of 9.60. The Camaro was running about .01 under his index. Travis's index was 8.0, and he was running .06-.07 under. The lights were set up to have Travis wait 1.6 seconds after the Camaro had left! This seems like an eternity when the car is sitting on the transmission brake screaming at you at full boost. Travis knew that transmission and engine heat could be a real issue.

This race weekend would bake the transmission, and they would have to rebuild it after the race. They used a special Power Glide, which Travis could rebuild in his sleep. Travis also knew the Camaro would have a "little extra" they would use if needed. He knew that they would need everything they could get to out run the AA/Altered.

Travis was 4th in line waiting for his elimination to run. They had lanes six and seven again. Travis had lane choice because he was low ET and he chose the right lane. When they introduced themselves to the Camaro crew, he was not surprised to see that it was a woman, a nice looking one at that. April had no reaction when Travis introduced himself to his competitor and shook her hand. She had nothing to worry about, Travis was professional, and she knew she had no real competition from her. Travis was about to bury the competitor. April knew he would do his best to blow the Camaro in the weeds, but tried not to get NCRA's attention. They would like to enjoy running that far under the index for a while.

Travis was first to do a burnout. He did not do as long of one this time as he knew the heat was going to be an issue. April guided him back into his tracks again, damn she looked good in those shorts. He then cleared the motor with a neutral throttle blip. The Camaro was done with her burnout, and they were both headed into the staging lights. Travis let the Camaro go in first. He would make her wait a bit this time. She could see what it felt like. First light on, power brakes up the turbos…Ease into the second light…it is on. This time Travis did not slam the throttle down but eased it down as he knew he would have plenty of time to get the motor to boost. He now had eyes on the second light. He saw the Camaro leave out of the corner of his eye. The engine is screaming now…Second light on and he let go of the transmission brake switch!

The Altered leaped out to the gate again, and just after he shifted to second, he caught the Camaro. Wow, that did not take long! Travis knew he would pull on her at top end. When the tach hit 6500 RPM, he backed off as he went through the traps. His win light came on, and all was good. As he got his helmet off, the crew was there. Zed said," Damn man, did you have to beat her that bad, she was cute."

Travis looked over at the Camaro driver, she was pretty dejected. She had her helmet off and had restarted the car to return to the pits. She did not even look at Travis when she drove by as she knew she was headed for the trailer and her day was over. Travis turned to April, who had a smile on her face, and asked," How bad?"

April told him, "Well, you ran a 7:40 and she ran a 9:45. Even with her 1.60 handicap, you had her by 100 feet at the end. You passed her like she was standing still about half-track."

Travis smiled, one down and on to the next round. There were 40 Competition Eliminator cars in this class. Now there were only 20 left. Back to the pits and check the car out. This round they had some time to check everything out. The next round was with half the cars. All classes would be faster. In the fourth round, they would again have more time as they would also run a round of Pro cars, Top Fuel, Top Funny car, and Pro Stock. Travis had a particular inspection process for the car. In fact, he had it documented. He had a sheet with steps to make sure every potential critical part on the car was inspected. He tracked the wear and tear so he could predict potential problem areas before they became problems.

He had done the same thing with heavy equipment, and it had proven to be a tool that customers loved. In many cases when he was still turning wrenches, his customers would pay field rates to have Travis do an inspection once a month on their fleet. He would still do that for a couple of his largest mining customers. He was also going to do fall inspections after the race season to help customers identify issues to be repaired, rebuilt, or replaced over the winter.

While inspecting the Altered, Travis did not like the smell of the transmission fluid. As he rubbed the fluid between his fingers it was gritty. He could tell that the fluid has clutch material in it! He turned to Zed and said. Let's get it up and change the transmission fluid and drain the converter. Zed knew exactly where to jack the car up, and where to put the stands. It took him less than 10 minutes to have it up in the air. Travis threw on a work shirt, started the air compressor, had the right tools out, and April had a new transmission filter and transmission fluid ready to go by the time Zed had the car up. Travis rolled under with a clean white towel and clean drain pan. He would remove the drain plug, and filter the old oil through the white rag to capture and inspect the particles that came out. He wanted to make sure there were no big chunks of metal indicating hard component wear. He also kept a sample of the oil on which he would have the dealer do a fluid analysis sample later, measuring oil condition and part per million elements analysis. This would tell Travis how his clutch material was holding up. No major particles, but the oil was very dark and burnt.

Because this was an Altered, a couple of quick fasteners and the team had full access to the bottom of the engine and transmission. Travis decided to go ahead and pull the transmission pan and clean it out. He had it off in seconds using a 3/8 impact and a ½ socket. April was already going after a new gasket. Travis came out from under the car with a pan in hand. He and Zed went into the trailer. The generator was running now, and the inside of the trailer had great lights. Travis and Zed inspected the pan looking for clues. Sure enough, there was more clutch material in the front of the pan then the rear. This meant the first and reverse clutches used by the transmission brake were the source of the wear. Travis decided to turn the clutch pressures up a bit to keep them from slipping. Zed asked, "Do we need to drain the converter?"

Travis replied, "No we are OK, the 6 quarts we put back in will raise the viscosity back to where we need to be. The filter should have caught any debris. We will change both the internal and external filters, however, just to make sure."

April headed to get a new internal filter and the red thread lock tight. This was one well-trained crew, and the new trailer was organized just right. In the old days, they would be digging through boxes or making mad dashes to whatever parts store they could find. They had the whole thing buttoned back up, and the car was running to circulate the new oil in 45 minutes.

Bubba had come by once, and he and Travis had a quick conversation. Travis said, "How did you do?"

Bubba said, "No worries .006 light, which was almost perfect and had him by about a car length at the end. I ran a 9:96, on a 9:90 index. I noticed you strapped it on the Camaro!"

Travis replied, "Yep, she will be home early today."

The next round they were up against a rear engine dragster, which would be closer to a heads up race. Travis had the dragster again at half-track, and had another 7:50 run. Inspections showed no issues. Now they were down to 10 cars. They had time to relax a little before the next round. Travis sat looking at the beautiful sunny day in Colorado, and his eyes drifted to the sun shining on April's hair and fair skin. She turned to Travis and asked, "What are you smiling about?"

Travis said, "Are you kidding me? I am living the dream. I am making a living doing what I love with who I love!"

Zed popped in and said." Awww Travis, I know I am good looking, but I am not marrying you." Travis threw his empty soda can at him, and they all laughed.

In the next round, Travis drew the record holder of BB/Altered which would be a real test. It was a pretty close race but Travis ran him down at the 1000-foot mark. He had decided he would use the water injection if needed in high gear in the upcoming races but it was not necessary. If he needed it this time he would use a manual button. Later, when they needed it, they would have it come on automatically. Travis would put a normally open switch in the high gear clutch port, and when the clutch pressured up, it would automatically close the switch and turn on the pump for water injection.

The inspection was good. The next round they ran another door slammer, a supercharged Mustang who had won on a red light. April had kept track of all the cars in the competition eliminator, and she reported that this car was right on the index all day. Even in practice rounds the car only had one pass under the index, and that was only a .01 under. They should have no trouble, but the team took nothing for granted.

The Mustang red lite, as they knew that a good light was the only way they had a chance. Travis still caught them at half-track. He let off at 6500 RPM and ran another 7.55 ET. This left five cars, and Travis was low ET of the cars left, so he got the bye round! In the bye round, (the only car running) they went through the same full exercise, but Travis did not run the engine up on the transmission brake as high. The car ran at 7:60. They had made the semi-final round! They had a lucky break as during the quarterfinals a rear engine dragster won, but broke in the process, which meant that there were only two cars left!

That meant that they were now to be in the final round! Even Travis was nervous. He had only made a dozen final rounds in the 20 years he had raced, and this one came too easy. They had plenty of time, as they were running another series of pros and the finals were not till tomorrow. Tonight, they would go over every inch of the car and then have some fun. The fun would be limited however as they had just looked at the ladder sheet. (A latter sheet is the track posting of who races who and who beats who). Their final round would be with another woman, but this one was also a national record holder in BB/Altered. April said she had been running .04-.05 under her index all day. It was a destroked alcohol powered big block Chevy. This was going to be a race.

CHAPTER 11:
THE FINAL ROUND

The team was on a natural high. They had beat off all competitors and even had a bye round! The car had performed flawlessly. As they closed up the rig, they realized their only real form of transportation was the golf cart! They would have to figure a way to get a couple of the bikes in there, so they had a way to get around. Bubba came over and offered to give them a ride and April came up with an excellent idea," Let me go with Bubba and get some stuff to have a barbecue in the pits." The rig had plenty of capability, as they had thrown on the propane grill. Zed switched on the outside work lights and cranked up the stereo. Next thing you know about 20 folks were hanging around.

Travis gave April a $100 and said, "get these folks some food and refreshments!" April and Bubba took off, and Zed started heating up the grill.

Chairs and people were gathering and the bench racing started. Travis and Zed covered the car. Hospitality was one thing, but no use giving the ranch away. Most of the technical discussions were about how to make a turbo car work. Travis shared enough to keep it interesting, but no discussion of timing retard in high or water injection. Those aces, he would keep in the hole. About 45 minutes later April and Bubba were back, and Zed started grilling. April was a good hostess, but Travis was right there helping to do what she asked. He was not going to take this beautiful lady for granted!

Denver Drag Way did not allow alcohol, which was no problem as everybody wanted to stay sharp for the finals tomorrow anyway. Travis was surprised to find the first round Camaro girl loser in the group! She said she decided to stay and see if she could learn anything. She was sitting with Zed who slipped Travis a sheepish grin. Yeah, he could teach her a FEW THINGS!

About an hour into this impromptu event the track owner showed up to make sure there was no drinking going on. His troubled face quickly went to a smile when he could see that it was, in fact, a clean affair with no alcohol. He ended up sitting next to Travis, and as he was stuffing a third grilled burger down, he asked Travis why it took him so long to stage. Travis explained to him how a turbo worked and that it took a few seconds for the exhaust gas to generate enough energy to get the turbos spinning. Travis explained that stalling the converter was the trick. The owner shook his head positively and said he would give the NCRA starter a heads up. Travis thanked him and asked if he wanted another burger? He said no and thanks and headed off to some other pit parties to make sure they were in line. It was his ass on the line with the insurance. He would let a few quiet beers inside the trailer slide, but nothing outside in the open.

When everyone was full, April plopped down in Travis's lap and put a blanket over them. The cold Colorado night air was beginning to bite at everyone's noses. About 10:00 there were yawns all around and all decided to get a good night's sleep? Zed said, "See you in the morning boss" and slipped away with Miss Camaro. No surprise there.

Travis said, "Be here by 7:00, Zed." Travis did not worry, Zed was very dependable, and he knew the drill on finals day. He would have Miss Camaro worn out by midnight anyway. Travis did not mind at all as it left the rig to him and April. April smiled as Zed left and began picking up and saying her goodbyes to all. She winked at Travis as he was picking up the last of the mess. She said, "Hey, I am going to go jump in the shower, will you wash my back in a couple of minutes?"

All of a sudden Travis had new energy to put into cleaning up the pit area! He thought it quite funny that the last song on the stereo was hard rock, something about her having her man by the Balls. Yes, she did, and it was OK with him. With the doors locked Travis was quick to peel his clothes off. He caught a glimpse of himself in the bathroom mirror. He still was not too sure what she wanted with an old fart like him. He had decided that he was not going to question a good thing. He had learned a long time ago that courtesy was the first priority, but when the candy store was obviously open, better make sure you left the candy owner with a smile.

Travis got into the shower with April, it was a little tight, but Travis had room to maneuver. He started by indeed scrubbing her back. He also washed her hair and took his time rubbing her head. He knew how good that felt to him. He massaged her neck and then worked his way down and around to her beautiful pert breast. He made sure they were really clean! April was making sure other parts of Travis were clean as well. There were some primitive groans going on, but Travis was not going to let this end in the shower. He dropped his hands to her bald beautiful love triangle, and he soaped it up real well. He slowly worked his clean fingers into her warm tunnel. He slipped his middle finger in and out slowly at first, then faster till he could feel her start her first of many orgasms. She pushed herself back on Travis's hard member. He could tell she was trying to line it up for entry! He diverted this trick as he wanted to make this a 500 mile marathon, not a drag race. Her knees buckled with the second orgasm and she turned around and gave him a deep wet kiss.

The warm water that had been pouring over them was starting to run cooler. They were running out of hot water. They had to remember they were in an RV! They shut the shower off and took turns playfully drying each other off. They retired to the sleeping quarters where they had a queen sized mattress. Matt has spared no expense to make sure his team got a good night's sleep. Zed would be sharing a sleeping bag in a tent tonight, but he would be just as happy. As they climbed into bed, Travis faced April, and stroked her hair with both hands and stared deeply into those beautiful blue eyes. He said quietly, "April honey, I love you more than air itself." With that, she buried her tongue deep into Travis's mouth. They could both taste passion and toothpaste ! Both always made sure they were kissing fresh. They kissed for a long time, until Travis began moving his kisses down her face, and then neck. He spent time there in the nook of her neck. He ran his tongue all around her neck, she tasted so good. She was moaning as he worked his way down her neck to her left breast. He filled his mouth with her breast softly at first but as he moved to the right he sucked harder, and she pulled his head deep onto her breast. Travis had worked his hand down to her now puffy lips where he had worked his middle finger up into her wet channel. He knew from this angle he was hitting the front G spot. He did not attack it, but instead caressed it and he began licking his way down her hard belly. He spent his time here too, as he could feel her building up to another orgasm. He timed it so that his warm tongue hit her clitoris just as her orgasm started. He made sure he used long soft licks on her crevice making sure he went the full length every time. Each time he hit her clitoris he could feel her arch her back and spasm in delight. Travis finally let the animal in him take over, and he buried his mouth into April. He was doing his best to lick her navel… from the inside. After several more orgasm, he slowed, and he could wait no longer. He was rock hard and red with fresh blood flow. He gave her one last wet kiss to make sure it was lubricated as she was very tight.

He eased up her body sliding his member into her hot hole just as he eased his tongue into her wet mouth. He could feel her moans now in his mouth. He started with slow deep penetrating thrusts. These quickly gave way to a more rapid-fire movement. His body was taking over. The animal in both of them was thrashing to make sure every thrust was as deep as possible. Travis rose up and grabbed her ankles, one in each hand. He spread her wide open and began pounding into her warm gushing body. He took one last look at her beautiful face, and the back side of her sexy legs and exploded into her with a powerful release. He could feel his hot orgasm blasting her insides. He could also feel their sex juices shooting out as April orgasmed each time he pushed in.

After what seemed an eternity of orgasm they both collapsed in a heap. Travis spooned April and held her tight. He could feel both their hearts pounding. He was going to do his best to make sure she was going nowhere. He did not have to worry, she was not going to leave this gentle but passionate bear. They slept like logs in a deep, peaceful sleep till morning. Travis always woke up early. He woke up even earlier on this race Sunday morning. He had been in a REM dream state, with visions of April dancing in his head. Fantasy quickly gave way to reality as he woke. He could feel his cock deep in a warm, wet place. Was he still dreaming? As his eyes blinked open, he quickly saw a beautiful blond head bobbing up and down on his hard pole. He did not even get time to protest. This was too one sided. He exploded into her mouth. He came with such force that he was concerned he would blow the back of her head off! April swallowed every drop of Travis's morning nectar. She came up with a smile and said, "Well now that breakfast is over, let's get to work."

She jumped into the shower, but this time it was all business. They both showered and dressed quickly as there was a lot to do. Zed had come back with Camaro girl in tow and breakfast sandwiches from the concession stand that was already open. Travis devoured his and a couple of donuts. He washed it all down with a Diet Soda. People teased him about always drinking diet soda. We have to save calories wherever you can! He had and will work it off today. He made sure to drink lots of water, and for some reason, he and April were both dehydrated!

They did another car inspection and checked everything over one more time. They had a discussion and all decided that they would leave the water injection in manual, but put it in the "armed" state in case Travis thought he needed it. The wiring was in series, set up with a toggle switch to arm and a push button to activate. The arm switch was on the power side, but the activate button was on the ground side of the circuit. This would reduce arcing during activation. They agreed however, that they would set the timing retard to come on when the high gear servo was activated using again a normally open switch that would close to ground from transmission servo pressure. This would give them a little extra the last hundred feet. Retarding the timing when the pistons are moving slower will give an increased torque rise as the fuel has more time to burn building higher combustion.

They waited patiently until they were called to lanes. Only two cars in his class this time and Travis was low ET, so he had lane choice. He went into lane 7, so they would have the right lane. The right lane gave him a slightly better view of the tree. Once in the staging lane, Travis started strapping on the helmet, got a quick good luck kiss from April, and Zed started checking tire pressures. Travis called to Zed and quietly said, "Hey Zed, what do you think, drop to 9 lb.? I believe we are going to need all the traction we can get." Zed agreed and completed the tire pressure settings. The team slowly pushed the car forward, and they waited their turn.

It was a bright sunny 70-degree day. The team's eyes were on the cars racing before them. No oil downs, and there did not seem to be any traction problems. The other Comp eliminator next to them was a very professional rig. Nothing but the best aftermarket heads, ceramic-coated headers, state of the art ignition… This was not going to be any push over. OK, Super Stock just finished up, so they were next. Travis pulled his belts tight. He received thumbs up from both Travis and April. Travis flipped on the ignition and hit the starter button. The engine barked into life. The turbo motor was not loud. The exhaust turbine of the turbos acted as a muffler breaking up the sound vibrations. Travis eased it into gear, and the car began rolling into his lane. Travis watched Zed and as he hit the water trough dip, he got the hand signal from Zed and Travis hit the throttle. Travis did a long burnout holding the engine at about 6000 RPM with a solid dry chirp when he lifted. Travis watched April back him up. He did not notice only her beauty this time, but also her professional concentrated guidance backing him into his own tracks. The people in the stands think that the pretty girl giving directions is just for show. In fact, it is critical to back into the hot rubber tracks that the car had just made for maximum traction. Travis noticed that he was the first to get backed up. The other Altered was playing some head games. He would be in the box first and would end up holding on the break a little longer as the competitor was going to try and "burn him down." Good thing they changed transmission fluid.

Travis stuck to his routine. He went into the first stage light, and then cleared the throat of the engine with a blip of the throttle. Travis waited till the competitor went into the first light, and the other Altered surprised him by lighting both almost at once. Don't let it shake you, Power brake up, bring up the boost and ease into the second stage light and then bury the throttle. All this took seconds but it seemed like an eternity before his tree started coming on.

The other car had a slower index and left first as they were in a slower class. They had the handicap. Milliseconds that seemed like hours to the last yellow light and then bang were out of the gate. Travis could see the other car in front of him as the second gear shift came and went. He was pulling hard now on the competitor, but he had still not caught him! POW, almost like another shift, the car leaped past the competitor! It was the ignition retard increasing the torque. A wild sense of high speed "Scoot" hit Travis. He was in the traps in an instant, and yes, his win light was on. Travis had a little more trouble slowing down and missed the second turn out. He had forgotten to use the water injection. Everything happened too fast. He had also noticed the chute seemed to hit harder. Had they packed it wrong? No, that was April's job, and she always got it right. Her man depended on it to slow down!

The answers came quickly as his team arrived yelling and screaming!!! Zed was jumping on the car like a monkey which kind of annoyed Travis for a minute, and then April was there screaming, "You won, you won and set a new world record doing it!"

It took a second to digest this, and he snapped around, but the lights were reset. Travis asked, "How fast? What ET?"

Zed came up with a smirk on his face and slowly said, "It was a 7.21 at 204 MPH! You passed them in the last 100 feet, and if they had doors, you would have sucked them off!" Holy shit!

The competitor also took the third turn out, and he had also set a new class record. He was a sandy haired guy and said, "Congratulations, but hell, I set a new class record and still could not keep you from coming around. I will get you next time after they adjust the index for this rocket ship. Good luck man." Travis thanked him and said the same.

He would have to remember this guy. He would not have to worry, April would have all the information, history, and times recorded by the end of tomorrow, right down to the guy's shoe, shirt and pants size! Travis started to get out letting Zed steer them back as always, and he said, "No man, this one is yours." Travis stayed in the seat and all his friends and competitors lined up giving him high fives all the way back to the pits.

When they got back, Matt was standing in the pits. Wow, when did he get here? When Travis asked Matt when he arrived he said, "We flew down this morning in the corporate jet with a couple of your favorite customers! "

Sure enough, a couple of Travis's biggest customers were standing there, and all had wide grins. Matt said," Damn man, do you have to let it all hang out and blast the record?"

Travis smiled and said, "That guy was too good to give a chance, and he set a new class record as well. Besides, who said we let it all hang out…?"

 They had won the race and set new ET and MPH records for their class. They would later find out that they were the only gas powered, non-Pro car to go over 200 MPH, ever!

CHAPTER 12: THAT'S NEXT?

It had been a wild weekend. Winning the race turned out to be the low point! They had set a new national record, for both MPH and Low ET for their class. Travis had continued to have the love of his life. She had not run away or changed her mind. Zed had found a new flame as well with another Camaro girl!

The trip back to the shop was a quiet one. It was like the events of the weekend had drained all the emotion and adrenalin from their bodies. Every ounce of energy was gone. It was all Travis could do to stay awake and keep their rig on the road. At least with this rig, they would not have to unload everything when they got home. It would all still be tucked safely away for the night. When Travis came to a stop to hit the automatic gate button, the crew still did not move. Zed and April were still fast asleep. It was not till Travis stopped the truck in front of the shop and opened the door causing the dome light to come on did they wake. Zed said, "Wow, we are here? Sorry man, I was going to spell you."

Travis replied, "No worries, but I am a deadbeat . Come on, April, let's get home and hit the sack."

April rubbed some sleep out of her eyes and said yeah, "That sounds like a plan." They drove home in April's truck.

As they entered the house, both just shed clothes as they headed to the bed. No showers even, they were both just too tired. April snuggled up into

Travis's back and had her arm around Travis. He had intentionally laid with his back to her so neither would be tempted. He did not have to worry about that, April was just as tired. The last thing Travis remembered was glancing at the alarm clock. The digital numbers said 3:15 AM.

The next morning, or really mid-morning, Travis woke to a ringing phone. It was Matt," Hey man, get your ass out of bed! KPower, the local radio station, wants to interview you this afternoon."

Travis was waking up slowly, "What…who...when… What do they want?"

Matt replied, "Wake up man, you're a local hero. There is a huge write up in the Denver paper that got pushed to the Cheyenne Star."

Travis was now waking up quickly. Travis said, "Really, wow I did not see that coming."

Matt replied, "Yeah me either. You better start thinking about what you are going to say."

Travis said, "OK Matt, I will put some thoughts down and send them over to you if you have time to look them over."

Matt replied, "You bet, you have all the time I can spare for the next couple of days. The customers we brought to the race ate it up. They are proud to say they have your engines in their equipment! Keep it up Trav."

April was coming awake now, "What was all that about honey?"

Travis filled her in and said, "Just sleep awhile, babe. I am going to jump in the hot tub and consider what the hell I am going to say while my bones soak a bit."

April replied, "OK, honey." Travis shed his jockey shorts and climbed into the tub. It was always the same, as you climb in the hot tub. There is always the mixed sensation of hot shock but relaxing heat of the water at 101 degrees. Travis had played with temperatures, and 102 was just too Hot and 99 too cold . 100-101 was perfect.

He kept the tub at 101 because he knew as soon as he lifted the lid, there would be heat loss once he got in. His body would act like an ice cube being dropped into liquid. He knew that the water would hold heat well, but he also knew that the heater running on 110 would take about an hour to raise the temperature 1 degree. There was about 500 gallons of water and at 2500 watts it drew 22 amps which was all the circuit could take. Travis knew that he could switch the heat and pump to 220 volts and cut the amperage in half. High voltage was much more efficient. He would have to get to that.

After Travis settled into the warm water, he began to consider what he would say to the disc jockey. His muscles were starting to relax, and the deep pain in his core was melting away. He sunk a little deeper into the tub and considered how he would open it . He would make sure that he gave credit first to Matt and then his crew. When pressed, he would talk a bit about how the efficiency of turbos is being overlooked and in the future turbocharging would be commonplace. He would then make sure that he described the feel of pure G force acceleration. He would try and explain the difference between speed and speed under acceleration.

Even if folks liked speed, or thought they liked speed, they would not understand that it really was not speed but acceleration that gave them the adrenalin rush. Travis fed on it. Not like a roller coaster, in fact he hated roller coasters. It was speed and G force that he could not control. He did not like the feeling of being out of control. He loved the feeling of being on the "brink" of out of control. He would have to be careful not to get too deep as most folks just started to tune out when Travis would go into detail. He had learned over the years to just stop when he saw folks start to what he called "Glaze Over." When he saw this in their faces, he knew they were done absorbing. He was the same way when he heard people start talking about looks or clothes. He would hear about the first three or four sentences and would drift off into some metal land. I guess, to each their own.

Travis had his thoughts aligned, when April arrived. He watched with great interest as she entered the Hot Tub. Her hair was messed up from sleeping and she never wore much makeup. Travis did not like a lot of makeup and she did not need it anyway! She gave a few pleasant groans as she slipped into the water and let her body relax. She threw her legs over Travis's and they both relaxed with their eyes closed for several minutes. He gently stroked her legs. He loved her smooth silky skin, and she liked his touch. He was careful not to move too high as he never wanted to take her for granted and wanted her to know that he just liked her company and closeness. She opened her eyes just a bit and looked into his eyes and said, "I love you honey, and love the life you have given me. I hope I can return to you as much as you have given me."

Travis blushed and said, "Honey your company alone is enough return for me."

She smiled and asked what he planned to say. He told her and she suggested a few things including to not be too technical. She then asked if she could go along and Travis replied, "Of course, you are welcome anytime, anywhere I go." He also knew that the pressure would be off him a bit because as soon as the disc jockey saw her, his interest would swing. KPWR (They called themselves K-Power) had a great morning team of a woman and a man, but he was pretty sure it was going to be the man that interviewed him.

They laid there for another half hour, and April was the first one to say," Hey, I am hungry! I have not eaten since noon yesterday !" Travis said, "Yeah, me neither."

They got up and after a quick shower threw on some clean race team clothes. They went and banged on Zed's door (He was sleeping in the spare room) with no answer. He finally groaned a couple of times and said "Go away." Travis and April finally gave up and jumped on the motorcycle.

They rode down to the local Drive Inn that had picnic tables. It was a beautiful sunny day and they wanted to eat outside and Travis liked that they served breakfast all day. After they ordered, they noticed that several folks were looking at them and smiling. Finally, a young boy came over to the picnic table they were sitting at and said, "Hey, are you the guy that is in the newspaper this morning?"

Travis blushed again and smiled and said, "Yeah, guess so." The kid then asked for his autograph. Travis grabbed his pin and said, "What is your name buddy?"

The boy said Mike, "Mike Gray."

Travis said, "OK, Mike, here you go," Travis wrote, "To Mike Gray, the fastest kid on the block, from Travis, the fastest man on the block." The kid smiled and walked away.

The waitress had come out and had their food. When Travis pulled out his wallet, she said, "Sorry sir, the manager said your money is no good here…it is on the house." Travis smiled and looked inside and the entire staff waved.

Travis looked at April and said, "Well, good news travels fast." He thanked her and made her take a $5 tip. They ate slowly and enjoyed an occasional handshake. Better savor this as no one knows what happens tomorrow.

They took April's truck down to the radio station so that Travis could have a little more time to think about what he would say. As they entered the front office of the radio station the owner came out to greet them, "How are you sir, my name is Fred Damion and I own KPowr. Thank you for coming in. Do I need to speak to your manager about the fee?"

Travis blinked. Usually he was one step ahead of most folks, but this one caught him by surprise. He recovered quickly, and said, "We have had a good week, this one is on the house. Maybe you could donate whatever you think it is worth to Saint Jude's Hospital, they do a great job for kids."

Mr. Damion smiled and said, "We will do that." Travis was in blue jeans, and had on a Biker Shirt from a local Cheyenne bike shop. April was wearing cutoffs and a Biker shirt like his. She made it look better than his. They were led into a room next to the disc jockey booth. He heard the disc jockey start a song and come out. Hey, we have about three minutes. Travis could now see the lady disc jockey sitting at the controls. They were both named Sam, the lady jockey was Samantha and they went by Sam and Sam in the morning.

Sam said, "Are you OK with an open discussion?" Travis nodded his head. Sam said, "Remember no cussing, but we have a 30 second delay in case you screw up!"

Travis introduced April and she started to sit in the adjacent room. Sam said, "Come on, you are coming in too! I don't think Travis will let you out of his sight, I know I wouldn't." Travis frowned a bit and looked stern at the disc jockey.

Travis smiled and replied, "Actually, she is part of the crew and might be able to explain things if you don't understand the technical jargon."

Sam smiled and held his hands up, "Ok, I can see you really are a tough competitor. We have about 30 minutes, but if it gets interesting we can drift another 15 minutes,"

Everyone went in, and Travis nodded at Samantha. She had a big smile on her face. He noticed April's grip on his hand tightened a bit which surprised him a bit. She had nothing to worry about, Travis was a one-woman man. Samantha was better looking than he had expected. Her radio voice was ruff and gravely so he had expected an older heavyset woman . Samantha was a short, slender brunette, with a nice rack on her. They were popping out of her top. She was wearing one of his team racing shirts. Where had she gotten that? Matt would have made that happen of course. Sam directed them to two seats close to the microphones. The song ended, and Samantha was the first to speak, "Well listeners we have a special event this morning! Travis Davis, the guy who set two national drag racing records in Denver last weekend has joined us. Travis, what does it feel like to be strapped into an 1800 lb. skateboard with a turbocharged big block Mopar?" Her knowledge caught him a bit surprised, but Travis was used to being under pressure. He had been in front of many large mining VP's before and she was not going to shake him.

Travis said, "Well Sam, it is kind of like really good sex the first time with your new flame. It happens fast and hard and is over before you know it!" April had her hand on Travis's knee now making sure Samantha knew Travis was hers.

Samantha, laughed loudly, and blushed a bit. Sam took over asking the questions and in the next 30 minutes Travis explained how competition eliminator Drag racing worked and just how competitive it was. He explained the advantage turbochargers had, and some of the obstacles they had overcome. Nothing too detailed, but it must have hit home as when they opened the phone lines, the question and answer portion had to be cut off at an additional 20 minutes. At the end, Travis made sure that he got a good plug in for Matt, his sponsor and then thanked his large customers by name for coming to the race to give a little free publicity. Large coal mining could use all the good press they could get. At the end, Sam and Sam turned the program over to the noon news and walked out with Travis and April.

Sam said, "Hey that was awesome, maybe we can make this a regular thing once a week and ask the expert racing mechanic thing."

Travis said, "Sure, I am always looking for new sponsors, just get your check book out. Next one is not free!" Sam and Sam laughed nervously and thanked them again for coming.

Travis made sure he had his left hand in April's back shorts pocket when he shook hands with Samantha. He wanted to make damn sure she knew who owned his heart. With Sam, he grasped his handshake with both hands and gave him a long hard look. He had noticed the sideways looks that April had gotten from him, but that was to be expected. That said, Sam got a taste of just how strong a grip this 20 year veteran mechanic had. The owner was in the lobby as they walked out and thanked them again. He said, "I just made a $1000 donation to Saint Jude in your racing team's name."

On the way back to the shop, Travis was a bit on the quiet side. April was not sure what was on his mind. Was he thinking about the car, the interview, or maybe Samantha! She decided to find out. April said, "Gallon of gas for your thoughts."

Travis kind of woke up and said, "Sorry honey, I was just thinking how best we could use this attention. I believe we should do some research and all of this type of revenue should be donated to some good causes. We will have plenty of sponsor revenue and race winnings. Matt could take care of the financial and marketing with his advertising and promotion group at the dealership. The Heavy equipment business could use some good press."

April was a bit surprised! She said, "Sorry honey, I thought maybe you were thinking about Samantha, she looked pretty sharp.

Travis laughed, "Honey compared to you, she was a four-door economy car. I have a Ferrari, why would I spend any time thinking about a Volkswagen." April laughed.

When they got back to the shop, Zed was there and ready to help unload the car and trailer. They started by rolling the racecar into the shop and then spent some time cleaning and restocking the tow rig. When they were done, Zed jumped in the rig and moved it to the side of the shop. Both Zed and April had gotten their Commercial Driver's License so they could drive the tow rig. Matt again made that an easy process. Zed and even April were naturals. It was already getting dark, and they decided to have a quick review of the race notes from the weekend and call it a night. It was then that Travis told the team that he had not even used the water injection! He told them that the pass just went by too quickly to even think about hitting the button. Zed suggested wiring it into the high gear servo as they had discussed and then April came up with even a better idea. She started by asking Travis to validate that the water injection was good for the engine. Travis replied, "Yes, it cools down the intake charge, which is better for the upper end." Travis added, "When the fluid evaporates it adds oxygen as well."

 April said, "OK, so why don't we use two nozzles? One smaller nozzle for low gear and a second larger nozzle to come on in high gear, when the heat is up in the engine and the pistons have slowed down?"

Travis and Zed blinked, and both said almost at the same time, "That is a damn good idea. They would add a pressure switch to the first nozzle and a second switch to the transmission high turn on the larger nozzle." Travis added, "We can add an override switch in case the extra power was not needed."

They would have to hustle. They only had two days to get ready for the four-day national event in Salt Lake. It would only take about 10 hours of driving to get there so they would leave Wednesday to be at the track and ready Thursday morning. The track opened at noon on Thursday for spectators. They all agreed to meet at the shop tomorrow morning at 6:00 AM.

CHAPTER 13:
DID NOT SEE THT COMING

Everyone was at the shop by 5:45 AM. We had to service the engine, transmission and rear end. Now that we had a sponsor, of course, we used nothing but the finest oils in all compartments. We had remote filters for both the engine and transmission and used Heavy Equipment filters off an excavator, which is much larger in capacity, and has a tighter micron element for quality filtering control. A complete engine service was 14 quarts. They cut the filters open to look for shavings and debris. They cut every filter open every time. People don't realize how much they could save themselves with a good maintenance program. Travis's customers always followed his suggested maintenance programs, and they often would exceed their PCO (Predicted Component Overhaul). Travis participated in "Valued Customer Days" once each quarter where they would display the car and Travis would put on talks about maintenance, systems operation, or high-quality PM (Preventative Maintenance) products offered by the dealer. These sessions were always standing room only. April suggested that at the next customer event they show video of the races. Travis laughed and said that they would come just to see her in her short shorts!

In addition to the service, they also pulled oil samples from the engine, transmission, and rear end. The dealership had a full oil lab and would track the history of wear metals, and oil condition, not so much for using up an additive package, as the oil was always new, but for contamination such as water or dirt. The oil lab could also trend how well the oil was holding up.

He had Zed pull them first and run them up to the lab so they could rush the sample. By noon the lab had called back and said just a little spike in the lead, but nothing to worry about. The lead came from the first layer of the engine bearings. It is what takes the pounding of the combustion cycle. The upper main bearings took some abuse as the engine RPM went so high the crank would over speed. When the engine was at 7000 RPM, Travis had calculated that the pistons were traveling over 700 miles an hour. This centrifugal force would lift the crankshaft into the upper bearings. When you disassemble most normal engines, there is almost no wear on the upper main bearings. The oil lab also said there was just a trace of high iron, Travis was not sure what that was from. The camshaft and lifters were usually the sources of this type of wear, so they paid special attention to the valve settings when they did them.

Normal wear would push the valve deeper into the head, especially with the special valve springs they were using that had over 300 PSI seat pressure. This meant normal wear would make the valve lash tight. If the valve lash is loose, it meant that the cam, lifters, rockers, or push rods were wearing abnormally. This logic was valid for all engines including the diesel engines that Travis worked on as well. All of Travis's customers set their valves at suggested intervals and sent all their oil sample alerts to Travis. This was part of the dealership's custom warranty for components overhauled by the dealer exclusively.

On his racecar, Travis used .032 valve lash clearance setting on his race engines at 4000 feet, which is the elevation of the next track they were headed to in Salt Lake. This will effectively reduce camshaft duration. Travis would use .028 settings at higher elevation as the air is less dense. By closing up the valve lash, it would add just a bit more duration of valve opening. Lift was the same, but the length of time the valves were open (duration) would be just a bit more to let the engine breath just a little longer. Travis and Zed had played with different settings on the dyno, and they also played with dyno room pressure to compensate for various elevation settings. Example, their shop was at 5,380 feet, which on a normal 70-degree day would yield about 11.6 PSI atmospheric air pressure. They could pressurize the dyno room at 3 PSI, which would make the engine think it was at sea level where atmospheric pressure is around 14.7 PSI. The tighter the clearance, the more duration the valves were open. At low elevations, they used wide gaps so the valve would close earlier. This would allow the engine to use more of the up stroke to build compression in thicker air. This did not give huge horsepower gains, but a hundred of these little things made Travis's engines have a slight edge on the competition who did not want to take the time to consider tweaks like this.

It was about midnight when the crew finally fell into bed. Of course, Travis and April hit the hot tub before getting into bed. It would help soak the paint and oil stains away. Tonight, April laid her beautiful soft legs in Travis's lap in the tub and she asked him to massage them as she was sore from running around all day. Travis was glad to accommodate! While the naked touching, of course, made them both feel passion, they were both just glad to be next to each other. They were way too tired for any more physical energy exercises tonight. That night both slept the deep sleep of tired, hardworking people that had a sense of deep satisfaction from a productive day's work, good health, and great lives.

Sometime before dawn, Travis had a deep sleep dream of April and himself making deep passionate love after winning the upcoming race. It must have left him hard as a rock, as he woke April up with his hard piston and rod poking her cylinder bore. She too was wet with anticipation. With both of them semi-conscious, they soon found Travis's piston beginning to stoke inside April's cylinder wall. It started as a slow stroke like going out for a Sunday drive.

They were both awake now, and April whispered, "Come on, race car driver, show me how you can shift gears and get this moving."

Travis did not need more encouragement than this. He saw it as a green light on the Drag starting tree, and he rolled both over so he was on top of April's back, with his hands wrapped around her body holding onto her beautiful full breasts. He began cranking his rod deep inside her, and he could hear animal sounds of pleasure coming to his woman. He heard her say the magic words, "Honey I love you, but can you go much harder and faster, I am about to orgasm!"

With that encouragement, he rose up on his hands on both sides of her body to support himself and began using his weight and every muscle in his body to slam his piston and rod into her. He first used hard, slow strokes, but then accelerated to a feverish pace where he could hear her moan. Sweat was gathering on his forehead from the work out. He considered slowing down till he heard April say, "Yeah, that's it harder, faster…"

Travis put it into overdrive, and he could feel his own pure lust giving this beautiful woman everything he had. She orgasmed several times but asked for more after each orgasm. Finally, as Travis could feel himself losing the ability to hold off, he decided to try and shove her into one giant orgasm. He loved banging her beautiful body. She cooed loudly, and said," Oh yes, yes, yes, deeper…harder."

Travis made one more massive shove with his pleasure tool and held it deep. April's body contracted and this put him over the edge and they both came hard with rushing gushes of mixed juices. The rush of their fluids combined with high pressure shots coming from the tip of Travis's injector caused human sex combustion with a final thrust of passion.

Travis collapsed on top of April, who pushed up into Travis a couple of final times to make sure she had drained Travis of his entire human nitrous! Travis rolled to one side pulling April with him so they would stay engaged for a few more precious minutes.

She whispered," Wow that was great, especially that last move you made. It surprised me, but felt wonderful to have you inside me!"

They both lay breathing heavily until both fell into another deep sleep. They slept for about another 40 minutes until they heard Zed's truck pull up. Travis was up first jumping into the shower, with April soon joining him. They both helped wash each other's hard to get to spots, and while their fun parts were too sore for further engagement, there were several wet sloppy kisses. They had to drive to Salt Lake for the next meet today.

They checked all the rig fluids, made sure everything in the rig was tied down and started out on the 10 hour drive. Travis drove the rig, and April sat in the passenger seat reading a business process book about business process improvement. Travis had read it and said it was one of the best books he had ever read as the knowledge in the book could be applied to any sequential process whether it was business or mechanical. Zed was passed out in the back seat. He said Camaro Girl was going to be at the meet in Salt Lake and he needed to be fully rested for her! It was a great trip, April by his side, and Zed their true comrade in the back seat. Music was blaring from the high-end stereo, and the rig rolling at 80 MPH passed everything in sight. Many of the Big Rig Semi's and even some cars would give them the thumbs up sign as they rolled by. About an hour outside of Evanston Wyoming East, they passed a State Trooper car hiding behind a billboard . Travis had let the speed drift to about 90 MPH! Travis saw it too late, and his eyes quickly went to the mirrors to see if he was coming out onto the highway. He held his breath a few seconds and then…damn, yep, here they come, lights on. Travis started looking for a safe place to pull off. He did so, turned off the engine, and April handed him registration and insurance card from the glove box, so this would take as little time as possible. The lady officer was out of her car now and looking the rig over carefully. She seemed to notice the "Not for Hire" lettering and the racing team name. Travis was in the wrong, and he knew it. The last song just had him running a bit faster than normal. The officer would have not even looked at him at 80 MPH as the speed limit was 75 MPH on Wyoming interstates.

When she came up to the door, Travis rolled down his window and said, "Sorry officer, we were going way too fast. Here is my vehicle information and license." He added, "Sorry again mam."

The officer did not say anything. She looked over the information and compared it to the information she had already received when she had called the plate number. She then said, "Well your paperwork is in order and your commercial license is up to date. She continued, "You know that a speeding ticket could put your commercial licenses at risk?"

Travis said," Yes mam I have no excuses, I should have known better."

She paused for a minute and then said something that surprised Travis, "Sir, we have been having some issues with drug smuggling, would you mind opening the trailer and let me take a peek? "

Travis was surprised, and said quickly, "Sure no problem." She was right, this would be a perfect cover for a drug smuggler! With that they all got out and instantly, Zed started checking out the cop's ass! Travis had the opportunity to whack him without the officer seeing him. A second patrol car came up as back up, and Travis was now getting a little nervous. It was also a female officer. The first one was a blond with a 9MM on her hip, and this one was a slender Redhead . She was also packing a side arm, but this one had a .45 caliber.

Travis was not nervous but also hoped Zed did not have a stash in the trailer somewhere. He never touched the stuff. They opened both the side and end doors. The Red head was the first to say something, "Wow, this is quite a rig." Then the Blond officer chimed in, "Man that car looks like it could fly."

Zed said without thinking or maybe too impressed them, "Yep, we just set the national record and we are getting ready to break it again this weekend …if we ever get there."

Travis frowned and quickly said, "Mam, do you want us to open anything up?"

Carol, the blond officer said, "No, but can you roll the car out, please?"

Travis quickly said, "Of course, Zed got the rear tie downs and I will get the front" in a tone that Zed knew it was time to quit messing around. Travis continued," April jump into the driver's seat and steer please."

April went into the trailer and began wiggling her beautiful tan body down into the seat. Travis could not help but watch her get in as he quickly undid the front straps. He noticed that both the female officers were watching April intentionally get in! In fact, neither of their eyes ever left April! They were whispering to each other with a slight knowing smile. Travis was surprised, amused and a bit miffed at this. He quickly said to April, "Thanks, baby." April gave him a quick smile and said, "Sure Honey." OK, Alpha male established.

The car rolled out into the bright sun and, of course, was polished and in perfect condition. The tires were huge, and the wheels shined perfectly. The sun was shining off the rear wing. Carol, the blond officer, said, "Who built her?"

Travis quickly said, "We did every weld, every nut, and every bolt."

The Red head with a nametag of Linda something was now looking down into the cockpit where April was sitting. She said, "Beautiful…every inch of her."

OK…Travis was starting to get a little steamed. April could see this and took control of the situation, "Hey girls, would you like us to take pictures of you in the car?"

This caught everybody by surprise! The officers hesitated for a minute, and looked at each other, and said, "Yeah, would that be alright?" looking at Travis.

Travis quickly picked up on April's move, damn he loved that girl. He said, "Sure, April help the ladies and put the belts on so they get a full effect."

Each of the officers took their turn getting in the car, and of course, they both needed extra help with the belts. The Red head went first, and April made sure she took extra time on the crotch and shoulder belts. The Red head even grabbed April's hand at one point and said, "Thank you so much for your help, beautiful."

When it was the Blonde's turn, she looked over at Zed and said, "Could you give me a hand in? I am a little bigger, and it might be a tight fit." Zed, of course, jumped at the chance. When he was helping her with the crouch belt, he said toying with her," Is that tight enough?" She replied, "Oh yes, I like a tight fit."

Zed knew not to push this little situation too far. They took several pictures, including one with the two officers, April, and Zed. Travis said, "Well ladies, we still have a long way to go and need to get moving. I have a couple of extra passes to the race this weekend if you would like to come to the race. They are VIP tickets and will get you in the pits so you can come down and see us in action."

The Blond got the hint but could not resist one more chance to demonstrate who was in control and said, "Well, that would be an attempt to bribe an officer unless you allow us to bring the beer?"

Travis smiled and said, "Sounds like a plan, let's get this loaded up and moving." The officers stayed till they were ready to go. The red head gave him back his license and registration winking at April. Zed was walking up on the passenger's side escorted by the blond. I could still see them in the mirror, however, and before getting in, I saw Officer Carol give Zed a passionate wet kiss and grab his ass with both hands! She sure told him who the boss was!

Zed climbed in, and Travis started to ease the rig back out, and the redhead yelled, "Keep it under 85 you guys and we will radio an all clear for you ahead." Travis waved and put the hammer down watching the ladies fade away in his mirror. He then looked at his teammates, and they were all speechless and wide-eyed.

Finally, they all laughed and Zed broke the silence saying, "Do you think they will really come?"

April jumped in, "Yep, and you are going to have your hands full, with a big smile on her face."

Zed replied "I think you are going to have your own problem. The Red head liked you quite a bit."

I thought April would blush and stammer at this, but surprised Zed and Travis when she turned to Travis and said, "Oh I don't know, Travis, how would you feel about a threesome?"

Travis damn near ran off the road and said, "Uh…Uh…I don't know…Uh honey, you are more than enough for me."

April simply said, "Good answer," and turned up the stereo to change the subject.

They arrived at the track and were one of the first cars to go through tech inspection. As always the inspectors asked some fascinating questions about the turbos and the extra nozzles in the intake. Finally, they made us show them the window washer fluid tank and explain the purpose. Of course, they made them swear to secrecy but knew that would never last. They passed the car, and it was midnight before we were set up and in bed. All were dead tired. As April and Travis lay there, April said, "You know honey I would do it for you." Travis said, "What the threesome thing?"

April said. "Yep… would you do it for me"?

Travis was shocked and at first did not know how to answer. Then he said, "Yes, if that is what you would want but not with another man. As long as it is lust and not love."

"April smiled and said, "Honey, there is only one love in my life…and they both drifted off to sleep."

CHAPTER 14:
A VERY CLOSE CALL!

Everyone was dead tired, so sleep came quickly. They were up and moving about 7:00 AM and time trials started about 10:00. Travis had some interesting dreams after the previous day's events! He was not sure he was ready to share his women with anybody even for a sensual experience. They finished setting up camp and did another one over on the car. A Camaro girl showed up late last night and had crawled into bed with Zed. Not sure either one of them had much sleep. After they were set up , it was about 9:00 AM and Zed said he was going to help Camaro girl get her car ready, but he would be back in 30 minutes. April and I sat in our pit chairs and had a few quiet close moments. April knew that Travis's mind was in the race now. He was mentally going through his checklist: Tire pressure, fluids, parachute, and he was going through where all the controls and switches were in the cockpit. He had to block all else out of his mind. It was a little chilly, so April had her bare legs tucked up against her chin with her arms around them to keep them warm. Travis had noticed the goose bumps on her arms and legs and without being asked, he went and got her a blanket. It was a motorcycle blanket from Sturgis and was soft and fuzzy. She said, "Thank you honey." in a sweet delicate voice. As promised, Zed showed up at about 9:30.

Travis was already in the fire suit and April had the golf cart positioned to hook up to the Altered. She hooked up the tow rope, and Zed got into the driver's seat of the golf cart. Travis eased himself down into the racecar cockpit. They towed the car up, and Zed timed it, so they were third in line to run. This would give Travis the opportunity to watch a few cars go down the track and get a feel. They would set final tire pressure just before they made a pass. April checked the safety belts to make sure there was no twist, and she pulled the safety pin from the parachute. They would run just before the semi-pro classes of Top Alcohol rails and funny cars. This meant they would see the Stock and Super Stock cars go down first. The stock class cars did not yield much information since they did not have much power and the track would bite for them with no issues. The upper classes (A and B) of Super Stock were another matter. These were high-end versions of the factory hot rods such as Hemi Cuda's and ZL1 Camaro's. Travis observed them, and April kept track of how they were running compared to their indexes. It appeared that they were all running a bit slow. They were 1 to 2 tenths off. They all seemed to get good traction, however. Travis asked April what the temperature was and she said it was about 70 degrees. Travis asked Zed to put the tires at 9.5 PSI. He knew that when he went through the burnout out box, they would come up to about 10 PSI from the friction heat of the burnout. Travis paid special attention to Camaro girl's car as she made her pass. He noticed that she made the same jig to the right that she had made in Julesburg.

Travis waved Zed over and said, "Hey, suggest she add just a little preload to the right rear coil over shock." Zed said, "Yeah, I was thinking the same thing. This would plant that right slick first and should correct the jig. About a half turn should do it. She will pick up a few hundreds of a second as well. If you're not going straight, you're wasting time and energy."

Soon Travis saw the cars in front of him move forward. He watched two rear engine dragsters take off and April said they too were slow on their index. They all seemed to bog off the line. Travis was confident that he had selected the correct tire pressure. He also decided to leave the water injection off the first pass to get a good baseline. Travis had his helmet on now and final check on the safety belts by April. She gave him a quick kiss on the top of his helmet and got a thumb up from both her and Zed. Travis turned the ignition switch on, and pushed the starter button. The engine rolled over about two revolutions and fired. He waited about 10 seconds for the oil pressure to get all the way through the engine. He was ignoring the burnout box guys who were waving him up. This car was his baby, and he would enter the water box when he was damn good and ready!

He eased the shifter into low gear and moved towards the burnout box. He saw the water box attendant put down a fresh water spray. He felt the bump of the front tires going through the box and then the rear dip of the tires. God, he loved this part. The show off came out in him. He knew every eye of the onlookers was on him. He had such a strange car. Turbos were just not used on American V8's in the 1980's. A soon as he felt the rear bump, he was in second gear to maximize tire speed without putting too much strain on the engine. He hit the throttle about half way . The engine roared, and he could hear the turbos spin up to a shrill pitch even in his helmet. The rear tires violently began to spin and bellow smoke. Travis was careful not to go over 6000 RPM. The car jiggled to the right slightly but was easy to correct. When he felt the tires beginning to bite, he let up on the throttle and allowed the car to coast to a stop. He glanced at the gauges as he eased it into reverse. All was well. The engine was at about 160 degrees coolant temperature. He started to back up and had only gone about 20 feet when April appeared from the center track just the way she was instructed. He watched her in her tight shorts guide him back. No time for mind drifting now. He had to concentrate on the race. He got the slow down sign from April, and he eased his hand brake on. Now the starting tree was on his left as he had taken the right lane. Once behind the starting line he stopped the car and put it into neutral. He blipped the throttle a couple of times to clear the engine and then put it into first gear again. He was running a rail with a big Chevy . It had a tunnel ram and two big carbs on it. Travis was sure the guy thought he was going to blow Travis away. He was in for a surprise.

He started to power up against the brake. The starter was waving him in impatiently as always. Travis lit the first pre stage light and quickly went into the second light. He then locked the transmission brake and buried the throttle. The boost was at 25 PSI when the last yellow light came on and he released the transmission brake button and instantly felt the car jump out of the hole. Just as fast as the launch was over, it was the last he saw the rail. Later April would tell him that he had covered the rail by about 100 feet meaning that if the rail had doors, they would have blown them off. The time slip validated the pass. They were two-tenths under their index, which meant they were three-tenths slower than their record. This is right where Travis wanted to be. The next day, time trials were more of the same. Travis did make a pass and tried out the first and second stages of the water injection, which gave them almost a nitrous like power. He let out early, however, as he did not want to give their secret weapon away! Even backing off early, it was their best ET, but slowest MPH. That had the competition raising an eyebrow. The day of the finals went as planned. They covered the first two races easily, and Travis had them both covered by 1-2 car lengths. In the final, however, he would be matched up against another very fast Altered who was running a blown Big Block Chevy. He was also the record holder of his class. Travis and the team decided to pull the stops out. Tires down to 8 PSI, water injection on and Travis had every intention of using both sets of nozzles. When he left the line, he could see that the other car had beaten him out of the gate! Wow, it was a girl driver, and she was good. She had a length on him, but when he hit high gear, he had the second stage water injection switch already flipped, and the high gear servo pressure valve told the second set of nozzles to come on. The car moved in front of the other Altered and continued to pull away all the way to the end. In fact, he covered the other car by almost three lengths, and they set another national record. They won the race but unfortunately the story was not over...

After Travis crossed the traps, he eased off the throttle, and before he could pull the chute the car began to vibrate violently! Next, the car seemed to hop into the air, and Travis realized that the rear tires were locked up! He was still doing over 150 MPH! The car came back down and the rear tires unlocked, but he was a bit sideways, and there was oil all over the car including the rear tires. He was in trouble, and sure he was going to roll. At the last split second he instinctively pulled the chute, which deployed and yanked him back to straight, allowing him to regain steering control and ease on the brake. The adrenaline had every muscle in his body tight and shaking. He made the last turn out and managed to stop the car. Inside the helmet, he could now hear his own rapid hard breathing. His heart was pounding so hard that he was afraid it would jump out his chest. He just sat there and gathered his thoughts. He did not move until he saw his crew show up in the golf cart. April leaped out of the cart, and Zed was right behind her. April's eyes were red, and he could tell she was crying and distraught. Travis quickly pulled off his helmet and said," It's ok, I am alright.``

Zed being Zed said, "Well you might be, but the engine is toast. There is a hole in the pan, and a rod is hanging out."

Travis got out of the car and hugged April assuring her that he was fine. When he turned his attention to the car, he could see that, in fact, Zed was right; there was a hole in the engine pan, and not only was a rod hanging out, but part of the crankshaft was still attached. The engine locked up and stopped the whole powertrain until the pressure in the converter could reduce and release the input shaft. When they got back to the pits, the two women State Troopers were there, but his crew was not in any mood for any new adventures. The ladies could see that there was trouble in wolf city, so said hello and went on their way.

The team quickly put the car in the trailer as Travis did not want anything touched so he could do a full failure analysis in a controlled environment at their shop. The team quickly packed up their camp and answered many questions with a, "Not sure yet what happened" answer. The trip home was tranquil, and April held Travis's hand the entire trip. Travis was in deep thought the whole time and pretty much had it figured out in his mind what had happened. When they arrived, everyone agreed it was best to just leave the car in the hauler till morning. Zed took off. Travis and April headed straight to the hot tub where Travis again held April's legs in his lap. After a short soak, they were in bed and quickly fell asleep in each other's arms.

The car was broken , but they knew they could fix it. Everybody was alive and healthy. The next day they hit the shop early again. Everything would have to come apart. Zed pulled the drive shaft which on this car had no u-joints. The shaft had splines to allow it to slide in and out but no u-joints. This was much stronger. They had used aluminum donuts in the main caps and a 2-inch steel bar to align the engine to the rear end. The fit was within .002 of an inch. They would have to do it again with the new engine block.

Travis had called Matt, the sponsor from the track and told him about the win, and the failure. He assured Travis that building a new motor would be no problem. They had two weeks before the next points meet in Kansas. Once the driveline was out, they could lift the engine and transmission out together. There was minimal wiring and four ½ inch bolts holding it in. They unhooked some plumbing, and wiring and the engine and transmission was out in less than an hour. This is one of the advantages of an open wheeled car. While Travis separated the transmission from the engine, Zed disassembled the rear end. It was a 9 inch Ford style. All looked good, but they decided to come all the way apart and Magna fluxed the gears. There was a Magnaflux machine in the dealer component rebuild shop. Neat process really. You put the item you were checking between two high-powered coils. The end brackets had brass end plates, and once you had the item in place, you stepped on an air pedal and the two end fixtures came together to hold them. Then you shoot electricity in to magnetize the part. Next, spray it with Magnaflow liquid. The liquid flows into cracks and shows up under a black light. They would disassemble everything first and do all testing one time. Next, they went to the engine. This took time as they had to discover the cause of failure. The top end looked great. No bent valves and even the camshaft looked ok. They put it in V blocks and checked for bend with a dial indicator. The cam only had less than .001 run out. The bottom end, however, was a different story. They were careful to lay everything out just as it was in the engine. The strange thing was even the rods that were mangled showed no real bearing wear. Just some impact damage from the failure. The main bearings were pretty good as well. Travis then noticed that they were shiny on the edges. The crank was broken into three pieces. Every break was on the main saddle. Travis checked the fillet radius on every journal thinking the crankshaft grinder had undercut a fillet. They were all perfect. They had three bad rods and three damaged pistons. None of this damage was the cause of failure. It was all consequential damage. They would all have to go, and the engine would need to be re-balanced. It was not until Magna-fluxed the crank that they had clues as to the failure. The crank had spider cracks all through it. It was Magna-fluxed before being assembled the last time, so something had caused the cracks.

Travis slept on it and came up with a hypothesis. With a few phone calls, other engine builders verified his conclusion. At that time the sanctioning body NCRA had a rule in place that racers going faster than 10:00 ET could not use a stock engine dampener. Some idiot down south had thrown his engine dampener into a caustic hot tank to clean it. Caustic cleans great but attacks the rubber making it swell. In this case, the outer ring of the dampener had come off, and the idiot had pushed it back on with a press! The dampener had come apart and actually killed a burnout box track official. Because of this, now engine builders had to run a solid aluminum dampener, which helped reduce weight, but did nothing to take out engine harmonics. There were some fluid dampeners being developed much like those used by marine diesel engines, but NCRA had not approved them yet. The aluminum hubs had allowed harmonics to resonate throughout the crankshaft allowing stress cracks to occur in the crank from all the internal harmonic vibrations. It would happen again unless they could get their hands on a fluid damper . Matt would find them a new NCRA approved fluid dampener. He would pull strings to get one of the first releases. Travis slept soundly that night. He was always more comfortable once he knew the cause of failure. If he knew what failed and why, he could keep it from happening again. Tomorrow they would tear down the transmission, and then start putting everything back together. They would also start building a new engine. Travis loved to build engines…and he had a few new ideas starting with a billet crankshaft and a fluid damper to make it even better. He would test how well and willing Matt was to help fund a new motor. Luckily, it would be three weeks until the next point's event, so they had time to rebuild everything if all went well.

CHAPTER 15:
A BREAK IN THE ENGINE GENERATES A BREAK FOR THE CREW

Everyone was at the shop early the next morning. Zed went after the transmission rebuild, and Travis called Matt to see if he was ready to go for funding for a new engine. He said, "You bet and transferred $10,000 to the race fund." He also said he would shake the trees to get one of the new fluid dampeners. Matt also said that Travis should get a billet crankshaft this time instead of a stock forged one. Billet crankshafts are forged crankshafts, but the raw steel is from billet steel, which has stronger chemical properties and has tighter control of heat-treating processes to make sure there are no or fewer inclusions (voids, or areas in the steel that have contamination). Inclusions are places where the steel can form stress risers and be the source of stress cracks, which lead to bigger cracks that can progress to fracture. In other words, billet steel is much purer, higher carbon content so it can be heated to a harder and stronger surface.

Carbon is the magic element in many things. The hardest form of carbon, of course, is a diamond. The key, in steel, is to get the right amount of carbon in the right spot. Too much and it will be brittle and break, not enough and it will be too soft and wear out fast or bend. They needed a crank in the 50-carbon point range, which would make the core hard but durable. They would also have the crank "Flame Nitrated " which would increase the carbon content of the surface of bearing journals. The foundry would also flame heat treat the crank, after grinding, to freeze the carbon in place on the surface, which would make the crank very strong and hard. The last heat treat process would be to "temper" the crank. In this process, the crank is again heated up to around 800 degrees (Blue color not cherry red), and then the crank is allowed to cool down slowly, which takes some of the stress out of the crank from the forging and heat treating processes. It relaxed the metal. It is kind of like doing a hard workout and then jumping into a hot tub which relaxes your muscles. That took care of crank planning, however, Travis still chose a used block. Used blocks have been out there a while and have "moved around" and found a steady state. Seasoned blocks are the best. If Travis had his way, he would buy a bunch of used truck blocks and bury them in the backyard for a couple of years to let them grow into seasoned blocks.

When Travis was selecting a block, he would first check the walls of the block for "core shift" by using a ball micrometer. When the block is being cast, (molten hot metal poured into a sand casting mold) sometimes the block is moved too quickly after being poured, and the metal will shift from one side to the other. The piston bore walls will be thicker on one side than the other. This, of course, could allow a weak spot or even a hot spot in the bore where the metal is too thin. After the crank and block were selected, the next step was selecting connecting rods. You often hear the term "blue printing" which is often misused. A true blue print build means taking every single piece of the engine back to exact factory specs. Not the plus or minus specs, but the exact specs. As an example, every rod must be the same length and weight. Travis would often have to go through several sets of rods before he would find eight that could be machined to the same exact lengths. If a rod and piston were too long or too short, it would affect that cylinder's compression ratio. At 7000 RPM you want everything working in harmony. Travis zero balanced his engines, meaning that each piston, rod, and wrist pin weighed the same as the blueprint specs. Once the components were selected the next step was to see how they fit as an assembly. He would have the engine roughly bored making sure every hole was 90 degrees from the main saddle. This took special equipment as most boring bars are just bolted to the top of the block. Travis used a machinist that had a machine that bore using the main bores as a point of reference for boring at exactly 90 degrees. Travis also had a company that made billet steel main caps. The main cap is the weak link in the block. This meant, of course, that the engine block would need to be line bored with the new caps installed. Main bolts were replaced with studs, and then the main saddle bores were machined to exact specifications.

The perfect main bores were the "point of reference" for the whole engine, just like a house foundation. You have to have a sound foundation to build a good house. Everything must be square. It is amazing how much can be done with a simple bubble level. Once Travis was to this point, he would install the crank and four pistons and rods one in each corner of the block. He then measured and moved each piston to the top dead center. (The piston is at its highest point in the stroke). He would then measure using a depth micrometer the distance from the top of the piston to the top of the block (called Deck Height) in four corners of each piston. He would repeat the process in all four-corner holes. Now he had a measurement picture of how square the top of the block was. He could then tell his machinist just how to cut the top of the block so that each piston deck height was exactly the same. Travis also measured the piston sidewall clearance. From this, he could give his machinist rough instructions of how much would have to be taken out during the final honing process. Travis had his engines finally honed with a deck plate. A deck plate is the same size as the cylinder head but has holes in it. This is bolted to the top of the block so that the block is pulled into place just like having the cylinder head bolted on.

The heads were not hurt, but Travis would disassemble them and check every part and check to make sure the sealing process and spring tension were exactly correct. Travis had put a seven-angle valve job on the heads. He started with the valve at 45 degrees base angle, and then back cut the valve using a 30 degree stone and then 50 degree angle cuts. In the head seat, he would start with a 70 degree, then 45, and then finish with a 50 degree stone. The final cut would be to top the head with a 15 degree stone. All of this was to allow the air to flow into the combustion chamber easier. The heads were not fully ported and polished as with turbos full porting is not required, but he did use an air grinder to clean up the pocket 1 inch into the seat. He would also put all the push rods in V-blocks and use a dial indicator to make sure they were not bent. Travis was amazed that with everything flying around in the bottom end that the top end did not appear to be damaged. The turbos were not so lucky, a piece of connecting rod came out of the pan and flew up into the compressor wheel of the right turbo. The left turbo bearings showed signs of lack of lubrication. The shaft bearings were smeared in the middle and had signs of heat. Travis was able to save the compressor housing and would order complete cartridges for both turbos. Cartridges contain all the moving parts of the turbo. All you had to do was salvage the turbine and compressor housings. Travis glass beaded (form of sand blasting) both housings and inspected them for damage. The failed turbo had a little damage from contact with the fin, but Travis was able to use an abrasive disc on a high-speed air grinder to clean it up. He checked clearance to the good compressor wheel, and it looked like it would be okay.

He would inspect all the roller lifters and the camshaft including putting it on the blocks to check for straightness. All seemed to be in order. He would take the rotating assembly (Crank, Rods, Pistons, dampener, flex plate…) and the block to his sponsoring machine shop and they would need a week to balance and finally hone the block. Travis had also built a block girdle that bolted on to the bottom of the block and tied all the main studs to each other, using the pan bolts. This made the block more rigid . After he dropped off the motor parts, Travis returned to the shop.

Zed had the rest of the powertrain almost completed. Travis commented to Zed, "Man, I hate waiting a week for parts!"

Zed said, "Travis, I will finish up here and go over and check on progress at the machine shop." Zed added, "Why don't you and April take a couple of days off and enjoy some downtime." Travis would have never thought of that, he could not do that…well, maybe he could. April deserved it. She really had not taken any downtime since her parents passed away. He would talk to her tonight and see what she thought.

That night, after they had a light dinner that Travis made for them, they headed for the hot tub. Once in the tub, and they were both relaxed lying there with their eyes wide open enjoying the stars in the Wyoming sky,

Travis said, "Hey April, would you have any interest in taking a couple of days off for a mini vacation? It is going to be a few days before the machine shop has our engine machined."

April could not believe her ears! Travis wanted to leave his shop and car for a few days. It took her a moment to formulate an answer! "Yes, absolutely, I would love to take a few days off. Where do you want to go?"

Travis replied, "Well, I thought maybe we would take the motorcycle and go up through the Wind River Canyon and spend a night in Thermopolis. The hot pools would feel great. Then we could ride up to Cody and then swing into Yellowstone through the East entrance. We could stay at Old Faithful Inn one night and then swing down through the Grand Teton Mountains and in Jackson a night. It would be a long but fast ride back home after that. "What do you think?'

April's eyes began to tear up. April said, "Travis that would be wonderful. I am going to start packing right now!" Travis smiled and said, "Remember pack light, we are taking the bike. I have checked the weather, and it should be good, but it will be cool at night."

The next morning they loaded up the bike and got ready to take off. Travis was pleased to see that April was in shorts. He would be able to reach back and feel those beautiful legs all the way to Thermopolis. The first part of the ride was a long straight boring prairie. Travis had to force himself to stay under 90 MPH. He could always tell when he was going too fast as the stereo was hard to hear above 90. They stopped for fuel and a quick bite in Casper and headed right back out. The sun was bright, and in a couple more hours they could see the beginnings of the little town of Shoshoni. He pulled into Shoshoni Drug for lunch. They had the best hamburgers and malts in the state. They both ordered a cheeseburger basket. Travis had a vanilla malt, and April had a triple chocolate one. They took their time eating, and not much was said as they were both too busy enjoying the food and their malts! Travis finished first, of course, and he went and paid the bill. He noticed a little-stuffed moose in the gift shop and picked it up for April. Man, he loved that girl. She smiled and gave it a quick kiss. She quickly named it Wilbur! She said, "OK, Wilbur, let's ride."

The next two hours were fantastic, and they were taking their time riding through the winding Wind River Canyon. April noticed all the different flowers and trees. Travis noticed all the layers of the various layers of rock representing all the thousands of years of erosion from the river digging its way down into the rock. He mentally commented how powerful a little water could be. They saw deer, antelope, coyotes, and wild horses. The Wind River area was of course where the Shoshone Indians lived for a hundred plus years until the evil white men drove them out. It was almost a disappointment to come out of the valley, except that they were now very close to Thermopolis. They pulled into the Hotel in the late afternoon where Travis had made reservations. It is right inside the Thermal State Park. They went in, threw their stuff in the very nice rooms and headed over to the water park. Travis liked the older pool in the park. It did not have as many kids fighting to get on the water slides. They both went into their respective dressing rooms, and Travis quickly put on his suit, and he wore a t-shirt as well. He was not very proud of his portly body. April, of course, put on a tasteful bikini and had a terry cloth cover up which she discarded as she got into the pool. Travis noticed that even the old men in the pool soaking up the minerals and heat paid close attention to this beautiful girl when she came out of the dressing room. Who could this goddess be with?

Travis was already in the pool as he had wasted no time getting in. The water had a bit of a sulfur smell but was a delightful 100 degrees. It felt good on his sore muscles from working and the long ride. She quickly grabbed Travis's large, strong arms and wrapped herself with them. Now the old men realized who she was with. Their wives and girlfriends were glad to see that she was taken, although they were not too sure what a cute young girl would want with the older man. Travis and April lay back wrapped in each other's arms…eyes closed and taking in hot water swirling around their melted body almost as one entity. They lay there for nearly an hour just soaking it in. Travis suddenly sat up and said, "Hey let's go down the water slide." This surprised April, but she was game. They both made several rides down the slide as there was a very little line and it was a real hoot. April screamed like a little kid giggling on every pass. Travis, of course, kept trying to streamline his large body in different ways trying to go faster on each pass. On the 6th pass, April came out of the end chute a little sideways which ended up with her getting a nose full of water. The mineral water was great to soak in but did not feel good stuffed up your sinuses. Travis and April had enough for the day and headed in to get dressed.

When they came out, Travis suggested pizza and TV next. April said that sounded great. They headed back to the room. They shared a cheese pizza and watched an old John Wayne western. Both fell asleep before the end of the movie. It had been a wonderful long day, and they slept very soundly wrapped in a spoon position. Travis had his hand wrapped around April, and she had his hand pulled close to her breast. Wilbur, of course, was with her as well. All was right with life.

The next morning April woke up first. Travis still had his hand wrapped around her and was holding her. She also felt his morning hard member pressing against her behind. Travis stirred a bit but tightened his grip on her beautiful body. He also pushed his member harder against her. He was still asleep but dreaming about the obvious. April reached to the table and pushed down a couple of times on the lotion container she had left on the nightstand. She quietly put some on her cylinder. She really did not need it as she was wet with anticipation. She then reached between her legs and guided his hard throbbing rod into her hot wet tight cylinder. Travis was not sure if he was dreaming or if this was real. He was still half asleep. Either way, he instinctively thrust hard into her hard wet space. It was tight, warm, and familiar. He knew it was the love of his life, April. He instantly moved his mouth to the back of her neck and began kissing, and licking her beautiful skin. She tasted so good. April moaned, and she said, "Bury yourself in me hard honey."

Travis increased his thrusts and quickened his pace. It felt so good each time he thrust up into her hot body. He squeezed her breast, and he heard her say, "Yes, yes squeeze the orgasm out of me." Travis squeezed harder and put her left nipple between his thumb and finger. Just as he did, he could feel her contract in orgasm, and he felt his manhood flood with hot female nectar. He bit her neck lightly and felt her orgasm again. He was awake now and wanted to pound her harder. He rolled on top of her back and positioned his hands next to her body to support his mass and give him maximum leverage to slam his eight-inch thick member into her hot body. He began making a slow, deep, hard thrust into her. He was starting to build up to orgasm deep inside, way down low, but it was rising fast. He began accelerating his pace. He slammed like he wanted to wear her out. He almost thought it was too hard when he heard April say," Come on baby harder, make me orgasm again." He rose up on his feet almost like he was doing pushups, but they pushed-in instead. Sweat was now rolling off his face. He began pounding her ass thrusting his member into her flooded hot body. She started yelling, "Yes, yes, yes pound me, Travis." After a final few thrust, he could not hold back any longer. With one final thrust he began pumping her full of his semen and was met with a flood of her juices. Her vagina was a river of cum. After a final few pumping thrust he collapsed on top of her. She turned her head and buried her tongue into Travis' mouth. After they broke their kiss she said, "Good Morning honey."

Travis quickly said, "Yes it is."

They then snuggled together and after another hour of sleep, they both got up, took showers and loaded the bike. The next stretch in their trip was a ride from Thermopolis to Cody. The road still had mountains for about 20 miles but then straightened out for a hundred plus miles. It was deserted, and the sun was out. April whispered into Travis's ear, "Let's haul ass, honey." The bike they were on was no stock bike. A stock motor had about 60 HP. Travis had taken the engine out and installed a big bore kit as well as a stroker crank. It now had 134 Cubic inches instead of 88. He also installed a bigger cam, port and polished the heads, installed oversized valves, stronger springs, a 44 MM carb, a two into one header, and an upgraded ignition system. It dyno'ed at 120 HP, but more importantly had 130-foot lbs. of torque. He also installed a stronger clutch spring and filled the clutch compartment with special power train oil that supports cohesion. The bike had an incredible bottom end and a thunderous roar when twisted wide open. After April whispered "haul ass," Travis slowly rolled the throttle on to full power. The bike resonated with the torque spinning the rear tire pushing the bike to over 110 mph. They covered 100 miles in less than an hour and never saw another vehicle until they were about 5 miles from Cody.

They stopped in Cody for brunch and both ate like they were starving. From Cody, they turned west towards Yellowstone. The ride now became beautiful. No more 100 mph, but now it was rolling hills and sweeping turns where Travis leaned the bike through. What a great ride. They passed beautiful lakes, Buffalo, Elk, Deer, and even got caught in a Bear traffic jam. The jam was caused by a momma grizzly Bear with two cubs. They went across the famous Fishing Bridge where there were hundreds of people catching fish, and then up to Yellowstone Canyon. There they got off the bike and walked up to both the upper and lower canyon falls. This was one of the most breathtaking sights April had ever seen. Travis and April held hands on the walk, and every time they stopped Travis took the opportunity to kiss her and tell her how much he was enjoying the trip.

April welcomed the walks as she was a bit sore from the morning's activity of riding each other and the bike. After they went to Yellowstone Canyon, they turned south towards Old Faithful. They stopped there and sat on the bleachers and waited for the next eruption. April sat on Travis, with her naked legs draped across his lap. He could feel the men around them carefully watching and secretly admiring him. After the Old Faithful eruption and a few pictures of April in front of Yellowstone Lodge, they headed further south towards Grand Teton Park. They did make a stop at West Thumb and walk the mud pots, April found them fascinating. Travis commented, "April can you imagine what the first trappers and explorers thought of this?" He then told April the story of John Colter who had split off the Lewis and Clark expedition. He was the first white man to walk through this land, and when he returned to St Louis and told his tales of Yellowstone's thermal activity, they did not believe him. Yellowstone in fact soon became known as Colter's Hell.

From West Thumb they headed south into the Grand Tetons. April was overwhelmed with everything she had seen. However, when she got her first view of the Tetons from the front she said, "Stop…stop…I can't take in anymore! It is too much, I can't see one more thing!" Travis had made reservations at Jackson Lake Lodge. He knew the maintenance manager there as he had worked on their standby gen-sets both at the Lodge and Colter Bay campground. His contact, in fact, had gotten them the Moran Room, which was a very nice room that had a direct view of Mount Moran. It was breathtaking. They had dinner at the Pioneer Grill and then set out in the lobby until dusk when they retired to the room where they had hot tea with Irish Cream liquor. They both fell fast asleep in each other's arms.

In the morning they got up early and rode down through the park, stopping at Jenny Lake where they saw a moose! From there they rode over to the old style barbeque at Moose Junction where they had breakfast. Old style pancakes and pan baked biscuits. They sat outside and enjoyed the view. April thanked Travis for the wonderful weekend. Then April made Travis very happy. She said, "This is great, but I miss the shop, and I am anxious to help you put the race motor back together. Can we drive straight home from here?" Travis blinked in disbelief as he had wanted the same thing but did not want to disappoint April.

Travis said, "April, are you sure you don't want to go to Jackson and spend the day?"

April did not even hesitate. "No, I really am ready to go. I would just buy a bunch of junk that I don't need. The pictures and memories I have of being with you are tokens enough for me. Let's ride."

They dressed in leathers for riding and April put on chaps over her shorts. They would be going over Togwotee Pass, and it would be cold. It was about 50 miles to Dubois. It took almost over an hour driving in the mountains. Once they hit Dubois, it was 190 miles to Casper. From Casper it would be 180 miles on the interstate to home. They were home by 10:00 PM, unpacked and in the hot tub by 11:00 PM. They would be asleep by midnight. It had been a great weekend. Tomorrow, they will be up early and start the final assembly of the race motor.

CHAPTER 16:
A NEW FIRE BREATHERS IS CREATED

They had agreed to meet at the shop by 6:00 AM. Travis was surprised to see that Zed had Camaro Girl in tow! Travis gave Zed an inquisitive look, Zed said, "Amy (New Camaro Girl) wants to know more about engine building. Is it OK?" Travis contemplated this a bit. Then Travis said to April, "April, can you draft some kind of nondisclosure document?" April said, "Yes, I think so. What would you like in it?" Travis considered this for a moment and said, "Amy must promise not to use the knowledge gained to directly compete against our race team in any class or category for the next five years. Also, state that she is free to use the knowledge acquired for her own personal gain unless it is direct competition of our race team." "Further, any contribution she makes to us is considered our intellectual property."

It took April a couple of drafts and a trip up to the Dealership company lawyer, but she had it done in less than an hour. The Dealership lawyer added some standard language that they use. In reality, Travis knew that knowledge is power, and what she would learn would be tough to protect legally. He was not upset however, as someone had to teach others, and he was honored that someone wanted to learn from his team.

All the parts from the machine shop are back. The Team carefully cleaned each part as if they were fine China. If they were to drop any piece of the internal parts and leave a dent or mark, it could create a stress riser in that part that could be a point failure later.

Travis took personal responsibility for the block. They had used a high-speed air grinder to make all the corners smooth, the internal walls had all the casting flash ground smooth as well. The goal was to remove all restrictions for the oil splash to return quickly to the oil sump. Oil that was clinging to internal parts consumed energy to spin. Zed had done this to the connecting rods and pistons before balancing. Travis had given the responsibility of inspecting the crank to April as she paid great attention to detail and he knew she would have it perfect. They had also paid the machine shop to "Knife Edge" the crankshaft. This cuts the counter weights in an inverse V, allowing the crank counterweights to cut through the air during rotation. It also makes the reciprocation mass lighter.

They took great care in cleaning every nook and cranny of each part. Travis insisted that each part be final cleaned with lacquer thinner and then sprayed with a combination of thinned down transmission fluid. They thinned down the transmission fluid with mineral spirits so it would flow through a spray bottle. Transmission fluid has a high amount of detergent additives in it, and in the thinned state has a viscosity of less than 5 WT. It would sink into all the pores of the metal. When the block was thoroughly prepped, Travis painted the inside with tan epoxy paint and then let it sit under heat lamps for two hours to harden. The paint was put on thick so it would fill all the pores. When everything was ready, the block was carefully put on an engine stand and all the internal parts were laid out on two layers of white sheets. The main caps were removed and again cleaned.

Travis then took great care to install the special full grooved main bearings being careful only to touch the edges. He knew that the oil and acid from his fingers would damage the bearing surface. Most main bearings only have a groove on the top half of the bearing, this groove allows oil to flow into the crankshaft and then to the rod bearings. By using full grooved bearings the oil would flow during the complete revolution of the crank. The new billet crank was also cross-drilled so that the oil receiver hole would feed the rod bearings from both sides of the crank journal. These new high dollar parts were going to make this new engine much stronger. The engine modifications and new parts had also removed almost a pound off the internal rotating mass. That was like taking 100 lbs. off the weight of the car.

The new engine would use less energy turning itself, and would rap faster. It was like a runner taking every effort to lean their bodies on everything but pure muscle.

Once the bearings were in and carefully lubricated with white assembly grease, the crankshaft was air cleaned one more time and laid in place. There was no need to check bearing clearance as the machine work of all the parts had been meticulously checked with micrometers and dial indicators for dimensions and straightness. The main caps were then installed and torqued with a two-step sequence starting from the center. All the bolts in the bottom end would be coated with an anti-seize compound. He would have to remember that this would show up as copper in the first oil sample. It happened once before and it freaked him out and he ended up tearing an engine down for no reason. After the installation, Travis tuned the crank once around to make sure it glided around with no restriction. He also struck both ends with a soft blow hammer, (Rubber hammer with steel shot inside) to remove excess assembly grease from the thrust bearing. Now he could use a dial indicator to check end play. All was good.

Now the engine was rotated on the engine stand to its right side to allow the pistons and rods to be installed on the right side. Travis carefully picked up one of the rods and piston assemblies which used full floating wrist pins retained with double snap rings, and placed it in a soft jaw vise (bench vise with rubber inserts so as to not damage road surfaces). He was careful to clamp the assembly high enough on the rod so that the piston skirts were supported, so they would not rock from side to side when he installed the piston rings. Travis used .015 piston ring gaps, which had already been set during the pre-assembly process. When he installed the rings, he was careful to keep the compression ring end gaps 90 degrees from the wrist pins. Most people don't know that a piston is not forged round. They are made a bit egg shaped. The wrist pin area and skirt expand at different rates. They change size when heated; hence , why the rings should be 90 degrees from the wrist pin. When heated in the engine, the piston would be perfectly round because of the different expansion rates.

Travis used special moly coated rings for quick break in. Before the ring compressor was installed, he made sure to squirt liberal amounts of transmission oil around and into the rings. He was careful to install the ring compressor on the piston rings making sure it was square to the top of the block. Next he rotated the crank, so the rod journal was at the bottom of the throw. Travis then put rubber caps on the rod bolts to protect the crank as he was installing the rod and piston. He then placed the piston and rod assembly into the cylinder and used the dead blow hammer using soft taps to make sure it had all lined up correctly. He also tapped on the top of the ring compressor to make sure it was seated on the top of the block. When he was positive all was well, he pushed the piston in using the handle end of the dead blow with one hand and supporting the rod with the other. He did this with one swift movement as he knew too many assemblers who used multiple small taps to push the piston in. All this did was allow the ring compressor to bounce and let the ring bounce out and break. Engine assembly must be done with confidence and skill to be done correctly.

Travis pulled and guided the connecting rod and bearing again with white assembly grease onto the crankshaft rod journal. He double checked that the rod number was facing out verifying that the piston was installed with the correct side out. Next he then placed the rod cap on numbers out and the bearing tabs facing each other. Sleeve bearings have a tab that goes into a groove, which does not keep the bearing from spinning, as most folks think, but instead ensures that the bearing is centered in the bore. Once the cap was installed and torqued, Travis moved the rod from side to side as a final check that all was well. This double checks the machine work. He repeated this process for all eight piston and rods. When the short block was complete, Travis used a torque wrench to turn the engine over as a final check. If all was correct, it should take less than 30 FT LBS to turn over. Travis put a plastic trash bag over the whole engine and wrapped it up with tape before he moved to check the rest of the long block assembly parts.

The next step was the top end of the engine including the cam and lifters. Big block Mopar has a lubrication problem when using a roller cam. High lift roller camshafts use a roller lifter that rolls up and down the cam lobe rather than sliding up and down the ramp. At some point when you increase the lift and duration, the edge of a solid/hydraulic lifter edge digs into the lobe ramp. A roller cam rolls up the ramp. The problem with a roller lifter in a big block Mopar in the 80's, was that the roller lifter is smaller on the bottom. When you use a high lift cam, it picks the lifter up far enough that the oil floods out to the point of losing oil pressure as well as flooding the top of the engine with oil, which wastes horsepower.

There are several complicated fixes including sleeves in the lifter bores, high dollar high volume oil pumps and several others. However, Mopar created a special mushroom tappet solid lifter camshaft with rounded edged lifters. These rounded edge lifters slide up the ramp. The lifters looked like mushrooms. Travis talked Mopar into letting him use a custom ground mushroom cam with longer duration and a grind centerline that allows for more valve overlap. This allows better cylinder fill when there is a boost from either turbos or a supercharger.

Travis needed a very special cam as turbos don't bring in boost right away unlike a blower, hence he needed a little more advanced center line than a blower cam. The center line is a measurable point that is the center in degrees between Top Dead center and max intake valve lift. A lower center line like 104 Degrees and the valve closes quicker in relationship to the piston moving up. A higher one like 108 degrees means the valve closes slower. Blower motors have instant boost so you use a later/ retarded degree. Naturally Aspirated engines are more advanced, like 104 degrees, to "fool" the engine into thinking it is high compression. Turbo charged engines need to be right in the middle. Travis used a 110 degree centerline. He also used a bit more lift than a blower, so the valve is wide open when the boost comes in. Travis also used a gear drive rather than a timing chain for better control. Travis did use roller rockers and 3/8 chrome moly push rods. All of this feeds air and fuel mixture through a set of special casting Mopar aluminum stage IV heads that Travis had modified. The heads had bronze valve guides, and he used big block Chevy oversized aftermarket stainless steel valves with 11/32 stems rather than the stock 3/8 stems. The smaller stems took up less room in the port so it made the port bigger!

On this build Travis heard about a process to put a brass O-Ring machined and installed into the head surface where it contacts the head gasket. This would allow more strength of a fire ring around the combustion chamber for the head gasket. The ring would allow more boost pressure, hence, more air for more fuel and bigger combustion. The bigger the boom, the more the down force of the combustion stroke. This was going to give Travis a big advantage as they could use more boost if needed. You can only use as much power that the individual tracks can handle. Travis built special intake manifolds for turbos that facilitated the injection system. Travis used a simple aftermarket 7-quart oil pan, and he had drilled and tapped out the block oil picked up from 7/16 pipe to a ½ inch hemi oil pick up. He also installed the special 1/4th thick steel block girdle between the block and pan. This will stiffen up the bottom of the block. All of this made a killer combination that also now had a SEMA approved fluid damper that would dampen out the harmonic vibrations of combustion. Travis made sure everything was clean and torqued to max measurements. This new engine would allow much more boost and would give his team a significant edge.

The dyno results were 15% higher than his last engine… In competition eliminator classes, this is a huge power gain. Most teams were happy to gain 5 or 10 horsepower . The increase in horsepower was fantastic but the rest of the powertrain had to hold up and the chassis had to put it down. You have to be more than fast…the car combination has to be consistent in delivering the horsepower.

After the dyno, he changed oil and pulled an oil sample and sent it to the dealer lab. In an oil sample, the lab analyzes not only the wear metals but the condition of the lubricant additive package. While knowing the status of the oil additives is important when managing heavy equipment, it was not too important in the racecar. The lubricants never have a chance to wear out since the oil is changed after every race. The wear metals, however, are a different case. They are measured in parts per million (PPM). The lab turned the sample processing in an hour, and most of the results were great. They also cut open the engine filters and they were clean.

Travis was not happy with the oil sample lead results. Lead is the metal on the main and rod bearings that is soft and protects the crank surfaces. The lead was only 6 PPM, but normal wear should have been 2 PPM. In other words, it was three times higher than normal.

They pulled the oil pan and checked a few bearings, and sure enough, there was some wear in the load area of the rod bearings. Zed agreed to roll in a new set. Travis called his oil engineer friend and asked him for his recommendations. The phone call resulted in a promise to airfreight a new mixture of engine lubricant that would have more zinc, and an increased viscosity from 20-40WT, to a new viscosity of 30-60WT. This should give the engine more wear protection. Travis's friend promised to send enough for the rest of the season. Once the oil arrived Zed put it in and did another couple dyno pulls. He sent the break in oil back up to the lab and the results came back perfect. They did lose about 2 HP and the oil pressure went up about 5 PSI from the thicker viscosity.

Now that the engine was taken care of, the team turned their attention to the transmission. The internals were in great shape, but the increase of horsepower came in the form of higher torque at a lower RPM. This means they would have to lower the stall speed of the torque converter. This required that they would have to send the converter off and have it "tightened up." They would shoot for a stall speed of about 4500 RPM. Or maybe they would just buy a new one and rebuild the old one as a spare.

This combination would make use of the extra torque now available out of the gate, if they could get the tires to bite. They would have to drop the pressure and maybe even go with a softer compound if possible. They would control the boost to not over power the track, and to not blow the record away too fast. They had made their wastegate adjustable by adding a bolt and lock nut to the end of the waste gate cover to adjust spring pressure. A wastegate directs exhaust gas either towards the turbos or directly into the exhaust pipe. The one they were using now had to be pre-adjusted on a bench. They played with the adjusting screws set up and one rotation seemed to raise the wastegate about 5 PSI in boost . Turbos are driven by exhaust gas, which is taking a waste product and turning it into energy. With the new

O-ring set up on the heads, they would be able to use more than 30 PSI of boost now. They would start with the 30 PSI that they have used before and bring in more power as needed. They had run the boost up on the dyno to 40 PSI and it was a huge horsepower gain. They located the wastegate on a cross over tube where it was easy to get to for adjustment. Travis had also installed a blow off safety valve set at 50 PSI, in case the turbos spool up faster than the waste gate could handle.

The team worked several late nights to get everything back together. The night they finished up, Travis had pizzas delivered and asked Matt to stop down to review their progress. The car looked great, and Travis assured Matt that it was set on kill. Travis had a favorite cartoon on the wall showing two vultures. One vulture said to the younger one, "Patience, my friend, we just have to wait for something to die before we can eat." The second vulture said, "Patience, fuck that, let's go, kill something." That was Travis's outlook on life. He was always ready to make something happen. After a few short passes in the parking lot and a long inspection of the car afterward, everyone agreed that they were ready to kill something.

CHAPTER 17:
READY TO ROCK AND ROLL

The next race was in Topeka, Kansas. The race car hauler was full of fuel, and the race car was ready to rock and roll. The track was much like Denver in that it was in excellent condition. It had a 1/8-mile concrete launching pad and was maintained and run by experts. Furthermore, the elevation was also only 3300 feet meaning they would pick up two-tenths of a second because of denser air. This along with all the changes made would be good except for one thing, traction. They had all agreed to drop to 8 ½ pounds of air pressure, and they had the softer compound slicks. Their sponsors, Big G tires, had also given them a second set of tires already mounted! The drive was long but uneventful. The team was too tired to facilitate any long conversations, they were all in their own private thoughts. They drove straight through taking turns driving so everyone was pretty rested when they arrived. They were so pumped with adrenaline it would not have mattered much.

The team was getting set up when Camaro Girl showed up. She had arrived at the track the night before. She asked Zed if it would be OK for her to ask Travis a question. Zed yelled at Travis, "Hey Travis. Got a minute?" That surprised Camaro girl! She did not mean right now, but when he had time. She underestimated how much Travis valued Zed. Travis replied, "Sure what's up?" Camaro Girl shyly asked, "Well, I am over revving the engine at the end of the quarter and keep breaking valve springs. Got any ideas?"

Travis asked what MPH and RPM she was crossing at. She replied that she was at 145 MPH, and 8500. Travis raised an eyebrow and said, "Yeah. That does not sound right. What size tires?"

She said, "14-32."

Travis inquired further, "What gears?"

She replied, "4:88."

Travis said, "Well 4:56 might help. But I think it might be something else. What RPM converter are you using?"

She said, "5500 RPM."

Travis asked one last question, "What is your total timing and do you have a retard switch?"

Camaro girl responded with a puzzled face before answering, "We use 40 total Before Top Dead Center and it is all in at 2000 RPM. I don't know about the retard thing."

Travis then said," OK Zed, what would you do."

Zed thought for a minute and said, "Well I would add a timing retard switch but not sure about changing to 4:56's. Her 60-foot times were 1.5, and taller gears would hurt her."

Travis gave a hint, "Zed, she is running a big block, is she using her torque well?"

Zed thought for a minute and then his face lit up, "The torque converter is too loose."

Travis smiled, and Zed knew he hit it on the head. "Yep, install a retard switch, use it in second gear, and go to a 4500-stall converter."

Camaro girl said, "Are you sure?" "I don't want to lose my whole shot."

Travis smiled, "Just try it. Also make sure your cam is on a 106-degree centerline. You will know if you have it right if your compression test indicates over 180 PSI or a little higher at this track. You have 11:1 pistons, right?"

She said, "Yes. Ok, I will let my crew chief (her dad) know."

She made one more pass with the old set up as a baseline and then her Dad put in all the suggested changes. They picked up a new converter from the vendors at the race track. Zed helped them swap it out. The next pass picked up 4 MPH, went three-tenths faster and crossed at 7300 RPM with no valve spring damage. Zed, Travis, and even April all got big kisses after that pass.

Travis's time trials the first day went a bit different. His first pass he blew off the tires, and he had to shut it down. The second pass they had dropped the pressure down to 7 ½, he did not use the retard switch, and he stopped at the first trap speed light and still ran the record! He had not used the water injection. After that pass, he had a crowd at his pit when he returned. Zed had already thrown a cover over the engine when they were hooking up to pull the car back to the pits. Nothing looked different, but this would keep them all guessing. They pushed the car into the trailer to set the valves to maintain the mystery. One of the valves was looser than normal. It was .005 more clearance than the others. Normal wear was to get tighter from the valve moving up in the seat. Loose valves means valve train wear. April recorded the adjustment in the logbook. They would keep an eye on it as it could mean cam rocker arm wear, which would slow the car down. They had already made the field, and there was another day of qualifying tomorrow. They decided to go up and watch from the stands for a while.

All of them had their team shirts on so Travis was stopped many times as they made their way into the stands for information and autographs. April had her cut offs on and looked spectacular. Travis noticed that she was getting plenty of attention, so he had his hand firmly in hers. As they went in front of the stands looking for a good seat, he put his hand into her back pocket. He gave her a slight squeeze. April turned and gave him a quick kiss on the cheek, and then Travis relaxed. He had established himself as the alpha male, and he knew that April adored him. How did he get so lucky?

Camaro girl, Amy, was in the lanes getting ready to make a pass, so they quickly found seats about half way up. April sat between Travis and Zed. April pulled Travis hand onto her inner thigh. It was warm and soft, and he was close enough to feel her internal heat. Travis was having trouble keeping his mind on the race.

His attention changed when a very cool 33 Willis came to the line. It had an 871 blower on it and was loping into the burnout box. The loping is caused by a massive air supply from the 871, which was most likely over driven as well. This means that the drive pulleys were sized to operate the blower faster than the engine manufacturing tons of boosts. The driver is an older white haired male. He had the car set up rich to make sure the pistons did not seize. Too lean and the pistons would burn. Too rich and the plugs would foul. This guy knew what he was doing. He did a great long burnout. He slowly backed up, and the engine surged all the way back. Damn this was cool! He also had a pretty brunette helping him back up into his tire tracks. He eased into the first light, and a big block Vega wagon was already in the second beam. The 33 put the transmission in neutral and cleared the throat before going into the second light. This old guy was putting on quite a show. He then pulled into the second light, locked the transmission brake, and he buried the throttle. The engine roared, and the light went green.

The Vega got out first, but the Willis exploded past the Vega before the 60-foot light. He banged second gear, and the car went sideways. This guy could drive! He eased the car back into the groove and finished the quarter mile. He ran a time that was about a half second slower than Travis! Wow, he would have to watch this guy as he was really competitive. Travis suspected he had more in it as well. What a show!

Next was Camaro girl and next to her was a rear engine small block dragster. Camaro girl got out of the dragster, and the dragster was having a hard time catching her! He finally caught her in the traps, but Camaro girl ran .04 under her index. This was time trials, if it had been a race, she would have smoked the dragster and he would have to spot her! The changes they had made really woke up the car and this chick could drive.

They watched for about another hour, and the cars all seemed first class. The last car they watched had a transmission failure that oiled down the track. It was going to take a while to clean up. They decided to go back to grab something to eat and go back to the pits. When they arrived back, Bubba was there. His car was running well also. His Vega defined consistent. They all sat down and ate a late lunch. It was a beautiful sunny day and with not even a whisper of wind. When they had finished, Travis gathered the trash and disposed of it. He went through the trailer and turned on the stereo and cranked it up. He went back and sat down. April sat down and threw her legs into Travis's lap. Travis massaged her calves, and she closed her eyes and let out a little moan. Bubba's eyes were locked on the scene. Zed said , "I think I am going to see Amy. She will be in a good mood after that last pass." The other three just lounged in the sun and discussed what tomorrow might bring.

Travis had decided to try the water injection tomorrow. The track was perfect, and the shutdown was very long. The shadows were getting long as the last car made the final pass. Several of the racers were gathering at their pit. The beer came out, and Zed broke out the grill. April started to bring out burgers and dogs, and Travis made baked potatoes by wrapping them in tin foil and throwing them in the coals. The bench racing started, and April came over and sat on Travis's lap. She put her arm around him and began swinging her legs back and forth. Travis found that his mind was drifting from the racing talk to watching April's perfect legs swing back and forth. Travis loved the way her knees looked. Perfectly even and her calves were perfectly shaped with enough muscle to be shapely and yet soft to the touch. Travis had his hand on her smooth thigh, and April caught Travis taking a long glance at her legs. April jumped up and started cleaning up to try and give others a hint. Soon the group broke up with everyone drifting off to their own rigs or the local hotels. Zed had come back to eat but now said, "Catch you later guys." Travis had not even finished putting the tools away before April was in the shower. Travis came in just as April was getting out of the shower.

Wow, the water was perfectly beaded on her skin. Travis grabbed her and said, "Let me lick you dry." He picked her up as they embraced in a passionate kiss. Travis kept his mouth firmly planted on April's mouth as he gently laid her down on the bed. He then worked his way down her firm breast spending ample time on each one not favoring one or the other. He then licked down the center of her belly, spending time at the beautiful navel. April was moaning with anticipation.

From there he worked his way down her to her naked, hot, wet womanhood and he began using his large tongue to give her long, broad licks. He was careful to cover here entire length with slow long licks always finishing on her clitoris. With each stroke, he got a little faster, and he soon began working primarily on her G spots. April grabbed Travis head and pulled his tongue deep into her as she began to orgasm. Travis lapped every last drop from her and rose up with a raging hard on.

April said, "Stick that hard tool into me now." He buried himself deep inside her with the first stroke, and April's mouth fell open. Travis eased out and looked deep into her eyes. He said, "Are you ready honey."

April just gave a low deep moan and he knew it was time to deliver. He kicked in the nitrous and began hammering her beautiful body. He next grabbed her by her ankles and spread her legs wide to gain deeper access. He loved the back of her legs and kept firm grasps but not too tight to hurt her. Sweat began building on his brow and ran down his face onto her beautiful legs. April opened her mouth with a loud moan and started to orgasm hard on Travis's hard weapon. Fluids flowed from her womanhood, and he felt it squirt into their love connection. Travis lowered her legs and moved them together as he climbed on top of her and buried his tongue deep into her mouth. Their tongues twisted and danced as Travis began pumping into her. April squeezed her legs together, and she could feel Travis's manhood rub on her soft legs. That friction was driving Travis wild with desire! She moaned into Travis's mouth and that was too much to take. With a final few deep thrusts, he began coming hard and deep into her tight, wet, warm womanhood. Afterward, they were exhausted. The kiss lasted longer than his orgasm. They both released their grasp and Travis rolled off of her, but she rolled with him.

They fell asleep still holding each other. It was a deep, deep sleep with no dreams, just peaceful bliss. Travis woke first the next morning .Travis then kissed April's soft eyes. He rolled out of bed and headed for the shower. In the shower he reminded himself just how great his life was. He felt like a million dollars, and it was going to be a great day. He had decided to open the car up, hammer down, and find out what wide open would do. He felt like he was on top of the world. The car was at full boost, water injection ready, and he could use the retard switch for a final push to get the most out of the ride. He would wring the rag out for everything it had to give.

CHAPTER 18:
PUT THE HAMMER DOWN

Zed was back early in the morning. April was already in the shower. Travis had been awake for a while thinking exactly what was needed to do to get the car ready. They were going to set the boost to 35 PSI and set the rear tire air pressure to 7 PSI. He was going to use the retard switch and the water/alcohol injection in high gear. The car was set on kill. All out, no holds barred. It was time to see if all this shit works.

After April finished getting ready, she made breakfast for all. Breakfast was a sausage and cheese muffin and a big Diet Soda. They were sitting next to the car, and Travis told them his plans. Everyone was quiet for a few minutes, and then Zed broke the silence . "Fuck'n a Tweety. Let's do it."

Everyone knew what to do. April set the initial tire pressure. Zed mixed and filled the water/alcohol injection system and adjusted the wastegate up. They had agreed on 60% window washer fluid and 40% distilled water. They used distilled water so no minerals would be injected into the combustion chamber. Travis made sure the retard switches worked correctly. It took about 2 hours to get all ready and warm up the car. Yep, they were ready. They could make up to three passes today. Travis knew that they should be more conservative, but fuck it, he was tired of waiting to prove to the world that turbos worked.

Travis was more nervous than normal as he knew too much about failure analysis. All it would take is one bad weld, a manufacturing stress riser, or just any of a thousand weak links. Screw it, he was going to put the pedal to the metal! It was time to go up for first round time trials. Travis had his suit on, and he was in the driver's seat. Zed was driving the tow vehicle, and April had her foot on the tow rope to keep the slack out. They were following their process to the tee. Travis was very proud of the team, they were performing just like clockwork. When they pulled up, they were three rows back from the front. Perfect, they could see how the track was holding up but not wait too long.

The knots in Travis's stomach were already getting tighter, but he was ready. He knew that once he was in the burnout box, he would be okay. Adrenaline would take over. He watched the cars in front of them, and the traction seemed excellent. It was 75 degrees, and even the sun was positioned correctly. The world seemed to be lining up for them.

Ok, it was time. He was starting the engine and warming it up. He eased the car in the water box after a quick kiss from April and a tap on the helmet from Zed. As Travis rolled into the water box he slammed the pedal to half throttle and the boost came up, and the tires began to fry. He was in high gear, and the tires spun wildly. Before he knew it, the car was at half-track. Travis eased the car to stop and dropped it into reverse, and he put slight pressure on the pedal just enough to start to move the car backward. He had gone about 75 feet keeping the center of the car in the lane when April appeared on the left side. He was in the right lane. April guided him back into his tracks, and they were perfectly aligned with his burnout rubber. He saw the lights on his left side. April signaled for him to stop and gave him thumbs up. He paused for a moment and gathered his thoughts. He did a dry hop to make sure the tires were ready and took a deep breath. Here we fucking go!

Then he eased the car into the first staging light. The car in the other lane was already staged, and the starter seemed impatient. Travis did not care. It was his time, and the team had worked too hard to rush this moment. He started to power break the car up to raise the boost. When he heard the turbos spool up, he eased the car into the final stage light and when it lit he locked the transmission brake and buried the throttle.

The lights started down and when the third yellow light flashed, he released the transmission brake, and the car exploded out of the line. The pull was incredible, and before he could even focus the shift light was on. No traction problem today. He banged second gear, and the car jigged a little to the right but stayed in the groove. Travis corrected quickly. There was that feeling of scoot, but the car then began to fly…literally. The front tires came up when he hit second gear! Luckily, they went right back down, and the car just gained speed incredibly fast. The engine was already at 7500 RPM, and they were in the traps. They may have to consider taller gears at low elevation tracks. Travis did not even look at the other car, which actually had gotten out of the gate first. In fact he passed him at half-track. Now he had to concentrate on slowing down. Wow, he was flying, and even the chute did not seem to slow him down as much as usual. He had used all the power adders. He knew it was the pass of his life. The car turned into the last turn out lane. It took a few minutes to pull his helmet off and get his belts unbuckled. He concentrated on slowing his breathing.

He heard the crew coming. Horns were honking, and the team was screaming. It was a little incoherent, but wonderful. April had the time slip, but he heard her before he read it. He heard her say…you ran a full second under the index and beat the world record by half a second. Travis grabbed the time slip, and he could not believe his eyes. They had broken into the 6.80's and ran over 205 mph! The new engine was a monster. Yep, the one-second under the index was going to screw them a bit but fuck it. The realization that everything worked was overwhelming. He was hugging both April and Zed when his eyes began to tear up. He could not help it.

They made one more qualifying pass that day and ran .010 slower but plenty fast to back up his new record. They decided to pass on the third run opportunity as it was not going to get much better than the first two. They would be the number one qualifier. That Saturday night was a bit of a blur. There were several car publications there, and Travis had interviews and well-wishers in their pit until after midnight. NCRA also stopped by and checked out the car, the fuel and had the team weigh the car. All checked out. When Travis explained the water injection it did raise a few eyebrows.

Saturday night passed slowly because of anticipation. Travis only slept about 3 hours. He spent most of the night laying there just watching April breathe.

In the morning, they pulled the valve covers and checked the valves again. This time there were no surprises. They changed oil and Travis inspected the cut open oil filter. No surprises there either. Finally, they changed transmission fluid just to make sure everything was ok. Zed filled up the water injection system and April topped off the fuel tank. They were ready. They went up to the staging lanes and checked the ladder sheet. (Final day cars are paired for close races) They pulled the 33 Willis with the wild blower. Travis knew that he was going to come out swinging. They would be the third pair up. This would be quite a race!

Travis did something out of character. He got out of the car and went over to the older man with the 33. He said, "Hey, man, I saw your pass yesterday and this is one cool ride." The older man at first stayed straight faced but then broke into a big smile. He replied, "Thanks, man, that coming from you is quite a compliment."

Travis smiled and was surprised the guy knew who he was. The older man then said, "Let's let it all hang out this pass."

Travis smiled and said, "Yep, completely agree," and shook his hand and then added, "Good Luck Man."

He climbed back in the car and pulled on his helmet and belts. April and Zed had pushed the car forward and they would be up next. Travis was all business now. Travis did another long burnout. April positioned him perfectly again. Travis heard the competitor's blower loping. Damn that car was cool. The 33 was first into the lights. Travis again took his time and concentrated on the tree. The 33 would be first out of the gate and he was running a slower index. Travis saw movement to his left but did not freak out. He was in the zone and he saw his last yellow come on and let the transmission lock button fly. The car leaped out the gate, but the 33 was really moving. Travis had still not caught him at the 1/8 mile mark. However, he was in second gear now and he was pulling very, very hard. The turbos were screaming, and the blower had the advantage out of the hole, but turbos pulled harder on the big end. It was all over at the 1000 foot mark. Travis had caught the 33 and was now pulling away. Travis decided not to use the water injection as it was not needed. He ended up beating the 33 by about a car length, which in comp eliminator was like a mile. He popped the chute and headed for the turn out lane. The 33 had taken the same turn out. Both drivers sat in their cars and waited for their tow vehicles.

Travis had his helmet off first and he watched the 33 driver pull his off and open the door for a bit of air. He looked over at Travis and Travis could tell he was a bit disappointed and not used to losing. Their eyes locked for a minute and then he gave thumbs up and a smile. Travis returned the thumbs up and had a really good feeling deep in his stomach. He had just beaten one of the best.

The next pass, the competitor had a red light as Travis's car was just too intimidating. Travis backed out at 1000 feet and coasted through the traps. They drew a bye round next as they were the low qualifier in Comp Eliminator. This was a single run, but Travis made a full pass to make sure the track was still solid. The pass was .0005 slower than the record pass. This meant they were in the final round.

The final was going to be against a six cylinder rail car. It was .080 under their index as well. The index for the six cylinder car was much slower so Travis would have to spot the slower car over a second in tree lights. This last race was going to be one to watch and a test of Travis's patience. Once again, the team worked hand in hand to get ready. Not much talk, just a few technical words and quick careful movements. The car was ready, the team was ready, and Travis was ready. The track was cooling off, however, and the traction could be an issue again. The team decided to put on the second set of fresh tires. Thanks Matt! Travis would have to make sure he did a hard, long burnout to break them in. The sun was lower in the sky when they were called to the lanes. Both cars pulled into the lanes about the same time. Both drivers looked straight ahead. It was all business on this pass. Travis had his helmet on and belts tight. The track official was waving them into the burnout box. April kissed him on the helmet, and Zed gave him thumbs up. Travis gave his team a nod.

He rolled into the water box, slipped the transmission into second for a high tire speed burnout and stepped down on the throttle half way. The tires lit up and grew high from centrifugal force. He did a half track burnout to make sure the tires were broken in. April was in front of him quickly to make sure he was lined up. Travis took his time to make sure he was exactly where he needed to be. He cleaned the tires with a dry chirp. He placed the transmission in neutral gear. He then blipped the throttle to clean out the engine. He eased it back into gear, and waited till the other car moved forward. He eased into the first staging light. This time he moved into the second light first. He buried the throttle with the transmission brake locked. The engine roared and the lights seemed like forever to come down. The other car was out there already and gaining speed. Travis was able to hold out till the last yellow light and then let go. Not his best reaction time, so it was all about power. Out of the starting gate and he was really moving now.

At 1,000 feet he had not caught the rail yet, but he was locked on like a guided missile now. The car was already moving like a freight train and then he hit the timing retard. It seemed to jump like hitting another gear and that is when he pulled ahead of the rail and his wind light came on.

They had won another race, and they were also way out front in points for the annual championship. The next several races were much the same. The car seemed to be getting more and more consistent. During time trials they did try and raise the boost but the tires would blow off as they could hold no more power. The mph was always great as the turbos always provided a fantastic top end. They had managed to win all the points meets in their Division and even one outside their division in Minnesota. They were in first place and ahead quite a ways in points. They did have a race in Denver where they had raised the boost and the car got quite a bit sideways during a qualifying run. Travis was able to correct it, but he had to pedal it and dropped a couple of tenths. He stayed number one qualifier, however, and they won the race.

They turned the boost back down after that pass. They were on the ragged edge every pass. They had to change tires after every race, but luckily with Matt and Big G Tires as their backers that was no longer an economic issue.

They were also having trouble keeping the turbos together. At the end of each pass they were shutting down and the turbos were still spinning very fast and they were also very hot. When they took them apart there were even oil quench marks on the shafts just like the drilling rig turbos Travis had seen. This was a telltale sign that Travis had seen on some of his customers' engines . The turbos were still spinning and hot and the leftover oil in the pressure galley dripped on the hot turbo shaft leaving a "quench" marks where it hit the hot polished bearing surface. They had to rebuild them after every race.

Travis had an idea to cure the situation by using a pressurized accumulator to help keep oil flowing after shut down. The accumulator has a diaphragm with nitrogen on one side and oil pressure builds on the other side. This maintains a reserve of stored oil pressure to be used after shut down. It does flood the exhaust a bit with oil, which will cause a puff of blue smoke on startup but is manageable.

The bottom line to all of this is that our team had a commanding lead in first place towards the comp eliminator championship. As the point's leader, they were automatically invited to the National event of the Fall Nationals in Indy. If they won there, they would lock up the championship and the record for both ET and MPH. They had two weeks before the Indy race, and it would take a couple of days to get there. They would have time to go over the entire car and make sure it was loaded for bear.

CHAPTER 19:
TAKING A BREAK

It had been a great season and the team decided to take one weekend off. Zed was off to see Camaro girl, Amy. Travis decided to take April on a motorcycle ride across Snowy Range. They would stay at a mountain lodge that Travis knew of that had Hot Tub rooms and no TV. Whatever would they do! They loaded up the Glide, and then rode about 3 hours through Laramie, across the Snowy Range Mountains and then to Saratoga to stay for the night. The leathers would protect them and keep them warm in the early morning hours and in the mountains. April looked incredible in the tight leather chaps over her jean shorts. There was just a peek of skin exposed that gave a hint of her satin skin under the leather.

The ride was pleasant. The pulse of the Glide seemed to vibrate their tensions away. They rode over the pass towards Laramie and had breakfast at a truck stop in Laramie. I-80 crossed Wyoming and the large truck traffic meant that they were great truck stops. Not always the healthiest food, but it sure tastes good. Travis had biscuits and gravy, and April had an egg and ham omelet. Their bellies were full as they took off for the mountains. About an hour out of Laramie the grade began to get steeper, and the Bike groaned a bit as they had it loaded down with luggage. The bored and stroked motor Travis had built handled the load well, since it had plenty of bottom end torque.

The landscape was beautiful. It was full of evergreens, wild flowers, and leafy trees. Travis loved the Blue Lupine flowers that were along the roadside. His Dad, who had passed away, had always loved them. As they neared the summit and the temperature dropped, the landscape changed to mostly evergreens. They would actually rise above "tree line" where it was too high and cold year round to support tree growth. Travis stopped on top of the summit, and he and April took pictures of the bike with a snowy background. They asked an older couple to take a picture of them on the bike, please. As the man of the couple handed Travis back the camera, he said to Travis in a low voice, "Damn you are a lucky bastard" as he admired April. Travis smiled and agreed. He knew he had it good. April was not only beautiful, but she was smart, and they had a common interest. She was also not afraid to get dirt under her nails. She was a natural mechanic and had a good foundation of physics. How could Travis have been so lucky to have found such a treasure?

They stopped for fuel and a stretch on the other side of the pass. It would take them about 30 minutes to get to the Lodge in Saratoga. When they got there, they had a warm greeting because the lodge was owned by one of his customers. The owner had several pieces of heavy equipment used for snow removal and continuing development and maintenance of his lodge. Travis was surprised that his room had been upgraded to a suite at no extra charge. The owner said," Hey, there is a bottle of Champagne in the room, cold and ready and that is on me."

Travis and April thanked them, and they unloaded the bike and headed for the room. It was getting chilly as they were still around 7000 feet. When they got to the room, they discovered that it had radiator heat, but it also had a lovely fireplace and fresh cut wood. It had a big leather couch and a king size feather bed. After they unpacked and Travis started a fire, they decided to head straight for the Hot Tub which was sunken into the floor. It was small but big enough for two.

April filled it while Travis tended the fire to a roar. Travis loved the feel of the hot water when he first got in. Both he and April gave sighs of relief, because they were both sore from riding all day. They sat close together and, of course, April soon had her beautiful legs in Travis's lap. He stroked her legs and even rubbed her feet, and she lay back and closed her eyes. Travis noticed that her beautiful body was shaved as she wanted to be ready for her man. He always tried to stay trimmed up himself, and it was not just a one-way street.

They took their time lounging in the tub for 30 minutes or so when April finally moved into Travis's lap. She buried her tongue deep into his mouth. She was not a shy kisser, and he liked that. They were hungry for each other, and they kissed for quite some time. April soon felt the rise of Travis's manhood pressing up into her. Without a word, they both got out of the tub and headed to the bed. Once there, Travis wasted no time in placing his head deep into her lap. He loved the way she tasted and the moans she expired when he was devouring her. He loved that she grabbed his head and pulled his mouth deeper into her. After her first orgasm, he held her legs high and wide so he could use deep slow licks that started at the far end of her crevice, and finished on her hard clitoris. Every inch tasted delightful. She squirted more orgasmic juices out which he quickly lapped up. He loved licking her juices that flew out onto her beautiful inner thighs. He would lick all the way to her beautiful calves as he savored her juices and her legs.

After several orgasms, he rose up and buried his now rock hard cock into her love nest. She was so wet that his first stroke went all the way into and bottomed out. She moaned loudly and said, "Yes Travis, bury yourself into me hard."

He did his best to pound her as hard as he could, but she kept saying harder, harder, please. He loved holding her ankles firm, but not so hard that he would bruise her. She loved being spread wide open, so Travis could pound to maximum depth. Travis varied his pounding. Sometimes hard and fast and then when she would start an orgasm, he would slow to hard and slow to maximize the duration of her orgasm. Her body was so tight, he was concerned that he would over stretch it and hurt her. She continued urging him on reassuring him that he was not hurting her.

He had lasted about 30 minutes, and at the end, Travis had her ankles in his strong hands, and he was pounding her for all he was worth. He finally shot a huge pulsating hot load that he was sure would blow the top of her head off! She answered back with gushes of girl orgasm of her own, and then they collapsed

Travis was now on top, with his mouth on top of hers and their tongues dancing in her mouth. Beads of sweat were on both of them as they had quite a workout. Travis was sure they were both spent, but as they broke their kiss, April said, "Roll over honey, I am in charge of round two!" Travis lay on his back and April started working on lapping all their mixed juices from Travis limp member. At first, it seemed that Travis crankshaft was not going to rise to the occasion, but she was patient and truly enjoying her love juice meal. When she started working on his balls, his member began to crank up! She began to lick her way up his belly and chest. When she reached his mouth, she buried her mouth in Travis's mouth. He was surprised to find her salty love juice tasted intoxicating.

April whispered in his ear, "Honey, if you will lick my sore pussy clean and make me cum again, I will let you put your hard cock in from behind." Travis's cock leaped to attention and Travis' strong arms lifted her warm body on top of his mouth. He buried his tongue into her and began to lick as deep as he could. April quickly reversed and returned to sucking and licking, deep on his stick.

Travis loved the taste, smell, and view of her beautiful ass and legs. When he was afraid her talented mouth was going to steal away his waiting surprise he grabbed her breasts and raised her up so he could bury his tongue deep into every hole. To his surprise, this gesture awarded him with an orgasmic rush from her vagina. This hot liquid was running down his neck and onto his chest hair. After she came a second time from this stimulation, April moved onto her stomach and said words Travis loved to hear, "Come on baby, put it in from behind." Travis's heart and head began pounding. He wanted to savor this opportunity and enjoy it. He first poured them some large glasses of Champagne.

April drank hers down and said, "Come on pound me, honey."

She again lay on her stomach, but this time she arched her behind up with her legs held together. The sight was incredible. Travis knew what he wanted next. He poured the rest of the Champagne onto her ass and legs and then began licking it from her beautiful sexy body. He worked his way up dragging his hard cock up her legs until nestled at the entrance to her beautiful vulva. He paused there to let the anticipation build. He put his mouth on the back of her neck. Her hair still smelled great.

To his surprise, April raised her body and pushed her wet love channel onto his raging hard cock. She gasps and then said, "Oh, there it is. I love your hard cock deep in me. Hammer me hard, honey."

He started slow and began to move hard but slowly . It was incredible, and it was taking every ounce of control not to orgasm into her beautiful body. April encouraged him, "Come on honey, harder baby. I like the way it feels, but I want you deeper before you cum."

With those words, all hesitation was gone. He rose up on his hands and looked down to the incredible sight of his body buried into her from behind. He began to pound her slowly , and low guttural grunts came from deep in her throat. April said," Yes honey, harder , faster, please." Travis began to ram deep into her as far and hard as he could. His speed picked up, and she just kept saying, "Yeah, yeah, and yeah!"

Finally, the inevitable explosion would hold back no longer. With a loud grunt, he buried himself as deep into her as he could and began exploding.

April said, "Yes, yes fill me up with your hot love." Travis shot every drop of his love juice into her hot channel with April pushing back into his rod. Travis rolled off after nearly passing out. He had ravaged April's beautiful tight body. They locked in a deep passionate kiss. They then spooned and fell fast asleep.

They slept for over 10 hours, which was uncharacteristic for both of them. They woke the next morning after both dreaming of their previous night's passion. Travis woke with normal morning wood, and as April awoke she reached down and guided his member into her somewhat sore body. Travis began to thrust softly up into her slowly. They were both a bit sore. April reached down between her beautiful legs and grabbed Travis's balls massaging them just right causing Travis maximum pleasure. Travis held off long enough to feel April orgasm. It was a calm but enjoyable way to start the day. They fell asleep for another hour and then showered together and packed up to get back to the shop and race car.

They went down and had a big breakfast and then headed out. They decided to go back through Rawlins, then Medicine Bow, and then take back roads to Laramie where they could hop on I-80 to Cheyenne. They took their time going through the mountains but once on the plains Travis ran hard. They were taking back roads and rode for a couple of hours and then stopped at Independence Rock, a State Monument. They looked at all the names that the settlers coming through had carved into the hard stone. It always made Travis think about the bravery of these folks seeking a new and better world. The Wyoming terrain would have been very rugged, and if they traveled in the winter, they would have been fighting subzero temperatures, biting winds, and blowing snow. He would have been one of those folks. April cried a bit after reading about a death announcement of a man's wife and child who were lost to sickness, probably due to bad water and extreme weather which was pretty common back then.

They made one more stop in Medicine Bow for a bio break, and then a hard, but beautiful, ride back through Laramie arriving home by 8:00 PM. Travis decided on a soak in the hot tub for the couple and early bed. They were both spent and sore, but it had been a wonderful weekend. Tomorrow they would hit the shop where Travis and Zed would get started on the car and April would get started making travel plans for the Indy event.

CHAPTER 20:
LOADED FOR BEAR

Travis and Zed were both in the shop by 6:00 AM. Travis asked Zed if he had a good weekend and Zed answered with a smiling "Yep, how about you?"

Travis just commented, "Yep, an experience of dreams."

The conversation then turned to the tasks at hand. They quickly had the power train out of the car, and after helping Travis get the engine on the engine stand, Zed started on the transmission refresh. He first pulled the converter and dumped the oil from it out on a clean white shop towel. He inspected the particles that were on the towel. No large pieces, just normal small wear material. He called Travis over when he checked the end play of the stator, and both agreed it was acceptable. Zed then filled the converter up with lacquer thinner. They would let it soak until it was time to put it back together, spinning it on the bench every couple of hours to make sure it would be clean inside. They would have to add thinner every day because of evaporation. Finally, Zed threw a clean shop towel over the neck to keep the debris from getting in. Zed then began careful disassembly of the transmission being careful to lay all out in order on clean towels.

Travis started the engine disassembly. Travis started by draining the engine oil again through a white shop towel. He also inspected the engine oil debris. He did find a few longer aluminum flakes that concerned him. He cut the filter open, and it confirmed a bit of bearing material. It was easy to identify as bearing material as it was not magnetic. Travis used tri-metal bearings which had a top thin layer of lead, then aluminum and last steel backed with a copper bonding in-between the steel and aluminum. Next, Travis flipped the engine over and used a 3/8 impact to buzz the pan bolts out. He carefully laid out all fasteners and parts after cleaning on white towels on the clean bench next to the stand. While not quite an operating room sterile condition, it was very close. Travis removed the deep sump oil pan, the girdle, and debris in the bottom and verified again that they had something going on in the bottom end! Damn, they did not need that now. Travis thought to himself, "Keep your cool and diagnose."

From the position of the debris in the pan, the issue must be in the center. Travis already suspected the thrust bearing because of the position and shape of the debris. He started with the center bearing cap and, in fact, the rear facing thrust bearing surface showed abnormal wear. Something was pushing forward on the crank. Travis went immediately to the nose cone of the torque converter requiring him to dump out the thinner. His inspection revealed that the converter nose was, in fact, showing some abnormal contact wear. He and Zed next measured the cone hub depth and compared it to another new spare converter. It was about .310 of an inch longer. He was mad at himself as they should have noticed this when mounting the transmission to the engine. Travis was pissed and gave all this information to April who called it into their converter builder. She would have much more finesse. They apologized and said they would overnight a new one at no charge and that it would be triple checked before shipped. They also offered to replace the crankshaft if it was damaged. They did not want a world record holder using their products upset! April would return the old one for failure analysis and then they would repair it at no charge and send it back for use as another spare. They would also pay double the contingency bonus should Travis become the national champion. Lastly they said, "As long as Travis remained the national record holder, there would be no charge for any parts they needed!" They said that they would include a master rebuild kit for the transmission at no charge.

Now that Travis had found the potential problem, he put the old thrust bearing and cap back on and torqued it so that he could proceed with the natural engine disassembly process. He would replace all the bottom end bearings during the engine fresh up. He rolled the engine back up to normal position and began disassembling the top end. He pulled the exhaust and turbos off and set them aside. He would disassemble the turbos later. It was more important timewise to get the engine apart in case there would be machine work needed to fix any additional issue. He then removed the intake manifold injection plenum, which on a Big Block Mopar only required eight bolts. He would disassemble all the injection valves and nozzles later. He did, however, give it a close once over to look for signs of leakage from boost. All looked well. He next removed the valve covers and closely looked for valve train damage. Nothing was evident. He checked valve lash to make sure there was no abnormal wear. He then removed the roller rockers and inspected them closely using a magnifying loop. They had trouble before with stress cracks under the rockers. Mopar used a rocker shaft, which was much stronger than the Big Block Chevy individual rocker set up. All looked good. He laid the rocker shafts down carefully to index them so he could put them back exactly as they came off. He then removed the push rods inspecting each for wear and straightness. They used a special chrome alloy 3/8 push rod. These were also laid out so they could go back in the same position. All were straight and no abnormal wear. The valve train all looked good. Next Travis removed the cylinder heads. He turned the head valves up and inspected the valve faces. The color of combustion carbon was gray which indicated proper air fuel mixture. White would indicate lean, black rich, and brown indicates oil burning. The valves all looked in good condition.

Travis poured lacquer thinner in each port to check for seat seal. One exhaust valve on the passenger side leaked a bit. Travis and Zed agreed they should do a valve and seat touch up. Travis then measured each spring height using a dial caliper. They kept them documented as if one gets higher by a large amount it would mean seat or valve wear. All was within their .005 tolerance they had set. He also checked all the valve spring seat pressures using their valve spring checker. It was a simple device that looked like a press with a ruler on the side. The process is to press the spring down to the assembled height using the ruler on the side and read the PSI gauge to see how much pressure is being generated to return the spring. The valve springs cycled thousands of times in one run so there was a high fatigue rate. The springs were all about 10 PSI lower than the last time. Both Travis and Zed agreed that they should change them out. They had three spare sets.

Last, Travis used a straightedge and a .001 feeler gauge on the head surface to check to see if they were warped. The heads they use are made out of aluminum and susceptible to heat warping . All seemed good. Travis made sure everything was laid out in order. This new shop was fantastic. Lots of bench space and climate control air. Travis then moved to the front cover and camshaft. They used a gear drive instead of a timing chain. It was much more accurate. The gear drive also had a cam thrust button to keep the cam from working itself forward. He removed the front cover and gear set. He had the engine upside down so the lifters were all in the open position to allow him to remove the camshaft. He then pulled the lifters and laid them out. They used mushroom tappet lifters to keep oil trapped in the lifter galley. Conventional roller lifters and the high lift cams rise too far out of the galley. When this happens, the oil pressure leaks off and drops the oil pressure to low dangerous states. They had discovered this the hard way. You could use a top fuel hemi oiling system to compensate but that was a waste of money and energy driving the large volume pump. The special mushroom cam worked great for their turbocharged application. The extended head surface of a mushroom style lifter allowed them to use higher lifts. He inspected everything one more time with a magnifying loop. Travis noted a little wear, but could not be measured as significant. He then checked the cam straightness in a set of v-blocks. There was less than a .002 run out which was good to go. Travis actually preferred used proven camshafts and lifters as they have already been broken in. You just needed to remember to put the same lifter on the same lobe.

Next, Zed and Travis moved to disassembling the short block. They removed each piston looking at each ring set. The rings have what is called a "witness lap" on the second ring. If you can see a line around the ring in the center, it means the ring was not worn out yet. They looked good, but would change them, and this time they were going to use total seal style rings. The rings overlap each other to eliminate leakage. Travis also checked to see if the piston ring lands had excessive wear. If the ring lands are worn, they could flex and flutter at high speed and leak or even break at 7000 RPM. Ring leaks are the largest loss of horsepower. All the pistons looked like new other than some light scuffing on the skirts. Travis used 600 wet and dry sandpaper with penetrating oil to clean them up. Next, they turned over the engine and removed the crank. They kept track of the main and rod bearings and laid them out and marked them, taping them together and cleaned them with thinner. Travis put them under the microscope and looked at the wear. No signs of lack of lube in the centers. The new oil was working. He did see some polishing of the upper main bearings indicating that the crank had risen from centrifugal force. This meant that the engine balance at high RPM was off a bit. They would have to shave the piston bottoms slightly and re-balance the engine.

Lastly, they inspected the block. The main saddles all looked great, measured correct and the line bore straight. The cylinder bores did show signs of light scoring. Travis checked his log book, and there was still .005 they could hone out using a deck plate and sunned hone. These tools were contributions of Matt and his generous sponsorship.

The transmission was much the same other than a little slippage on the high gear clutches. They would put in new plates and discs, as well as new clutch piston return springs. Zed and Travis agreed that they would not reseal pistons and servos. They looked good, and it is too easy to cut seals. They disassembled the valve body and all looked good. They both agreed to open the discharge port for the reverse a bit more. This would allow the transmission break to release just a few milliseconds quicker. They now knew what they had and there were no major surprises. They also knew there would be several late nights getting it all done.

It was almost midnight before they turned the lights off and they headed for a shower and bed. April was already asleep when Travis got home. He took a quick shower and jumped into bed. It was good to know that there were no major problems found during disassembly. Travis only slept a few hours and at 4:00 AM he decided to get up and go to the shop. He liked working in the early morning when building engines. He could concentrate without getting interruptions. Travis started with the block hone work. He first measured all the pistons so he could make the piston to wall clearances the same for balanced power. He then set the block up on the hone using the main journals to set up on making sure the bores were exactly 90 degrees. He then put on the deck plates. Deck plates are torqued on with head gaskets, like heads, and have holes in them to allow the hone or bore the block. The plates pull on the block just like the cylinder heads. By 6:00 AM he had all honed and had perfect cylinder walls. The final finish was with 1000 grit so the rings would seat quickly on the dyno. Travis then put the block in the tank of solvent that had an air lift agitator. They would leave the block in the solvent until they were ready to reassemble it.

Travis next moved to the heads. He started by cleaning the valves with solvent and a brass wheel on the shop grinder. In a normal rebuild, he would use a glass bead blaster, but the debris was light, and the brass wheel is a softer cleaning tool. After the valves were all clean, he then measured all the stems and inspected the margin on the valve faces. All was good. Next, he put the valves in the valve grinder and set the angle to 44.25 degrees. He used this for just a bit of interference angle so there would be a small but crisp sealing seat between the valve and valve seat. All the valves cleaned up with less than .002 grind. He did not have to re-do the other two angles. Travis then moved to the heads, which he had also put in the solvent soak tank last night. They were already spotless. He carefully measured all the bronze valve guides which had less than .002 wear. He then chose a valve guide pilot and a new fine grain stone. Once the stone was installed on the grinder, he dressed the stone to a perfect 45 degrees. He used two stones, one for the intake which was bigger in diameter and one for the exhaust. He just touched each seat using the fine and a high speed grinding motor. Travis dressed the stone after each seat. After he had finished the first head, he put it back into the solvent tank and moved back to the other head. He did those seats, and he put them in the solvent as well. They had kept track of all the valves to make sure they went back into the same holes.

It was now after noon, and he was hungry. He went into the office where April had a couple of grilled cheese and some canned soup for all of them. Zed said he was ready to reassemble the transmission. Travis finished lunch and filled up his big cup from the soda machine that Matt had put in for them. Man this was the life.

He then went out and pulled a new set of springs off the shelf and started to check them for seat pressure using the titanium retainers. He had told April at lunch, he was going to use them so she could remove them from inventory and they would automatically get reordered. They all checked in the spec, and within 2 lbs. of each other. He then pulled one of the heads from the solvent and aired it off. He then started putting the valves back in using a little lapping compound on the face and a small suction cup to seat the valve. He spun the suction cup with a wooden handle between his hands, which would lap the valve into the fresh seats. After a few spins, he used a magnifying loop to check the seat seal. This was old school, but it ensured that there was a perfect seal. With the ¾ degree interference angle the seat would be narrow but very crisp. Also, as the valve moved up and down on the seat it would "pound" itself in evenly for a better seal. The logic is, if the seat is too narrow, it would not seal and if too wide, it would transfer/retain heat and burn. This process took a few hours. After Travis was satisfied they were all perfect, he sprayed everything clean with lacquer thinner and reassembled using all new valve locks and a little 50 WT oil on the valve stems so they would not run dry on start up. They did not use valve seals as the stems would run too dry and possibly seize. It was a race engine and they did not care if it used a little oil during runs.

It was after 7:00 pm when he completed the heads and bagged them up in plastic bags to keep them clean. He had also sprayed them down with some penetrating oil to maintain the steel pieces from rusting. Travis decided to call it a day. April had already left, and she was sound asleep when he got home. He did not want to wake her so decided to watch some video from the last race. Many of the track owners provided VHS video taken on the starting line of the cars. Travis looked at the tape for a couple of hours and observed many of the racer's launches. He made mental observations in how many of the cars could have been set up better. Each time the Altered came up, he watched the launch several times in slow motion. On the third pass, where the car made a jig to the right, the cause was apparent to Travis. The left rear tire was wrinkled a bit more than the right. The pressure must be a bit lower.

He would have to show this to the crew. It might be that the sun had expanded the tires from sitting in the staging lanes.

At about 10:00 PM, he had enough and took a quick shower and crawled into bed next to April. She stirred a bit and backed up to a spoon position pulling Travis's hand onto her breast. He gave it a little squeeze and then they both drifted off into dreamland . It was interesting that Travis's dreams were now not as good as real life! The next morning Travis woke before the 6:00 AM alarm and decided to get up quietly, turn off the alarm, and let April sleep. He jumped in the shower and was out the door in 20 minutes. He stopped at the gas station and grabbed a big diet soda and apple pie. He was in the shop before 6:00 AM.

He started by pulling the block out of the solvent and air blew it off. He then sprayed it with penetrating oil to keep it from rusting. The penetrating oil soaked into the pores of the metal. He then put the engine on the stand using one of the jib cranes. Wow, this was an excellent shop. He had the tunes going, and he was soon into the zone. He started by checking the cam bearings. They were in great shape. This was a relief as installing cam bearing is time-consuming and always a risky pain in the ass. Zed was already at the machine shop with their rotating assembly for rebalancing. They had already taken 5 grams out of the bottom of each piston and they needed to rebalance the crank respectively. This should fix the crank lift issue at 7000 RPM. After checking the rest of the block over, Travis got out the 360 grit ball hone. The ball hone did not remove any metal and is used to rough the surface for quick ring seat. It was kind of like putting primer on a perfect surface. After he had honed the block he cleaned it again first with warm water, then lacquer thinner and finally sprayed it down with penetrating oil again. The next step was to put in the camshaft and lifters. For a mushroom tappet cam, the lifters have to go in before the cam. After getting the lifters in with the block upside down, he eased it into the cam bearing using white grease and made sure it rotated easily. He was stalled now until he had the crank and number one piston, which was needed to dial in the camshaft. He got a new clean trash bag and used it to cover the motor.

He decided to look over the chassis while he was waiting. You can't rush machine work. He was confident that Zed would make sure everything was right. He started by checking all the Heim joints on the suspension. He was looking for loose lock nuts, elongated eyelets, and in general checked all exposed nut and bolt tightening procedure. He inspected all the welds and braces. He also decided to rotate the front two tires side to side. They used a 1/16 inch tow-in alignment setting, to help the car stay straight could cause a minor amount of tire scuffing. Rotating them would keep it even. The castor and camber is set permanently as the front end is part of the frame. These angles were set when the frame was built in a jig and non-adjustable. He also checked front tire pressure. They ran 45 psi in them, and one was a little high. Travis also repack the bearings and set the preload. They were spindle mount wheels and once he had them on and cleaned up, he moved to check the rear end.

They had just rebuilt the rear end with 4:10 gears so he just drained the oil and inspected the drain plug and the bottom of the drain pan for debris. All looked great, only minor particles from normal wear. He pulled an oil sample, and he would have April run it up to the dealer oil lab where they would check it for parts per million wear metal trends.

Travis insisted that all his customers use oil sampling as it was an excellent way to track wear and maintenance practices. This good, consistent inspection process along with good oil and filter changes using good products, allowed his customers to get the maximum life of the equipment they own.

Travis next checked the rear tires for abnormal wear, cracks, and to see if the screws that secured the bead to the rim were not broken off. Drag racers had to drill through the rims and install sheet metal screws through the rim into the bead of the slick. Without this, the wheel would spin inside the tire and, of course, loose seal. The inertia at takeoff from a standing start was incredible. Travis found one screw had broken off. He used a left handed drill bit and center punch on it. As predicted, as soon as he started drilling the screw, the bit caught the metal and the screw came right out. If this had not worked, he would have tried an easy-out. The last resort was taking all the screws out and removing the tire to get access to remove the broken screw. That would have been a real time consuming pain in the ass.

Travis had just finished checking out the rest of the chassis when Zed came in with the crank. Zed then went and got the piston and rods.

Travis asked Zed, "Any issues?"

Zed shook his head no and said, "Nope, all is good." Travis then cleaned the crank with thinner and installed it using plenty of white grease. He, of course, used new bearings and torqued the main caps, starting from the center out, and torqued them twice. He then installed the cam gear drive and front cover. They would leave the keyway so the cam was on a 110-degree centerline. This is a way to index the position of the cam lobes in relation to piston top dead center (TDC). This is called valve timing. Valve timing profile is how much, and how long, the valves are open and closed in relationship to the piston travel of each respective cylinder. The more advanced or smaller the number, the sooner both the intake and exhaust valves close before TDC, the more compression pressure is built. Travis liked the 104 -106 degree centerline for naturally aspirated engines. With over pressured engines (Turbos or blowers) you can afford to leave the valves open a bit longer for increased cylinder fill. He installed the number one piston with no rings so he could check the cam centerline .

To degree in the cam is a pretty complicated process, but the short version is that you set up a dial indicator on the piston, and another indicator on the number one intake lobe via a lifter. You also have a degree wheel on the crank with the 0 mark indexed at TDC #1. They were not using a degree wheel this time but using the new fluid damper which was marked 360 degrees. They could check and make sure the dampener was marked correctly by comparing it to the piston TDC using a dial indicator during the cam dial in process, killing two birds with one stone. The process then was to record the reading on the degree wheel at .050 before the max intake lobe lift and .050 after the max lift. The center between these two numbers should be 110 degrees before the top dead center. Travis ran through the process twice, and both times it came up with 110. They were good to go.

Travis took the number one piston back out, and he then installed all the new rings on all eight pistons after cleaning them with thinner. It was late afternoon, and April asked if they wanted to stop for dinner. Travis replied that they were on a roll and asked her if she would mind just going and picking up some pizza.

She smiled and said, "Sure around 7:00 PM be ok?"

Travis looked at Zed, and they both agreed that would give them plenty of time to get the short block assembled. Neither tech liked stopping in the middle of a process. Travis and Zed carefully, and methodically, installed all the pistons and rods using transmission fluid as a lubricant on the rings, checking torque and ring alignment multiple times. They finished installing the last piston about 4:00 PM. Travis checked turning resistance using a torque wrench. Travis knew that if all was well, it would take less than 30-foot lbs. He started with 10-foot lbs. and it turned at 25-foot lbs. All was well. They then installed the top end, and set the valves. They primed the oil pump with 50W oil and installed it on the block. They then installed the clean oil pick up screen, windage tray, and main saddle girdle. The girdle added bottom end rigidity and the windage tray kept the spinning of the crank from whipping the oil and robin horsepower. The last step was to install the pan with 5/16 bolts. They torqued the pan bolts twice.

They added oil and pre-lubed the engine with a reversible drill and a pump priming shaft Travis had made out of an old distributor drive gear. It was interesting to listen to the drill as the pump picked up prime and the oil pump as it pushed oil into the galleries and crankshaft. The drill motor would almost stall when everything was full. This was an indication that there were no major leaks in the system. This process also pushed oil to the top side of the engine so everything was lubricated before starting. They were able to build 70 PSI oil pressure with the drill motor. Skipping this step was a common mistake by rookie engine builders. In this case all was oiling well. After they finished building the engine, they hung the transmission and new converter back on and installed it back into the Altered. They then installed the intake and completed the hook up of all the fuel lines, wiring, and water injection systems including testing to make sure all was operational.

April had showed up with pizza and the crew just ate as they worked. They were on a roll. They did not dyno the engine this time as there were no major changes. This meant that they needed to do a startup, let the engine get warm and then do several converter stalls to build boost and make sure the rings were seated . The engine fired up within two revolutions. They let it warm up a bit and then repeated the converter stall process three times letting the engine cool down to touch each time. After the third warm up and stall, Travis and Zed did an engine leak down test, which verified the ring seal. The cylinders had less than 2% leak down which is the best they had ever seen. They also checked boost, which was right on spec. Boost was in direct correlation with horse power. If you have a boost , you have horsepower . If you grafted it out, it was a one on one relationship. The crew, including April, made a complete inspection of the car to make sure everything was just right. After a joint discussion, the crew agreed, the car was "Loaded for Bear."

CHAPTER 21:
LIFE SHIFTS INTO HIGH GEAR

They had four days to load up and make it to Indy for the US Nationals. If they made it to the quarter finals, they would stay in first place. If they won, they would have the Comp Eliminator Championship locked up. Travis also thought they could reset the national record one more time. The team agreed that they would let it all hang out one more time. It would be unprecedented to have a Competition Eliminator rookie team end up as the National champion and record holder in the same year, but no one had tried turbos on a drag car at this level before either.

Travis also had a surprise in store for April. April had secretly told Zed that she wanted to drive the car someday. Travis had just obtained health care insurance for the team, and he used this excuse to ask the team to take physicals. Travis arranged to make the physical for April to be a Class 3 which is what is required for an NCRA driver's license. He offered to do the same for Zed, but he said he was going to stick to turning wrenches for now. Travis had also gotten April a hot pink fire suit and helmet without her knowledge. He had already contacted the track officials, as well as the racing officials and they had agreed, time allowing, letting April do her qualifying passes on the second day of time trials. April already knew everything she needed to know about the car cockpit. He would tell her on the first night of the four-day race, and they would have her practice cockpit orientation. Travis also had a seat bottom and backrest pad made to adjust the seat for April's figure, which was much smaller than Travis's girth.

Travis had planned quite a surprise for April, but little did he know an even bigger one was in store for him. It took them 6 hours to load the trailer with spare parts, the spare short block, converters, and spare transmission. They were very grateful that they did not have to load tools. They loaded the bikes, food, water, clothes, tow vehicle, and lastly, the race car. They checked all the tie downs, and they were ready to rock and roll. It was about midnight, and they were in the shop. Travis said, "OK guys, guess we should head out about 6:00 AM."

Zed looked at April and then back to Travis. Zed then said," I am too wired to sleep. Let's go now."

Travis blinked and looked at April. She nodded her head yes, and Travis shrugged his shoulders and said, "Ok, I am out voted, but I get the sleeper first."

They headed out on I-80. They stopped outside of Cheyenne at a truck stop and topped off with fuel and a bio brake. Travis was still out and slept through the stop. Zed and April had talked nonstop about Amy, Camaro girl, and every aspect of the racecar. Zed had the rig singing at 75 mph. He was being careful to avoid a ticket as there were only two things in Nebraska, corn fields, and police. When they passed the corn palace about half way across Nebraska, the sun was coming up, and Travis was waking up with it. He rubbed his eyes awake and said," Hey, I am hungry."

Just outside of Lincoln, they stopped at a large truck stop. Zed topped off the rig with fuel and April, and Travis went in to find a seat at the dinner. April was wearing daisy duke shorts and a "Moon Eyes" T-shirt with no bra. Travis could feel all the trucker's eyes on April, but he was confident in their now more mature relationship. They walked holding hands and she put a little extra swing in her walk just to tease the truckers a bit. As Travis and April sat down in the restaurant, they began discussing the final prep for the car and what competition might be in Indy. The truckers sitting close to them were shocked at how much April knew about the details.

One of them finally said, "Hey is that your race rig out there?"

Travis let April answer, "Yes it is, and we are headed to Indianapolis for the US Fall Nationals."

The trucker then asked, "What is in the rig for power?"

Travis again let April answer, "Turbocharged and after cooling 3408 Cat running 40 PSI of boost when it is wide open. We have to be careful not to open it up in the lower gears as it would pop the transmission or rear-end because of too much torque."

The trucker blinked and was a bit dumbfounded at her knowledge. April questioned, "What is in your rig?"

The trucker responded, "Cummins, not sure of the details but I know it has a turbo."

April finished the conversation with, "Oh, well competition is not a dirty word," and smiled. Travis was also smiling inside.

Zed was walking in the door and could tell from the smile on April's face something was going on. He caught on quickly and said, "Hey April, can you drive the next leg? I am getting tired."

April, who had just gotten her CDL (Commercial Drivers License), said, "Sure, as long as Travis is ok riding bitch" with a smirk on her face.

Travis laughed at that one and said, "OK you guys, let's get some grub," as the waitress walked up. Travis ordered flapjacks and hash browns with American cheese, Zed had a meat lover's egg omelet, and April ordered steak and eggs. The food arrived quickly and disappeared into their mouths even quicker. Zed and April hit the head and Travis paid the bill.

As he was leaving the trucker, who had been talking with April said to Travis, "You know you are a lucky bastard don't you?" Travis just smiled and nodded and started to walk away.

He paused after a few steps, turned and then replied, "You should see her after she makes a pass in the race car or when she is riding her motorcycle!" The driver's jaw dropped, and Travis headed to the bathroom himself.

They all grabbed sodas and chips for the drive and headed out to the rig. April climbed in the driver's seat, and Zed jumped into the sleeper. Travis looked back as he got in and sure enough, the truck drivers were all watching to see if April really was driving. She turned and looked at them before she closed the door, she made sure they all had another good look, and she winked. The driver she had been talking to just shook his head. April wheeled the rig out onto I-80 easily, and she skipped shifting the rig up to road speed. She really was a natural. When she hit 75 she settled back for the ride. She had noticed Travis, however, watching her legs as she shifted. Each time she pushed the clutch her calves would tense and show off those beautiful lower calf muscles. She looked over to Travis and commented, "Like what you see baby?"

Travis looked up and said, "You know I do!"

April replied, "Well, they are all yours honey." Travis reached over and gave her inner thighs a rub up and down.

They then they heard from Zed in the back, "Come on you fuckers, I am trying to sleep not listen to porn." With that, they all settled into their own worlds. The stereo was kicking out some ZZ Top and it just happened to be the song "Legs." April concentrated on the drive, and Travis looked through the latest Drag Newspaper checking records and class indexes. They made good time and did not stop until they were almost all the way across Iowa. Another bathroom and soda break and back on the road.

By nightfall, they were close to Peoria where Mother Caterpillar was located. Travis had some friends there that worked for Cat, and they had asked if Travis and crew would stop in for the night. They were a day ahead of schedule, and it would be an easy drive from Peoria to Indy, so they stopped. Travis's friends, Jeff and Linda, were glad to see them. They had acreage outside of town and had plenty of room for the rig. Travis had called ahead, and when they got there, they found a full blown barbecue waiting for them. Jeff had never met April or Zed and was impressed with April, the crew, the rig, and the race car.

When Linda saw April, she commented to Travis, "Not bad, old man" with a smile on her face.

Travis blushed and said, "Yep, pretty great life right now."

Linda added. "Good for you, you're a nice guy, you work hard and deserve it."

Travis spent most of the night in a chair next to the fire pit they had started with April in his lap. April always fit in with whoever they were with. She was smart and had not let her beauty go to her head. Jeff, Travis's friend, was impressed at how much she knew about the car. Linda was even more impressed at how she jumped up to help and did not seem to have eyes for anybody but Travis. Zed hit it off with Mike Black, one of Travis's Peoria friends. Mike was a Jeep guy and had a CJ5 with a supercharged 454. They had been ripping around Jeff's acreage all night. You could hear both of them laughing above the roar of the motor. Mike did not drink, but he was high on horsepower. They damn near tipped the thing over a couple of times. The party lasted to about midnight and then all said their goodbyes and drifted off to bed.

Travis and crew just slept in the rig as all their stuff was already there and it was very comfortable. They said their goodbyes that night as they would pull out early the next morning. It had been a great but long day, and everyone fell to sleep quickly. Travis took a bit longer to fall asleep, he was anxious to get his first look at the track conditions. He took one more deep breath of April's wonderful smelling hair, which was a mix of perfume and smoke from the fire and fell asleep. He was truly a lucky guy.

The next morning, Travis woke up to the wonderful feeling of having his member buried deep in April's warm wet love tunnel. He had his normal morning stiffness, and she had woken and just simply pushed herself back on to his shaft. Travis had slept with his right hand around her breast. He gave it a little squeeze to let her know he was awake and began pumping his shaft deep into her. She pushed back to match his strokes to get maximum penetration. It only took about 5 minutes of this action for April to orgasm, flooding his crankshaft with female lubricant. April then reached down and caressed Travis in the area just behind his testicles. She used her fingernails lightly which felt incredible for Travis. Travis made a few more slow but deep thrusts into her and could not help but to lightly bite the back of her neck as he squeezed her breasts. He had both of them in his hands now. This combination must have hit April's trigger as he could feel another rush of her warm juices flood his crankshaft. This was all it took for Travis to start a violent orgasm shooting his male lubricant deep into her.

He came hard, and April said, "Yes, Yes honey, fill me up." Human combustion! After they took a minute to let their hearts slow down, April turned her head, and Travis gave her a morning kiss.

April said, "Come on, let's get a shower and get on the road old man." Travis lightly slapped her on the ass as she rolled off the bed and said," Thanks, Honey, you are the best thing that ever happened to me."

They showered and jumped in the rig. It was still early enough that Jeff and crew were not up yet when they pulled out. It was still dark in fact, and Travis remarked at how beautiful the Peoria lights were as they headed up the hill on I-74 headed towards Indy. They were on the road for about an hour and a half and at the halfway point. They stopped at Champaign at their favorite breakfast fast food place. It was a quiet breakfast on a cool morning as everyone was buried in their thoughts. Travis was calculating the air fuel ratio changes they were going to have to make for Indy as it is only 1500 feet. April was recalculating the championship points so they were sure what it would take to lock up the championship. Zed had his eyes closed in the sleeper and was dreaming of his night to come with Camaro girl! She was coming to Indy as well. Her combination that Zed and Travis had suggested, had her number two in points for her class.

Around 9:30 AM, they were pulling into Clermont, which is on the East side of Indy and where the US Nationals were held. It was busy but not too full yet. They only set in line for 30 minutes waiting for check in and then another 20 minutes for tech. The officials knew the car and the only special thing they asked for was to have them weigh the car. They could go ahead and set up, but come back and pick up the weight slip from the official scales. They had to pit by class but were able to get a spot close to the return lanes. It was a beautiful day but a bit humid. Travis would have to factor that in his calculations for the injection set up. They set up camp making sure to give proper access to the fans that bought pit passes. April had made up new team shirts that were very bold and attractive, and she had made up about 100 more for sale to the public. She had them priced at $10 which Travis thought was too much, but they could always go down. By noon they were all set up and had the car weighed. It was 150 lbs. over which was fine. They had a ballast box built in the back of the car to adjust weight. The crew thought it was a bit strange that Travis wanted to leave it heavy. Secretly he was planning for April's license passes. The 150 LBS should make up the difference between his and April's weight.

Next, Travis removed the injection valves and disassembled them to put in the smaller return line jets which would increase the injection pressure and richen the mixture. They would pull the plugs and make sure after they made the first pass.

At 1:00 PM, they called their class to the lanes and Travis and the car were ready. April topped off the fuel and Zed checked tire pressure as Travis was putting on his suit. He then climbed into the car and April and Zed brought the golf cart around and hooked up the tow rope. April was wearing her Dazy Dukes again. She had several pairs as she knew they drove Travis wild. She liked pleasing him and the attention from everyone else was OK too. She put one of her beautiful legs and foot on the rope taking up the slack. Zed carefully started towards the lanes. Zed timed it so that they were 4th in line. This would let Travis see several cars go down the track and observe the traction and bite on the starting pad. The first car left very hard and in fact pulled a wheel stand high enough that the driver had to "peddle" the car. It came down hard, but did not seem to acquire much damage. No clean up.

Zed looked at Travis and said, "What do you think?"

Travis thought for a minute and said, "Let's try 9 PSI." Zed set the tire pressure to 9 and checked them twice." Zed gave the car a once over and gave Travis a thumbs up. The rest of the cars had no problems. April had been recording the times and checking them against the records and indexes.

She came back and said, "It looks like they are running about .02 under except the first one which did the wheel stand." The wheel stander was way over his index. Going up is not going out. Too much wheel stand robs time. It looked cool but might cost you the race.

The car just in front of them was running and pulling into the burnout pit. It was a B Gas rail. Travis watched the burnout and then turned his attention to getting the car started. April gave him a kiss on the helmet and he eased the car into gear. The other cars in front of them were staged and lights were coming down on the tree. They left hard and then the starting official was waving them in.

Travis eased forward and he noticed the temperature gauge had come off the 100 degree mark. They were going to make the first pass without the water injection for a baseline . He felt the rear tires bounce in the water box. He hit the throttle about half and the engine roared to life. He could feel the tires roast and the car slide sideways as usual. He did a long burnout to make sure the old rubber came off the tires. He then started to ease backward keeping the centerline stripe in the center of the car until April came into view. April guided him back, and while Travis noticed her beautiful golden legs, he also noticed that her shoes were sticking to the track. The track was so sticky that it almost pulled her shoes off! This looked to Travis to be the best traction they had ever seen. They might be able to turn it up a bit. Now he could see the tree to his left as he was in the right lane. April gave him the stop sign.

He halted the car and put the transmission in neutral. He blipped the throttle to clear out the motor. The engine sounded perfect and he could hear the low whistle of the turbos. Travis did a dry tire blip. The car in the lane next to him was a rail and he was finished backing up. Travis started forward in first gear as he needed time to spin the turbos up. He started power braking the engine a bit using the hand brake to get the exhaust generated to start spinning up the turbos. The boost gauge began to rise and eased into the stage lights until the first light went on. He pulled hard on the hand brake and increased his pressure on the foot throttle and the boost rose again. The rail had the first light on now so Travis eased the throttle down and let the car slip into the second light where he then engaged the transmission brake and he buried the throttle. The engine was screaming now and the turbos were spooled up. The rail was staged now and the lights started coming down. When the second yellow light went out, Travis let it fly and the car roared out of the gate as the green light came on. Travis was surprised a bit by how violent the car left and he noticed that the front end was up about 6 inches and carried them for a bit. The car had left straight so this was not an issue and before he knew it the shift light was screaming, "Shift!" He banged second gear and the car did not slide right but the front end popped up again! The car stayed straight again and it began to scoot…really scoot. Man it was pulling hard. Before he knew it he was through the traps and pulling the chute. He felt the belts tug hard at his shoulders and the car slowed quickly.

He never saw the rail. He took the second to last turn out and let the car coast to a stop. He had not used either the timing retard or the water injection, the crew arrived and had big smiles on their faces .

Zed waited till Travis had his helmet off before he said, "I thought you were going to wait to use the water injection?" Travis blinked with a questionable face? Zed smiled and said," You were within a .01 of the national record." Travis and April both had big smiles. One run and they were dialed in! That afternoon they turned the boost up a couple of PSI and made two more passes using the timing retard. They set new records with each pass. The front end was carrying to the 60 foot mark but the car was holding nice and straight. This was a kick in the ass. They would save the water injection till race day. They were done and had the car under cover by 6:00 PM.

They had comp eliminator number one qualifier locked up on the first day. They broke out the barbeque and folks were starting to gather in the pit. Indy was out of their division, so there were lots of new faces. There were lots of curious peaks under the cover. A couple of racers even asked Travis to take the cover off.

Travis just smiled and said, "No, sorry, we better keep it under wraps for now but I would be glad to answer questions you might have." Travis did his best to respond to questions, but once in a while he would answer with the word "FM which stood for Fucking Magic." It was a great evening.

Around 10:00 PM, April was sitting on his lap. There were plenty of lights from the tow rig.

Travis said, "Hey Honey, I need to get something out of the hauler, can you let me up." April kissed him and jumped up. Travis winked at Zed. There were still several folks sitting around bench racing. April sat down in Travis's chair and was talking with Zed who had moved his chair closer to April to keep her occupied. Her back was to the rig so Travis could get the new hot pink fire suit and helmet out without April seeing it.

She was heavily engaged in conversation when Travis said," Hey honey, you look a little cold. Do you want to put this on to stay warm?" Her head turned slowly, and it took her a second to realize what Travis was holding.

She looked carefully at the suit eyes blinking and then looked up to Travis and said, "I don't understand?"

Travis responded, "Honey, I have cleared it with the track officials and tomorrow afternoon, time allowing, you are going to make your license passes."

A huge smile came to her lips, and she made a very unusual comment, "Are you, fucking, kidding me?"

Travis replied, "Nope, try it on." She put it on reverently including the boots and gloves. She finally slid the helmet on, and all fit perfectly. After April had everything on Travis went over and kissed her on the helmet just the way she did when he was about to make a run. He pulled the license paperwork including the Class III physical from his back pocket and handed it to her. She stood there several minutes taking it all in.

She pulled the helmet off, and Travis said, "Honey you will make four passes. Two half passes to get comfortable, then one easy and one full pass if time allowed. I have arranged for a couple of Pro Stock racers to observe so they can sign off on your license if all goes well."

Travis was standing, and April came over and pushed him up against the rig and put a lip lock on him that lasted long enough that everyone got the hint. When the kiss stopped, folks were already saying their good nights and heading towards their own pits.

Zed said, "Hey, I am going to find Amy." She had made several passes earlier that day but was having some traction issues.

Travis started putting things away, and April went inside to take the suit off. When Travis went into the rig, she was standing there with just the helmet, gloves and fire boots. It was quite a sight to see. Travis' mouth fell open, and he just stared at the beautiful image in front of him. She shoved him onto the bed and then slowly did a fire suit strip tease. She pulled the gloves off first and then bent over backward to remove her fire boots making sure that Travis had a great view and what a view it was. The last thing she removed was the helmet and when she had it off, she gingerly placed it inside the helmet sock and then attacked Travis with wet sloppy kisses.

Travis could feel her excitement and passion coursing through her body. When their long, passionate kiss broke, she started ripping his clothes off. When naked, April buried her warm mouth deep onto his crankshaft, which was already at attention. After she had him at full attention, Travis pulled her on top of him to the 69 position. He buried his tongue deep in her already wet body. He loved the smell of her. She tasted like sweet fruit juice. The concentration of giving her a tongue bath kept him from exploding into her mouth. He kept it up until she had flooded his face and neck twice. She repositioned facing him up on the balls of her feet. She slowly lowered herself onto his hard crankshaft and then slowly started stroking his cock like a piston in a cylinder. When they had found a rhythm, Travis grabbed her breast and made sure he timed his massaging pressure to her down strokes. She was coming down hard on every stroke. He could hear and feel her beautiful ass bottom out on his legs with a wild slapping sound. This lasted several minutes, and he felt several warm gushes of warm girl orgasm flood his crankshaft. Finally, she crushed her mouth down on his and buried her tongue deep in his mouth and began rapidly increasing the RPM of her piston action on his crank. About 30 seconds of this action was all he could take. She was speed humping him! She could feel him engorge as his orgasm built inside his body. She let her last warm flood of orgasm flood his crankshaft. They both explode violently. She continued to kiss him and slowed to a stop. She rolled off but maintained a tight embrace with her leg up on his body. Their hearts were pounding. She finally broke the kiss but moved her head next to his ear.

She whispered, "Please don't move. I don't want this moment to end."

He replied, "Me either honey, I love you and tomorrow will be a great day." They fell asleep that way and remained like that for quite a while before finally moving to a spooning position. Tomorrow was truly going to be a great day.

CHAPTER 22:
AN UNEXPECTED SURPRISE

They awoke early, and both were anxious about the upcoming day. After they made the bed, April laid her fire suit reverently out on the bed. It was a beautiful sunny day but humid. It was going to be a bit sticky, but the race car would love the thick air.

Travis had the car uncovered and was starting to go through his race day checklist carrying a 7/16, 1/2, 9/16, 3/4 and 15/16 wrenches in his work apron. He was going to do a nut and bolt tightening session on all critical parts of the car. If the love of his life was going to make runs in the car, he wanted it perfect. April wiped down the entire car making sure it looked perfect. She was wearing her favorite red hot pants and a V neck sleeveless T shirt.

Travis said to her, "Honey, put your helmet and gloves on and jump into the cockpit so you can go over all the controls. I have a track official coming over at the lunch break to sign off on the controls review for your license. Just run through the process as if you were making a full pass."

April, still a bit stunned, put on the helmet, boots, and gloves. She still had on her short shorts, so it was quite a sight! She climbed into the car and continued to practice the process. Ignition On, push the starter button, check all gauges, pull on the hand brake, pull shifter crisply into low gear, ease into low gear, move to the water box and stop, and place the shifter into high gear. Perform the burnout and be prepared to correct for rear tire drift. Ease hand brake on making sure the engine does not die. Once you are stopped, place the shifter into reverse and start backing up keeping the centerline of the track in the center of the car and watch for Travis from the center of the track. Once Travis appears, slow down reverse speed and follow directions to retrace tire tracks. Stop, and place in low gear. Check gauges and blip tires to clear off debris. Put the shifter in neutral and clear out the engine with a couple of throttle blips. Place the car back in low, power brake to build boost and carefully move into the first staging light. Ignore the competitor. Once pre-staged, pull the hand brake on hard and power up turbos easing into second stage light. As soon as the second stage light comes up, lock the transmission brake and bury the throttle. Leave when the second to last yellow light goes out. Watch the front end lift and car drift. Hit high when shift light comes on. Hang on till you are in the traps and then pull the chute, and engage the hand brake when comfortable. Shut off the fuel valve and ignition and slow to a stop. She went through this process about 30 times. She also made sure where the on-board fire extinguisher button was located.

At about 12:30 PM the track official came over, and she went through the process describing it to the official. Travis observed and was not sure if the official was watching the process or ogling April even though she was in her full fire suit. The results however were that April passed, and the official signed off. April got out and was a bit shaky.

Travis commented, "No worries honey, I was watching and you have it down pat."

April replied, "Travis, I can't wait!" They ate lunch but April could not eat much. She was too excited. She had butterflies turning in her stomach. At 1:00 PM the track announcer called for special time trials to come to the lanes.

Travis said, "OK baby, here we go. Get your suit on." April dressed and when she came out Travis took several pictures with his 35 MM camera. Even in the bulky 7 layer fire suit she looked hot. They already had the seat cushions to fit her beautiful body. She put on the belts and Travis made sure they were tight. She put on her helmet and gloves and opened her visor. Travis could see that she was shaking a bit.

He reassured her, "April, honey, calm down. You got this baby."

She looked up, smiled, and said, "Travis, I am not scared…I am excited!" Travis smiled and hooked up the golf cart. Zed was driving the cart, and Travis took his new position facing backwards with his foot on the tow rope keeping it tight. They headed up to the lanes.

There were only a few cars in the lanes for time trials. Bubba and Camaro girl were there to observe as well as the two Pro Stock drivers so they could sign off on her license runs. It only took about 10 minutes for April to be next to make a pass.

Travis leaned down to her and said, "Remember, honey, the first two passes are just half passes. Concentrate on doing a good burnout and take you time. Don't worry about the water injection. Shut down after you hit second and you won't need the chute," He finished with a kiss on her helmet and a quick, "Love Ya Babe, have fun." April did not respond as she was in full concentration mode.

The starting official was signaling her now to move forward into the water box. April started the car, pulled on the hand brake and pulled the shifter into low. The vibration of the engine was pulsating through her body. She eased the brake off and the car moved forward. It was a single run as it was a license pass. She felt the car roll into the water box and as soon as she felt the rear tires dip into the water trough, she shifted to second for more tire speed. She then snapped the throttle to half and the engine roared. The turbos spooled up and the rear tires instantly started blazing smoke and with centrifugal force causing the tires to grow. Oh My God, this was fantastic! The butterflies in her stomach had exploded! She was scared and exhilarated all at the same time. The car drifted left and it was like power sliding on snow! She loved it! She has ridden high powered snow machines with Zed and this felt much like that except on a much higher plain. Before she knew it she was almost half-track . She eased off the throttle and after the car stabilized, grabbed the hand brake. Once the car stopped, she paused to gather her wits. Fuck, this was great!

She eased the shifter into reverse and started backing up, being careful to keep the center strip in the middle of the car. She was in the right lane so watched for Travis to appear on the left. About 100 feet out Travis appeared and had a big smile on his face. He first gave her thumbs up and then guided her back into her burnout tracks. He gave her the slow down sign and then saw the starting tree appear. She stopped the car and put it back into neutral. She checked the gauges and the engine temp was just starting to come up. She blipped the throttle to clear the motor as she had rehearsed with Travis. Travis came up to the cockpit and pointed to both the oil pressure and temperature gauge reminding her to check them. All was good to go. He went back up and gave her the blip signal to clean the tires. She popped the throttle but now the tires were sticky and she felt the hard G force and heard the loud chirp of the tires. This freaked her out a bit causing her to go a bit far and cross the starting line again. No worries, it was a practice run.

Travis guided her back and she again put the shifter in first. She eased the car up using the hand brake while starting to power brake the turbos up. The first staging light came on and she pulled harder on the hand brake and pushed down a bit more on the throttle. She could hear the turbos spool up to a loud scream. The second staging light came on. She locked the transmission brake button on the steering wheel and buried the throttle as she and Travis had practiced a hundred times. The engine roared and the turbos were screaming. She could feel the whole car tension up, ready to launch. She had huge butterflies in her stomach again. The anticipation of the launch was incredible. Would she be able to handle it?

She saw the yellow lights come down and then the green came on. She knew it was a late light, but as Travis had instructed her she was concentrating on making a clean pass. The car exploded out of the hole and butterflies exploded in her stomach. The adrenalin rush was incredible. All she could think about was, "fuck me, this is wild'. Her head slammed back and April was holding on to the steering wheel for all she was worth. Before she knew it, the shift light was screaming at her to shift. She banged second gear and the car took a jig to the left. She quickly corrected but did not oversteer. She fucking loved this! She was at the 1000 mark before she backed off. She did not want to back off as she loved the pull of the car. She did not want to risk going too far as the race officials were watching. She just let the car roll out through the traps and then she pulled back on the hand brake.

She had no problem making the first turn out. She brought the car to a stop and only then could she feel her whole body shaking and hear her rapid breath inside her helmet. She fucking loved this!!!! What a rush. She could not help but scream with joy. God all she wanted was more of this! She just sat there waiting for HER crew to show up. Travis and Zed soon appeared with the golf cart and they both had huge smiles! She pulled her helmet off and Travis and Zed both gave her thumbs up.

Travis came up to her and said, "Wow honey, your 60 foot time was better than mine this morning! You crossed the traps at 120 MPH!' That shocked April a bit and a big smile crossed her face. They hooked the car up and pulled it back to the pits.

Once the car was parked, April leaped out of the car and attacked Travis wrapping her legs around him and putting him in a lip lock! She broke the kiss and said, "I love you honey, thank you, thank you, thank you."

Travis replied, "You bet honey, let's get you ready for another pass."

They checked the car out and Travis asked Zed to go up and see if she could make another pass. By the time Zed came back, they had added fuel and had the car ready to go again. Zed gave thumbs up and April quickly put herself back into the seat. No butterflies this time. She could not wait to make another pass. The cooling system had the car back down to 100 degrees so they were ready to go. They pulled the car up to the staging lanes and Travis went over to the race officials. April could see that he was having an active discussion. The officials were shaking their heads, which confused her, but finally she could see they agreed and Travis shook their hands. Travis always used handshakes as he knew that it was a very personal touch. A firm handshake just makes you feel good. She was puzzled.

Travis came back with a big smile on his face. He leaned down and said, "April, they have agreed to let you make a full pass because of your last performance." She blinked a bit in shock. Her stomach did a flip.

Her next comment made Travis laugh. She said, "I gotta pee."

She leaped out of the race car and headed over to the tower restroom. The race officials laughed. April was quickly back in the car. Now she was all business. She did an excellent burnout again, and this time she did not cross the start line with her dry chirp to clean the tires. She staged the car perfectly and left under full boost. The car went hard and straight and this time she carried the front tires about 30 feet. She hit second gear a little early but the turbos were fully spooled up and picked up the load. The Altered roared through the lights and she was .02 under the index!

The race officials gave thumbs up. Travis went over and discussed the pass, and they said she only needed one more pass for her license. They would try and get it in before the end of the weekend. Her reaction time was still a bit slow but was something that she could work on. Travis had the beginning of an idea starting to form in his mind. They still had time for Travis to get a run in before the lanes closed. The team went over the car and the only correction needed was an increase of two PSI tires on the left front tire. April documented the change in the log. They kept track of everything. At 200 MPH a low tire could mean disaster. If it came up low again, they would pull the wheel and do a water bubble test. The car was ready, and Travis was excited to get a pass in. It was towards evening, and the air was cooler.

The announcer called," Last call for time trials for comp eliminator."

Travis was getting his suit on and planned to use the water injection. Once he had the suit on, he eased himself down into the seat and then put on his helmet. He was not nervous as the car had proven itself with two drivers now. This was just fucking fun. Zed drove the golf cart, and April was in her shorts and had her foot on the rope. She still had a huge smile on her face as the excitement of her last pass had stayed with her. She said it was as good as sex! Travis had competition…the race car! They were fourth in the lanes, which meant that Travis could watch a couple of passes. It looked like the traction was excellent. Zed double checked the pressure, and it was still at 8 PSI. Travis started the engine and was waved into the water box. When he felt the dip of the rear tires, he nailed it and did a very smoky long burnout. Damn, he liked doing that. He started backing up and soon saw April on the right side this time as he was in the left lane. He stopped when April indicated and put it back into 1st gear. He blipped the throttle and cleaned the tires. He was going to let it all hang out. He was going to push the car to the limits.

He cleaned out the engine and then eased into the 1st staging light while building boost. He then pulled harder on the hand brake to ease into the 2nd staging light. He did not even know or care who was in the other lane. As soon as it came on, he hit the transmission brake and buried the throttle. The boost gauge snapped up, and he watched for the last yellow light to come on and let the transmission button fly. The car exploded out of the gate, and the front end came up about 6 inches. Travis grunted a bit from the pull not sure if it was testosterone or the G force. He was waiting for the jig, but it did not come. The shift light came on, and he banged 2nd gear and then reached over and activated the water injection. The car leaped forward with incredible pull, and jiggled slightly which was easy to control. The car was pulling very very hard. It went hard and straight right through the traps. He was really moving. It must have been a solid pass. He used the last turn out, and in a few minutes, his crew was there with smiles and thumbs up. He had Run .01 under the record.

They only made two passes on Friday and the car performed flawlessly. It repeated the .01 under record performance, which would in fact reset a new record. Travis tried to get April her final pass but the track had several oil downs so there was no time for license runs. Friday night they decided to celebrate a bit and broke out the barbeque grill and asked several of the fellow competitors over for a meal and drink or two. It was a warm moist night in Indy and the music was flowing out of the tow rig's ample stereo. April spent most of the night on Travis's lap. The bench racing was hot and heavy and the conversation about the water injection system actually gave Travis an idea. It took a few tenths to activate the water injection button after the shift. After everyone had left, Travis drew out a quick schematic of an automated system for the water injection. They could run the power wire to the pump but wire the ground wire first through a pressure switch placed into the high gear transmission servo test port and then to a micro switch placed on the throttle so that it was only closed when the throttle was wide open just like a well set up nitrous system. They would keep the current toggle switch in series as an arming switch. The water injection would come on automatically when they hit second gear. Zed said he could get a micro switch from Camaro girl as they use something like this on their nitrous system when they were bracket racing.

They pushed the car into the hauler to work on because it had better lighting and would be more secluded. Travis had a pressure switch that was normally open but closed with 50 PSI. The transmission high gear servo pressure was over 200 PSI. April ran the wiring and installed the 1/8 inch pipe thread switch into the transmission servo. Travis worked on fabricating an adjustable bracket for the micro switch. Zed was back quickly from Amy's pit and tossed Travis the micro switch. He then helped April run the wiring. Travis finished up the small bracket and installed it and the micro-switch on the injection linkage so that it closed only when wide open. This would allow the water injection pump to ground and energize. April jumped into the cockpit and they tried the system several times. It worked like a charm. This would automate the energizing of the system, which might help them pick up a tenth or so. This should make a hard hitting second gear. Very cool, and the team was satisfied with the new solution.

It was about midnight and Zed said, "Hey, Amy is waiting for me, can't keep a girl waiting!"

After Zed was gone April said, "Hey, buddy, did you hear him? I am feeling pretty randy myself, how about some help?"

Travis smiled and said, "Well, how about we wash each other's back?"

It did not take long for the pair to strip down and jump into the hauler shower. The water felt warm running over all of their sore muscles. After a quick soap up they were soon locked in an embracive kiss with their tongues buried deep into each other's mouth. They both had their eyes closed letting the water splash over their heads and also giving their tongues maximum concentration to explore the partner's mouth. They kissed for a long time and Travis could feel his crank get harder the longer they kissed. Finally, Travis broke the kiss and climbed out of the shower. They quickly dried off and ran naked up into the bedroom where April attacked Travis forcing his hands down. He did not fight the effort. She again buried her tongue deep into his mouth. His crankshaft was at full mast now. April's cylinder was dripping wet so without breaking the kiss she raised her body up and placed her love channel right on top of his crankshaft. She lowered herself down onto his shaft with a quick shove which caused a deep guttural moan from her throat. She held it there with Travis buried deep in her for a few seconds and then broke the kiss.

She said, "Hang on Travis, we are going to try and set a new record!"

With that, April rose up to the balls of her feet and then began accelerating her up and down movement on Travis shaft. Travis looked down at the incredible sight and he could see her tight cylinder milking his member with each stroke. She was moving rapidly now and the sound of her ass slapping down on his groin was incredible. She was speed fucking him again! It was so quick it was almost like a crowd clapping. He was going to orgasm too fast! He had to slow down…he tried to concentrate on the wiring they had just done, but when he heard her orgasm and felt the mass of warm fluid flush down his crotch he could not take it. He made a thrust of his own up into her and came with a violent stream shooting lubricant up into her cylinder. She groaned and orgasmed again, flushing their juices down their connected genitals. She made a few more strokes to make sure she had milked his rod for all it had and then rolled off next to him.

He could see her breast move up and down with her rapid deep breath. Finally Travis said, "OK new record. You rocked my world and drained me in 10 minutes!"

April smiled and curled up into his arms and said very softly, "Love you honey. You are the best thing that has ever happened to me in my life."

Travis responded "Likewise babe, we have a great life don't we?" April nodded and they were both quickly asleep.

Saturday there was one round of time trials, and Travis made a short pass to make sure the new water injection setup worked well. It worked perfectly and gave second gear a real kick in the ass. Travis did not want to let the cat out of the bag so backed off of it at the 1000 foot mark. Even letting off early the car ran the index. They would run the first round of eliminations that afternoon. After the test pass, Travis and the team went over the entire car one more time to make sure they were ready. When they got the first ladder sheet (Ladder sheets present who runs who), Travis noticed that the car they were running against was just under their index and it was a slower class so Travis would have an option to use the water injection only if he needed it. The other driver knew he would have to "Tree" Travis even to have a chance. The first race was over before it started. The competitor red lit which was predictable. Travis launched and then made an easy pass. He still caught the guy in the traps even with a red light and an easy pass. They were number one qualifiers and because of that had a bye run for the first round on Sunday unless a round winner broke. That meant they were one easy pass and two hard passes away from the event win, and class champions! Tomorrow was going to be a great day. They would burn the midnight oil tonight making very sure everything was perfect. Hell, no one could sleep anyway.

CHAPTER 23:
A SUNDAY TO REMEMBER

Travis was up at 4:00 AM on race day. He just could not sleep. He was beside himself with excitement. He knew the car was right on the money and was confident that the new set up on the water injection would give them another tenth or two. He let April sleep and after a shower went for a walk. The pits were pretty quiet except for those who had worked all night thrashing on cars to get them ready. The air was thick with humidity which made wearing a fire suit uncomfortable but the race car would love the thick, dense air with lots of oxygen. There would be some records set today. He headed up to the staging lanes and tower. He was surprised to see several of the race officials at the base of the tower. The officials were chatting and eating breakfast. He was walking by with the intention of letting them be. They had much on their plates, and he did not need to bother them. Just as Travis was passing, Tom, the starting official that had witnessed April's time license passes yelled out. "Hey Travis, come over here for a moment if you have time."

Travis smiled and replied, "Sure, anything for you guys."

He could not believe that they knew him by name.

Travis then commented as he walked over, "Hey, this is a great event. How can I help you?"

Tom surprised him by saying, "We all just want you to know how impressed we are with your car and your new driver! Not only is she smart and beautiful, but that gal can drive!"

Travis replied, "Yeah, I am a lucky man."

Tom added," Yeah, we would all like to have daughters like that one."

Travis now flushed red, a bit embarrassed and even angry. He held his cool, however, and said, "Thanks, guys, but she is not my daughter…she is my girlfriend."

All the officials had stopped eating and were now all listening intently. It took Tom a second or two to digest that but then said, "Wow, you really are a lucky man. Damn smart too. You have a record setting car and a hot girlfriend!" He then added, "Hey, we have been talking and if you are willing to stick around till after the finals, we would like to let her make her last pass so she can get her license."

Travis was now very glad he had not reacted negatively to their surprise about April being his girlfriend. Travis replied, "Yes, we would be glad to stick around. Thanks guys, that would be great!"

They gave him a thumbs up and said, "Good luck today. We expect you in the finals!"

Travis thanked them and headed back towards the rig to give April the good news. When he arrived back at the rig it was after 6:00 AM and April was dressed and sitting out in a lawn chair. She was wearing a team shirt and matching shorts with white tennis shoes. She was sitting Indian style in the chair. It hurt Travis's knees just looking at that sitting position. Travis could not help the big smile he had on his face.

April said, "Wow, you are chipper this morning. Are you ready to win or just glad to see me?"

Travis laughed and said, "Well, yes, on both counts, but I also have a surprise for you."

April looked at Travis and said, "Oh yeah, what ya got for me big boy," with a coy smile. Travis flushed for a third time this morning! He sat down next to her and put his hand on her knee and then told her about his conversation with the race officials.

April blinked a few times and said, "I gotta pee!" Travis laughed. They both got up, and Travis saw Zed walking up just as she had made her urgent announcement. Zed had a puzzled face, and so Travis filled in the blanks.

Zed then said, "Travis, I have to talk with you."

Travis had been dreading this. He was sure that Zed would be upset that he had not done some time trials as well. What came next surprised him.

Zed said, "As you know, Amy and I have really hit it off. She has asked me to be her crew chief, and I have asked her to be my wife!"

April heard the last part and ran and gave Zed a big hug. She said, "That is great!"

Zed then said, "Wait there is more." Travis just knew he was going to say Camaro Girl was pregnant but instead he heard Zed say, "Travis we want you to be the best man, and instead of me leaving the team, she would like your permission just to pit next to us."

Travis paused for a moment and then said, "Well, hell, yes and, hell yes!" Wow, this was turning out to be quite a morning!

After a few more congratulations, April said, "OK, boys, let's get this rocket ready to ride. We have some racing to do."

They took the cover off the car and started wiping it down as the sun was coming up. The humid night air had left a layer of dew on the car. The team was not used to all this humidity as Wyoming has an arid climate. Competition Eliminator is a very competitive class. The technology and effort to keep a car current is costly and stressful. Competition Eliminator (CE) is also considered a sportsman class, not Pro, so while the competition is extreme because of the non-break out rule, the competitors are limited. There was just too much mental and financial resource required for the average sportsman racer. Due to these factors, there were only six cars left in the CE class this morning.

Because of all this, Travis decided that he would pull all the stops out on the first race today. He wanted this win and the championship bad. If he beat the first competitor and also stayed low qualifier (farthest under the index) for

CE, he would get the bye run. If he does not break in the bye run, he would be in the finals. If he wins the final, he wins the championship. He felt he had to prove to himself, the car, his crew, his sponsors, and to the world for that matter that turbos were here to stay.

The team moved the car to the lanes when called. This time Travis was first up. This was alright with him as they would have more time to fix anything if something went wrong. He knew the track would be perfect. Travis pulled into the water box and did a moderate burnout. They had the tires at 8 PSI, and there was no reason to tax the power train too hard for a burnout. The car had to hold together a couple more rounds. April was backing him up, but he did not notice her short shorts today. He watched her shoes sticking to the track instead. He had a laser focus on the race today. He did his dry chirp to clean the tires. He pulled into the first staging light, while starting to build boost and then waited for the rail competitor to turn on both stage lights. Other than someone staging next to him, Travis was not even aware there was another car on the track. It was like he could see the whole race in front of him much like a quarterback throwing a pass. He could see the touchdown. The rail moved in and Travis pulled harder on the hand brake and eased the throttle pedal down hearing the turbos scream. He eased into the second staging light, locked the transmission break, and buried the throttle almost in one motion. He was a machine driver today.

He had tunnel vision and launched on the third yellow light. The car jumped out of the gate. Travis did not realize it but he actually had a .01 spot to give to the competitor. His concentration had been so intense that he actually left the starting gate first. The wheels came up and carried about 20 feet. They set down straight, and he saw the shift light come on. He banged second gear, and because he had the water injection on, the wheels jumped up again for a bit. The car pulled harder than Travis had ever felt before. The speed proliferated now, and Travis was through the traps very quickly. He hit the chute and enjoyed the hard pull on his shoulders validating that it was a high MPH pass. He let the car roll out till the last turn out. He sat quietly just listening to his breathing in his helmet. He could hear the engine popping as it was cooling down. He was unusually calm. His crew did not have to tell him. He knew he had just made the quickest pass the car had ever made. The crew arrived in a very jubilant state. He had, in fact, set a new record over .09 under the index, which had just been adjusted! The rail, which was in an almost equal class, ran under their index, but never even came close. He blew them into the weeds. Travis climbed out of the car and April drove the racecar back to the pits.

Travis drove the golf cart, and Zed kept a foot on the tow rope. The crowd was going wild. You would think that they had just won Top Fuel from their reaction. When they got back to the pits, Bubba was there. It was quiet, and all Bubba said was, "Fuck man, that was incredible. I can't believe you can keep making this thing go faster and faster."

They would in fact get the bye round. Travis and the crew went over the whole car. Zed noticed that the screws holding the tires to the wheel on the right side were bent. He carefully worked them out without breaking them and replaced both sides with new stainless steel screws. They filled the car with fuel, and were ready for the bye run. Travis did not stall the turbos up and he only made a half pass on his bye run. No use risking something to break before the final. He still ran over 120 MPH. He did not even pop the chute.

The crew again went over every inch of the car. Travis even ran the valves to make sure everything was perfect. They agreed to leave the existing set up on the car for the final round even though Travis thought the track would handle more turbo boost. They refilled the water injection bottle and topped off the fuel. They were ready. Travis researched his competitor this time. It was an incredibly fast door slammer. It was a small block Chevy with massive compression and a motor that had every spec perfect. The car was set up perfectly as well. The driver was a very talented woman, and she was very competitive. April had done the research, and the competitor was running .07 under the index! This would make this an even touchier situation as she was in a much slower class. Travis would have to spot her a full half second in the tree. It was going to be quite a race.

They watched two Pro classes which were quite impressive. Several records had been fractured at this race, including theirs. The races were very close, no one went up in smoke and there was a national record set in Top Fuel.

They went back to the pits when Stock and Super Stock finals came to the lanes. Travis put his suit on and just sat in the car until they were called to the lanes. There was a nice breeze. Travis looked at the American Flag and he could see the breeze was blowing down track which was perfect.

Their class was called. The crew took him up to the lanes. Both competitors had their eyes glued forward. They both started the engines about the same time. She was a cool competitor and in fact had been a national champion a couple of times already. She was ready to put this rookie away and win her championship. They both pulled into the water box at the same time, and she surprised Travis by doing a short burnout. He knew that her team had done their homework and realized that staging a turbo car was a bit time-consuming. She was trying to get in his head. In drag racing, it is called "psyching out" your competitor. Travis was not going to fall into this trap. He knew that the starting official was aware that this was a final round and would give both competitors a reasonable amount of time to get set. The official had also seen Travis run before. He did his normal burnout, and April backed him perfectly into his tire tracks. The other lane had already moved into the pre-stage and stage light! She was not at the converter stall yet, however. He ignored them and eased into the first stage light, put it in neutral and cleaned out the motor and dropped it back into gear. He then used the hand brake to start to build boost and ease into the second stage light. Once in he locked the transmission brake and nailed the throttle. Out of the corner of his eye, he did see the other lane leave, wheels in the air. The long spot time made Travis careful not to red light so he left a bit late. In fact, it was his worst light of the day. She had gotten to him.

Now it was time to see if the massive power plant in front of him could pull it out for him. The car left hard again carrying the wheels about 20-30 feet. It left so hard that he gained about a length back right out of the gate but she was out there. Would the turbos have enough to catch her? We would know in just a few seconds. The shift light came on, and Travis banged second. Again the water injection shot made the car leap forward, but it stayed straight. Now the engine was roaring, the turbos were spooled up, and the engine was building massive power. He could feel the car pull harder and harder. The timing retard came on and the other car was getting larger to him. He could tell that he was reeling her in very quickly. Would it be enough? The car was flying now and the turbos were screaming. He actually caught her before they hit the first line of the traps. At the finish line, he was a full car length in front. This was considered as a blowout loss in the Competition Eliminator. Yes, she had cut a great light and made a record run…but the Altered had run another record time and was just too much for anyone to beat. He had won the race, set a new record, won the event and locked up the Championship.

After pulling the chute, Travis let the car roll out to the last return road. It was like the car and Travis both had a sigh of relief. The crew arrived, and they were very jubilant. Travis was amazingly somber. He quietly and carefully took off his helmet, set it on top of the roll cage and got out of the car. April, of course, came running and jumped into his arms wrapping her beautiful legs around him and locking him in a lip lock. Travis lingered in his kiss holding her by her ass to stabilize her. He was truly a lucky man.

When they finally broke the kiss, Zed said, "Well, now what old man? You broke the record, won the race, and locked up the championship!"

Travis said, "Well, I guess the only thing left to do is watch the rest of the finals and then get April ready for her last license run."

It took a second for that to register with April, but then she stopped in her tracks and turned around and stared into Travis's eyes and said, "Did you just say that I am going to get to finish my license passes today?"

Travis had a smile on his face and said one word, "Yep."

April did not even know what to say, and she sat down on the back of the golf cart. Her beautiful legs seemed like they did not want to hold her up. She was going to get her last pass, and then her license. She was not too sure what would happen next. Just the thought of running in the competition excited her. Zed jumped in the race car, and Travis drove the golf cart while April made sure the tow rope stayed tight. On the way back there were lots of thumbs up from both the fans and racers. The track announcer had made a big deal out of Travis's final pass. Everyone knew that he had won the race and locked up the championship.

Travis had a familiar funny feeling in his gut. He had this experience many times when building cars, engines or just winning a card game. It was an inner sense of completeness. It was a great feeling, but it had another tone to it. In his mind, he was done! He was ready to move on. After all, how could he top this? He had another idea brewing in his mind. After they had the car back to the pits and had it prepared for April's last run, they went up to the stands to watch the rest of the finals. Travis had changed out of his fire suit and into blue jeans and a race team T-shirt. April had put on her fire suit pants and shoes and had a Race team T shirt on as well. They went up to the stands and found seats close to the starting line. Usually, Travis was done and ready to roll after his final pass, but it was nice to get a chance to see the race instead of loading up the car and heading out right away. Travis took a special interest in Top Alcohol Dragster (TA/D) as he had some ideas on how a Turbo car might do in this class. Many of these cars still ran a two speed Power Glide. This meant they still used a converter, which is what would be needed to stall against to build turbo boost. All the cars in this class were still using superchargers. This gave Travis food for thought for sure.

They missed Top Fuel Funny Car as they had gone back to the pits to bring the Altered up into the staging lanes so that April could make her last pass after the last final had run. She did not seem all that nervous. She had a very intense look on her face, and she was watching every movement of the pro teams to see what she could learn. The last class, of course, was Top Fuel Dragster. The final round was a couple of well-known racers Keith Brown and Grizz Harley. The underdog of the two was Keith Brown. Travis had met Grizz several times, and he knew him to be a very cool character. They called him "Grizz " because he was a bigger, husky man and had white hair and beard and looked a bit like a Grizzly bear. He was in his sixties and had been in hundreds of races. Keith was younger and hungry to prove himself. Travis leaned over to April and Zed and said, "Watch, I bet Brown will go up in smoke. I am betting he has the engine set on kill and the track is cooler because the sun is going down."

The cars left together, and neither had red lights , but as predicted at about 60 feet, Brown's tires began to haze and were soon going up in smoke. Grizz went on to win and run a number just a .01 over the national record.

The crowds were heading towards their cars to begin the mass exit from the race track when the announcer made a surprise announcement. He said, "Folks, you may want to stick around. We have a young lady by the name of April who is going to make her final license run today in an AA Altered Turbo) (AA/AT). This is the same car that set a national record, won the race, and locked up the class championship earlier today with a different driver."

Many of the fans just kept moving, however a great number decided to stay and watch. They were in for a real surprise. Travis and Zed were in for a surprise as well. Travis was not sure if the extra attention would shake April up. He hoped not. When he kissed her helmet, he noticed she said nothing. She was in the zone and had a laser focus on what she needed to do. What would happen next would shock not only the remaining crowd but Travis himself.

April made along smokey burnout. As he was backing her up into her tire tracks, he noticed she flipped on the water injection and retard arming switches. This surprised him a bit as she did not need to go that fast to get her license. He said nothing and gave her thumbs up when she was far enough back. Her beautiful eyes had a very determined look in them. She was all business. She made a dry chirp to clean the tires and then eased the car into the first staging light. Other than the sound of the engine and turbos, it was pretty quiet! All eyes were on April.

April knew she was going to give them a show. She slipped the transmission into neutral and cleared the motor out with a couple of quick blips of the throttle. She took a second to make sure she had focus. God, Travis loved her. She eased the shifter back into gear. She was using the hand brake to build boost, and Travis got a huge smile on his face, and he said to Zed, "Watch this Zed. It is going to be something to see!"

April eased into the second staging light, locked the transmission brake and buried the throttle. The turbos were fully spooled up and screaming when the last yellow light came on, and April let the car fly. The car leaped out of the hole, and the front end came up about 6 inches and stayed up. She had cut a .505 light, which is .006 from being a red light. At about 40 feet the tires set back down and stayed down until she hit second gear when they popped up again for an instant. Travis knew that meant she had used the water injection. She was flying now. She was the only car on the track and it seemed like everyone left watching was holding their breath. All you could hear was the roar of the engine and the screaming turbos all the way down the track. She roared through the traps and then the chute opened. There was a slight pause after the ET and MPH came up on the scoreboard .

The announcer went wild as he said, "Ladies and Gentleman… April has just run a new Track and World record for AA/AT!"

There was a loud roar from the remaining crowd. Then the announcer added that they may have just witnessed the beginning of a new up and comer.

Travis was thinking the same thing. He and Zed climbed into the golf cart and drove down the track to retrieve their NEW DRIVER…

Please send feedback and ideas for book two:

More Love, Lust & Combustion @ Mingomoran.com

Printed by Libri Plureos GmbH in Hamburg, Germany